CW00554232

# Circle of Blood Book Five:

# Lover's Atonement

**Other books by R. A. Steffan**

# Circle of Blood Book Five:

# Lover's Atonement

R. A. Steffan & Jaelynn Woolf

Circle of Blood Book Five: Lover's Atonement

Copyright 2018 by R. A. Steffan

All rights reserved. Printed in the United States of America. No part of this book may be used or reproduced in any manner whatsoever without written permission except in the case of brief quotations embedded in critical articles or reviews.

This book is a work of fiction. Names, characters, businesses, organizations, places, events and incidents either are the product of the author's imagination or are used fictitiously. Any resemblance to actual persons, living or dead, events, or locales is entirely coincidental.

ISBN: 978-1-955073-44-8 (paperback)

For information, contact the author at
http://www.rasteffan.com/contact/

Cover art by Deranged Doctor Design

Second Edition: December 2022

# INTRODUCTION

This book contains graphic violence and explicit sexual content. It is intended for a mature audience. While it is part of a series with an over-arching plot, it can be read as a standalone with a "happy ever after" ending for the two main characters, and a satisfying resolution of the storyline. If you don't intend to continue the series, you may wish to avoid the epilogue.

# TABLE OF CONTENTS

# ONE

There was a special kind of clarity that came from knowing you were one tiny slip away from certain death. As a CIA undercover operative and former US Navy SEAL who'd completed multiple hazardous missions over the years, Chan Wei Yong had spent enough time walking along that razor's edge to recognize its dangerous caress.

Now, he stood at the back of the raised stage set up in front of the Buddhist Thean Hou Temple in Kuala Lumpur, Malaysia. Chan looked out over the assembled crowd as the monk standing at the front of the stage whipped them into a frenzy of anti-Muslim hatred.

*"It is time for followers of the true religion to rise up! We must cleanse this city of the infectious parasites that have been sucking us dry for so long... this is our domain now, and we must claim what we deserve!"*

Thunderous roars of approval accompanied the monk's words. The crowd stood in the torch-lit courtyard, naturally forming little clusters of people within the larger pattern of the mob. As the shouts died down, disgruntled murmuring remained audible under the speaker's booming voice. The onlookers almost seemed to sway together, as though mesmerized by the words pouring across the open space of the courtyard.

The natural reverberation from the temple and the surrounding palm trees magnified every word the monk spoke. It was a fascinating phenomenon that allowed him to speak powerfully to large groups without the use of electronic amplification equipment.

It also allowed Chan to record the assemblies discreetly from his place in the shadows, using the wire hidden his sleeve. He stood straight, his shoulders back—his dark gaze looking out from a stony face. Every now and then he moved his eyes over the assembled people, searching the crowd for anyone with malicious intent. He needed to maintain his cover, after all. And his cover right now was the role of a hired security man, paid to protect the self-proclaimed warrior monk, Tengku Asal.

As ever, the danger of possible discovery made Chan feel more alive, even with the knowledge that his death could fall upon him at any moment. He was focused. Centered. His attention, sharp and steady.

It might have been that same craving for danger which had kept him in the service of the Central Intelligence Agency for so long—and in the Navy SEALs, prior to that. It was as though risking his life made everything feel more real to him. More immediate. As long as he was risking his life, he could set aside his feelings of failure and self-loathing for all the shitty things he'd done in the past.

*Focus on the moment.* That was his motto these days. Because when you stopped worrying about the here-and-now and let your thoughts wander down the path of might-have-beens…

He blinked, bringing himself back to the present, the tightening of his lips the only sign that his focus had wavered momentarily. *No. I am not going down that rabbit hole tonight.*

Tengku's voice still rang out, whipping across the crowd. *"…and the Divine spirit within us will wash these lands clean with the blood of our enemies! I call on each of you tonight to fulfill your oath to me. Give yourselves in honor of the nation that we will build from the ashes! We will watch the bastard offspring of the evil that has overrun this country burn alive, and they will know death at our hands!"*

Chan very carefully held in the sigh that wanted to escape. Zealots were the same the world over.

*Ten points for enthusiasm,* he thought. *Minus several hundred for logic and rationality.*

He'd been deep undercover in Malaysia for almost eighteen months now, serving Tengku as his joint chief of security. Chan had moved up the ranks of the so-called Brotherhood of the Cleansing Flame thanks to an informant who'd vouched for him. Shortly after Chan was made co-chief of security, that informant had died of a mysterious illness. Chan would never know for sure, of course, but he strongly suspected poison. The man had seemed perpetually haunted and fearful whenever he and Chan met—as though he were always looking over his shoulder.

*This life isn't for everyone. You have to watch your back every moment, and if you can't handle that, you have no business playing the game.*

To be truthful, the informant's loss hadn't hit Chan all that hard. As cold as it sounded, it was simply one less loose end — one less person who might possibly blow his cover within the ranks of the Brotherhood. It saved him having to deal with the man at a later date, and now no one in Malaysia knew Chan's identity. His cover was deep enough to withstand almost any scrutiny… unless he fucked up, of course. Then all bets were off.

The Malaysian government might have known that the US had a man on the ground within the Brotherhood, but they could no sooner identify him than they could lay hands on Tengku. And Chan had no doubt whatsoever that the authorities would *love* to lay hands on Tengku. Unfortunately, they knew full well that he and his cult were gaining in popularity by leaps and bounds. At this point, with all the instability and political scandals going on in the region, taking Tengku could well spark rioting that would tear the country apart.

So, with few other options, the Malaysians simply watched and waited, hoping that Tengku's cult wouldn't continue to grow at its current pace — all their hopes riding on one unknown American agent in the midst of the nest of lunatics.

And didn't it just sound completely ridiculous when you put it in those terms? They couldn't even be bothered to embed their own damned spies in their own damned back yard… or at least, they hadn't done so as far as Chan knew. If nothing else, a bit more international cooperation here would lessen the load of paperwork Chan faced once he returned home. *If* he returned home.

"The government soldiers will soon be coming for us!" called a voice from the crowd, interrupting Chan's thoughts. "We must take care, my brothers!"

He gave the speaker a closer look and moved strategically forward, ready to protect Tengku if the guy made a move toward the stage. Almost everyone in the crowd was either a Chinese national or a naturalized Buddhist immigrant, including the man who had spoken.

"And even if the soldiers do not come, the Malay Muslims will fight to the death, just like their brothers in the Middle East!" the guy continued, gesturing with both hands.

"We will not bow to those swine," Tengku replied in a deceptively calm voice. "Come forward and join me, brother."

Chan watched as the man blanched, clearly not expecting to be called up to the stage. He shuffled forward and stepped onto the raised platform with Tengku, looking like someone who was abruptly and seriously reconsidering his life choices.

"What is your name?" The monk asked, placing a hand on the speaker's shoulder.

Chan could see the man swallow hard. "Loy Cho."

"Why do you doubt the cause, Loy Cho?"

Loy chewed on his lower lip, obviously sensing the danger in Tengku's voice. "I'm... merely concerned for your safety, Honored One, and the safety of all the Brotherhood."

Chan could tell Loy was lying through his teeth, but he did not speak. He moved closer to

Tengku, ready to intervene if Loy tried to attack the monk physically.

"Such deception," Tengku purred. Slowly, he withdrew a dagger from his waistband. Loy jerked backwards even as Chan stepped forward, grasping his shoulders from behind to hold him in place.

"You will pay the price for your lack of faith," Tengku whispered. Menace radiated from him, palpable in the still night air. No one in the crowd moved or made a sound. They scarcely seemed to be breathing.

With a flash of the blade, Tengku ripped open Loy's shirt with the knife, nicking his chest superficially with the tip of the blade. The wound was not life threatening, yet blood streamed from the shallow gash.

The man gasped and tried to pull away. Chan tightened his grip and hissed for the man to remain still.

Tengku paced back and forth, a predator toying with his prey. He fingered the blade in his hands, tapping it gently on his palm. It left bloodstains on his skin.

Using the tip of the knife, Tengku flicked the shredded pieces of fabric away from the man's chest, exposing more of his flesh. The heat of fear was rising all over Loy's body, and Chan could feel sweat forming on his skin under his grip. Loy flinched away every time the knife was brought towards him.

"I think he is beginning to learn, don't you?" Tengku asked Chan.

Chan knew better than to respond. Instead, he maintained his flat stare at the leader, as any faithful security chief would do. Tengku smiled and shook his head.

"All work and no play, Chan?" he asked.

The western proverb was stilted and out of place in the Malaysian dialect of Mandarin Tengku was speaking, and Chan was too old a dog to fall for such an obvious ploy. He allowed a slight expression of confusion to pass across his features before they settled back into a blank stare.

"Oh, never mind," Tengku said with a wave of his hand. He turned back to his victim, who used the momentary interruption to speak.

"Honored One," he croaked, his voice harsh, "I will never doubt the cause again. I meant nothing by my questions, I was simply seeking to ensure that everyone remains safe. I hear rumors on the streets day and night; I thought I could serve you in this warning!"

The monk raised an eyebrow. "Rumors? And what exactly are the contents of these *rumors*, my conflicted friend?"

The man swallowed, and Chan could feel him trembling. "People speak of government crackdowns. They are saying that the police may start mass arrests in some of the Buddhist enclaves."

"What do you think, Chan?" Tengku asked. "Should we believe him?"

Chan stared into Tengku's eyes, his expression betraying neither worry nor any other emotion.

"Caution is always prudent," he replied, keeping his voice low.

"Well said," Tengku acknowledged. He turned back towards Loy, who was now sinking towards the ground as his knees went weak. Tengku raised the knife, and Loy let out a terrified squeak.

"Never question the goals of the Brotherhood again," Tengku said, and struck a crushing blow across the man's jaw with the hilt.

Chan felt the strike reverberate through Loy's body, but made no attempt to support him as he fell. Rather, he allowed the man to stagger out of his grasp and collapse onto the wooden platform. Another man, his hands raised in a gesture of peace, inched forward and grabbed Loy's arm.

"Respect to you, Honored One," the man quavered, his voice strained as he pulled his comrade off the edge of the stage and led him away, staggering.

The crowd parted and let the two men pass, recoiling as though they were diseased... as though their treachery might be contagious. Clearly, no one else wanted to incur Tengku's wrath today.

"No more doubt, my friends," Tengku insisted, his voice rich with persuasion.

With that, he lifted his hands in farewell and departed the stage. Chan followed a few steps behind him, scanning the crowd of people nearby. Tengku's entourage, or his henchmen as Chan preferred to think of them, followed as well. They smiled and waved, basking in the reflected glory from their fearless leader.

After Chan escorted Tengku safely to his quarters in the temple and ensured that guards were stationed to watch the door, he was ordered to return to the large building nearby, where the Brotherhood maintained most of their operations. The place had originally been a condominium complex one street over from the temple, though it had since been repurposed as an office building before being abandoned completely.

Chan had already reported its location to his US handlers. Should Tengku start making attacks on a larger scale, they were contemplating a joint mission with the Malaysian government to attack the facility, just as the unfortunate Loy Cho had tried to warn. A military operation so close to the historic temple grounds would no doubt incite outrage among the populace, but with luck, collateral damage would be minimal and there would be few civilian casualties.

Chan, of course, was in considerably more danger than most in the event of such a strike. He accepted this knowledge. He had come to terms with the idea of his own death years ago. Right after his divorce, in fact.

Ever since then, he'd found that living had lost quite a bit of its appeal.

# Two

Damn it, Chan chided himself. This was not even *close* to a good time to rehash that particular part of the past. He tried to push the memories of his wife and daughter back down into the darkness, where they belonged. Nevertheless, as he walked along the dimly lit street, he couldn't stop his mind from replaying the memory of the woman he'd pledged to love, honor, and cherish climbing into a car and driving away forever. All because Chan had done something unforgiveable.

He shook his head sharply. *For better or worse, for richer or poorer, in sickness and health. Forsaking all others.*

What a goddamned joke.

The aftermath of the divorce was when he'd decided to accept a position with the CIA as an undercover operative. Because at least that way if he died, his benefits would go to his daughter and she would be well provided for by Uncle Sam. God knew that was a better future than he'd been able to manage for her on his own.

And if he lived…?

Honestly, Chan never considered that option too closely. It was probably only a matter of time before he was compromised—his cover blown during a delicate operation, to fatal effect. Why should he plan for a life well lived when he'd already destroyed every possibility of a happy ending?

That was the real reason he wasn't afraid of death. Why subject another operative to the most dangerous missions, when Chan himself was not worthy to walk the earth?

*Focus, Chan. This is the kind of self-indulgent shit that leads to mistakes.* He could practically hear his grizzled old CIA trainer speaking in his ear, giving him a hard shake of the shoulder for good measure.

He let out an audible sigh as the yellow lights of the complex came into view. Two of his men stood blocking the gate as he approached, but they immediately leapt back when they recognized him.

He'd trained the Brotherhood's guards to expect harsh punishment for every mistake. For a band of guerillas with no formal military background whatsoever, they were remarkably easy to mold. Several of them could have enjoyed very fruitful careers in their country's army, he suspected, had they not chosen the path of extremism instead.

"As you were," Chan murmured as he walked through the open gate. The two security guards nodded to him respectfully as he passed, then resumed their positions near the gate, watching the dark road leading into their base.

Chan had been informed that the Brotherhood had recently taken several more hostages, including one American reporter who'd been snooping around for information regarding recent terrorist bombings. Chan was confident that Tengku was behind the bombing attacks, but he knew better than to ask for outright confirmation. His job was merely security within the complex and the nearby temple. Any intel beyond the day-to-day running of the Brotherhood, he needed to seek out on his own—*discretely*.

He walked into the ground floor of the large building and made a right turn. There, he entered a dingy office with multiple computers crammed onto dated desks. He shut the door behind him, hearing the click echo all around the room. As he flipped on the light, he was startled to see another one of Tengku's lackeys sitting with his feet up on a desk in the corner, waiting. Chan covered his reaction and betrayed no hint of surprise as he surveyed his co-chief of security with a steely stare.

Time seemed frozen for a moment before Chan broke the stillness. He pulled out his battered wallet and a ring of keys from his pocket, tossing them down on a nearby desk.

"You're here late," he observed as he sat down across from the other man.

"I've been waiting for you," his co-chief replied.

"What do you want, Pula? Just here for a pleasant midnight chat?"

Pula smiled, more of a sneer than a look of pleasure. "I wanted to brief you before I left. There are some new security measures that Tengku wants enacted."

"Funny," Chan replied in an icy tone, "I just left Tengku and he made no mention of anything like that."

Pula glared at him for a long beat. There was no love lost between the two of them, and Chan suspected that the entire point of having two security chiefs was so that they could keep an eye on each other. It was practically Rule One for cults—make sure everyone was spying on everyone else.

"I believe it is the wish of the Honored One that we address this project together," Pula said eventually. "I was given the information and instructed to pass it along to you."

"Right," Chan shot back, "so, get to it. What is this new plan, exactly?"

Pula massaged his chin with one hand, a thoughtful gesture.

"Tengku is beginning to fear that our ranks have been infiltrated," Pula finally said, his tone businesslike.

Chan did not react outwardly.

"Oh, really?" he asked Pula. "What gives him that impression?"

"The government often seems to be one step ahead of us. That is all I am permitted to say."

Chan shrugged. "That's true enough. I suppose it makes sense. Does he have any thoughts on who the traitor might be?"

Pula considered him again. "He's got a vague idea."

After several moments of silence where Chan looked at Pula expectantly, the other man finally continued, "We have a local arms dealer that we do business with sometimes. He's been off the grid for several weeks. The last time he met with the Brotherhood, he was given very generic information about some of our targets so that he could help us acquire the weaponry that would be most effective."

Chan raised an eyebrow. "Well, that was stupid. Surely Tengku would never…"

"*No*," Pula interrupted, his voice sharp. "Of course not. You should be whipped for even suggesting such a thing. This was a security breach by the low-level contact person who met with the dealer."

"So, you think this contact person could be the leak?"

Pula shrugged. "That's what Tengku believes. It's our job to tighten security within the ranks to prevent any further… *slips*."

"And the suspected mole has already been dealt with, I presume?" Chan asked, already knowing the answer.

Pula smirked. "He will no longer complicate matters."

Chan leaned back in his chair and cupped his hands behind his head. He felt his back pop in several places as he stretched tight muscles.

"Well, at least we aren't stuck dealing with a manhunt," he finally said shrugging his shoulders and trying to loosen up. He did not want his internal tension to alert Pula that anything was amiss.

"Agreed. This breach of security is to go no further, however."

"Understood," Chan said with a nod. "So, what is Tengku proposing?"

Pula quickly outlined a new plan that would further isolate the Brotherhood's prisoners and hostages. They would only have contact with a small number of trusted guards, and all supplies would be delivered to an off-site location before being brought in on the opposite side of the compound from the cells. The security of the hostages was now one of Tengku's highest priorities.

"So, any questions?" Pula concluded.

"No. That all seems quite clear," Chan answered.

It made perfect tactical sense, too, but inside his heart was sinking. This would make getting information even more difficult than it had been before. To date, Chan had been relying on loose-lipped cult members discussing rumors and plans. Tengku was a master at keeping any incriminating documents or other hard evidence close at hand. If that had been his only source of intel, Chan would have had to pry the information out of Tengku's cold, dead fingers.

Now there was an appealing mental image.

Chan chewed the inside of his cheek. He would have to contact his handler soon. He was overdue getting her a report on the status of Tengku's plans. The CIA was also hoping to learn the numbers and identities of the hostages.

Pula stood up with a grunt and headed toward the door of the office. Chan got up as well.

"You just got here. Where are you headed?" Pula asked, his voice growing suspicious.

"I make it a habit to do a security walk of the building every couple of hours. That way, I always know what's going on and where my men are.

While they, in turn, realize that I might appear at any time."

"Ah," Pula replied with a knowing look. "Well, I'll leave you to it, then."

He left by the same door through which Chan had originally entered.

Sighing in relief, Chan walked quietly to the other door, which led to a large storage room. At the far end, there was a door opening onto a flight of stairs that led down to an old basement bunker. It was originally built as a storm shelter for the condominium residents, but it had become very useful to the Brotherhood as a prison for their most valuable hostages and dangerous enemies.

Chan pitied the poor souls who were kept down here. The ones held in the main part of the building had it bad enough, but these people? They'd been sent down here to disappear, he suspected. He'd spent an inordinate amount of time recently trying to figure out their identities without tipping off the Brotherhood that he was more interested than he should be.

Now, though, it was time to stop fucking around. He crept down the steps, exhaling silently each time one of his feet landed — an old SEAL trick that helped him move around without making a sound. The darkness in the hallway was absolute, so he flipped the light switch that he knew was located on his right side, from his previous expeditions down here.

The single bulb burned yellow in the center of the large space, casting a hazy light all around. The prisoners were held in small cells along the edges of the room. Iron bars formed the front of the cages. The sharp smell of fecal matter and decay hit his nose like an assault. Checking the gag response that threatened him, Chan narrowed his eyes and took inventory.

As a highly trained observer, Chan immediately began cataloguing basic information about each of the prisoners, along with any changes to their numbers. He recognized several of them from his previous trips. Some of them had been held here for months now. He'd gotten a few names during that time, but the basement was under constant surveillance, so he couldn't speak freely. Unless they volunteered the information while trying to wheedle him into letting them out or getting messages to their loved ones, it would be too suspicious for him to speak with them.

At the back of the room, a prone figure caught his eye. Since he'd joined the Brotherhood more than a year ago, that particular cell had remained empty. It seemed ominous to him that the figure inside did not stir in response to his approach as the others did. For the most part, his journey down the row of cells was met with blank stares and shuffling limbs. A few of the newer prisoners still maintained enough spirit to glare suspiciously at him, clearly fearing that they were about to be subjected to some new torture.

It disgusted Chan that he could do nothing to help them, but he knew that it was only a matter of time before the US and Malaysian governments got impatient and organized a raid on the warehouse, potential riots be damned. He tried to tell himself that when it happened, these people would be extracted safely and returned to their families.

On some days, he even believed it.

As Chan moved through the semi-darkness, he noted that the prone prisoner still hadn't moved a muscle. There was no sign of breathing, or any other suggestion of life.

*Just great, all I need is someone down here dying on my watch,* Chan thought. Despite his natural compassion, he was almost frustrated that this guy — whoever he was — couldn't have held on a little longer. *A few more weeks, and maybe you could have gotten out of this shithole, you poor bastard.*

Placing his hand on the cell door, he rattled the bars.

Nothing.

"Hey!" he called to the prisoner, who still made no movement.

"Wake up!" he said in an even louder voice.

The man's face twitched, the movement so slight Chan wasn't totally sure he'd seen it.

*Fuck, I guess he's alive after all. Good.*

Even so, the guy looked more like a goddamned mummy than a living person. Emaciated, as thin and ragged as if he hadn't eaten a solid meal in months. Frail. Covered in burns and odd scars. Chan flinched as the figure's head rolled toward him, skin stretched tightly over sharp bones like cracked parchment. Eyes pinned him, cold and distant, as ancient as the moon in the sky, but dark like night.

Those eyes chilled Chan's marrow, making him feel as though his legs had been paralyzed by the power of a mere glance.

*What the – ?*

Chan blinked several times, trying to mentally shake himself free of the hypnotic gaze. He opened his mouth to speak; yet no sound escaped him. The figure before him made no move, took no breath, and his lips remained pressed closed. Yet Chan heard a voice in his mind. The tone was deep and arresting, though he detected no malice in it.

*Is it really you?* The voice asked inside his head, sounding distantly curious. Those hypnotic dark eyes blinked once, slowly, before the voice continued. *How strange, and yet how terribly apt.*

Chan could no more answer than he could make his feet move. His legs and his tongue might as well have been paralyzed.

*I have a message for you to relay,* the voice continued. *I fear I will soon lack the strength to deliver it myself. I will give it to you, and then you will forget it until the time is right. Do you understand?*

Chan had undergone years of training in resisting psychological manipulation, and part of him thrashed under the weight of the hypnotic presence pressing down on him. But the rest lay quiescent, waiting to be told what to do—eager to hear the message.

"I… understand," he heard himself whisper.

*Good,* the voice murmured, *now, listen closely…*

# THREE

"Duchess?" Abby whispered through the crack in the door.

Duchess, who had been checking email on her laptop in the spare room graciously offered to her by Mason's brother, glanced up and saw a pair of lips pursed next to the small gap. A faint smile tugged at one corner of the vampire's lips. She left the computer and crossed the room with silence worthy of a nightwalker, her feet making no sound on the bamboo floor. Before Abby could grow impatient enough to call again, Duchess was poised on the other side, gazing with veiled affection at the little fingers gripping the doorframe.

"Hello!" Abby whispered, even louder.

"Yes, Abby?" Duchess answered in a normal tone, right next to the child's ear.

Abby jumped and squealed in surprise before collapsing into delighted giggles. With the corners of her eyes crinkling from the smile she was suppressing, Duchess opened the door and allowed the light from the hallway to stream inside.

"It's very early, Abby," she observed, mock severe.

The small, dark haired child stood before her, looking faintly apprehensive in her pink pajamas. Her father's storm-blue eyes peered out from a tiny version of her mother's oval face.

"I know. But will you brush my hair?" Abby asked, producing a predictably pink hairbrush from behind her back.

Duchess let her features soften as she opened the door more fully.

"Of course I will, *petite oiseau*. Come and sit on the bed," Duchess answered. She stood back a step and allowed Abby to pass in front of her.

"You make your bed really fast every day," Abby observed. "I hate making my bed, but Daddy says I gotta."

Duchess glanced at her bed, which had not been slept in since she arrived. "It is a good habit to cultivate, even if it isn't very fun."

Abby made a noise in her throat that suggested she didn't think too much of Duchess' opinion on the matter, but she clambered onto the bed in question without further protest. Once settled, she sat expectantly with her legs crossed.

Duchess perched behind the little girl and gently brushed tangles out of her long raven locks, starting at the ends and gripping the hair so it would not tug. Before long, she was able to pull the brush through effortlessly with long, smooth strokes.

"How long are you staying with us?" Abby asked in a soft voice.

Duchess considered her words for a moment. "I'm not certain, *ma petite*. Until your parents get tired of us and ask us to leave, I suppose."

*Or until the next crisis calls us away.*

"They won't do that," Abby replied with supreme confidence. "They say that it's important to always make guests feel welcome."

Duchess chuckled and tweaked the girl's ear. "Well, until *you* get tired of us, then."

"No way!" Abby insisted, clearly offended.

Hurried footsteps passed along the hall outside the door. Duchess paused, sensing Mason's retreating presence. He was worried about something.

Abby, noticing nothing amiss, clapped her hands together and said, "Oh, good! Someone else is awake! It must be time to get up!"

Unfolding her legs, the little girl leapt off the bed in a single bound. She spun and held her hand out to Duchess, who laced their fingers together and allowed Abby to tug her out of the door.

The house was dim and silent, the sun only barely peeking above the horizon—not yet high enough to pass through the large windows. Duchess took a moment to enjoy the glittering beauty of Singapore beyond. It was refreshing to be surrounded by such brilliance, after the darkness they had experienced in Damascus and Haiti. Here, there was no outward sign of Bael's presence—so far, at least.

The reprieve was a relief for all of them, pouring much-needed life into their battered souls—even if Duchess was finding it increasingly difficult to be with the happy couples around her. When it was just Eris and Tré who had reunited with their mates, she and Oksana could sequester themselves to privately bemoan all the love floating around in the air. Now, though, she was starting to feel very alone in her aloneness.

*Well, alone accept for Snag… assuming he still lives.*

That sense of isolation pulled heavily on her, and for comfort she squeezed Abby's fingers. The little girl looked back at her and flashed a dazzling smile. She was missing two of her teeth, making her grin look lopsided, like a cheerful jack-o-lantern.

The warmth that spread through Duchess at the sight almost made up for everything else. Since she'd been barely more than a child herself, Duchess had adored children and dreamed of being a mother. Bael snatched that opportunity from her before it ever bore fruit, however. Even some four hundred years later, the pain of that loss was almost more acute than the loss of her soul mate.

And what did that say about her?

"Who's Uncle Mason talking to?" Abby whispered, tugging on her hand.

Duchess had been so lost in thought as they entered the kitchen that she barely noticed Mason having a tense conversation over the phone.

"What have the local authorities told you?" he asked, his tone grim.

Mason stared blankly at the cabinets, clearly not seeing them. He held the phone in one hand, while his other hand gripped the edge of the marble countertop, white-knuckled.

"And they could tell you nothing useful at all? There are no suspects? No clues?" he demanded.

"Abby, come away for a few minutes," Duchess said quietly, about to pull the child from the room.

Abby resisted, planting her short legs shoulder width apart and pulling her arm back. "No—Uncle Mason is upset. He needs me!"

"Let's allow him to finish his phone conversation in private, *petite oiseau*," Duchess murmured, but the little girl shook her head stubbornly.

"You don't understand," she retorted with a glare in Duchess' direction, "I'm his little bird. I can always make him smile. You'll see!"

Before Duchess could stop her, the small child had pulled her fingers from Duchess' grasp and hurried towards her uncle.

She took his hand and looked up at him.

"Uncle Mason," Abby whispered, shaking him.

He flashed her a brief, strained smile, but shook his head at her with a soft shushing sound, still listening to the rapid speech of the person on the other end of the line.

*This is bad,* Mason sent along the bond, a bit too loudly. Though his control of his recently acquired vampiric powers had improved immensely in the past few weeks, he still struggled to control his mental volume at times, especially when under pressure.

*Mason, we aren't deaf,* she replied in kind.

His eyes flickered to where she was standing in the doorway, and he sent back an apology. Chagrin briefly crossed his expression, but then he was once more focused on the phone conversation.

"I understand. No, I think the clinic is fine with a substitute physician. I'm sure, given the circumstances, that Doctors Without Borders will send extra help."

He listened again. "Of course. But keep me posted, okay?"

He chewed at the inside of his lip as the person on the other end spoke. "All right, Gita. Please take care of yourself and let me know if there's anything I can do to help from my end. We'll talk soon."

He hung up the phone and stared at it for a moment, his face blank.

"Uncle Mason, don't be sad. I can chirp like a bird!" Abby offered, smiling up at him.

Despite his obvious preoccupation, he smiled back and brushed her hair away from her face. "That makes sense, since you are my little bird. Now, though, will you fly away and find Oksana for me? I need to talk to her and Duchess for a minute."

Abby stuck out her lower lip. "Adult talk?"

"I'm afraid so, sweet thing," he said gravely, "but it shouldn't take long."

With a dramatic sigh, Abby shuffled away muttering, "That's what grown-ups always say."

After the little girl left the room, Duchess sat down at the table and lifted an expectant eyebrow at Mason.

He sighed and scrubbed a hand over his face. "So. That was Gita Belawan—my old partner. The one who took over the clinic in Haiti when I left," he said, and sat down next to Duchess. "She just got a call from the Malaysian authorities."

"Oh?" Duchess prompted.

"Her son, Haziq, has been kidnapped. He's a doctor in Kuala Lumpur."

Duchess' eyes narrowed as tension took root in her chest. "Kuala Lumpur. The same place we've been getting reports of religious unrest and escalating violence."

Mason nodded. "Yup. Spot on. I mean—there's always been a fair amount of civil unrest in that region. And while kidnapping isn't uncommon, it's usually drug-related. Not respectable professionals being nabbed off the street."

"Did the authorities have any idea why Dr. Belawan's son was targeted?" Duchess asked. "Or was it random?"

Mason sighed. "It's not clear. Maybe he offended the kidnappers in some way? Or they thought he'd be valuable? Hell, he may have just been in the wrong place at the wrong time. There's no way to know for certain right now."

"What *are* the authorities saying? What did they tell her?"

"Basically, they told her to sit tight. They suspect a particular group, and they're supposedly doing everything possible to recover the group's hostages, who they believe are still alive. Apparently Haziq is one of several that are being held right now by this... cult, or whatever you want to call it."

They were both silent for a moment. Duchess sent a tendril of thought across the bond to Oksana, questioning.

*I'm listening, ti mwen*, Oksana replied. *I'll be down in a moment – just let me get this blasted foot attached.*

Duchess gave an internal nod and spoke again to Mason. "Did the police say anything else specific about this group they think is holding hostages?"

"They did," Mason replied, sitting back in his chair. "Surprisingly, they're Buddhist extremists." He flickered a wry eyebrow. "I suppose there's something to be said for bucking stereotypes."

Duchess shook her head. "It's not unheard of. It might not get much play in the news media, but there are plenty of Muslims in Myanmar who would be happy to tell you about abuse by Buddhist militants."

"Good point," Mason allowed. "And I should know better, really. I had some colleagues in Myanmar, and I heard how much of a mess it was there for a while."

"Malaysia is majority Muslim with enclaves of Chinese immigrants, most of whom are Buddhist," Duchess mused. "It could be a similar dynamic. Cultural friction artificially magnified by the general slide into chaos."

Mason sighed and said, "Yeah. It could be. Seems like everything that was already bad is getting exponentially worse in the last few months."

"And now your friend's son is caught up in the mix," Duchess said, her voice fading away as she considered the situation.

"Just so," Mason agreed glumly. "Haziq Belawan specializes in pediatric medicine, of all the damned things. Just like his mum."

Duchess felt her blood burn. Always, it was the children these days. The children, and those who tried to protect and care for them.

"Savages," she whispered.

Mason nodded but did not speak. She could tell that the news was weighing heavily upon him, especially since they were very close to Kuala Lumpur. Close enough to get involved, in fact— should they choose to do so.

The sound of soft, slightly uneven footsteps caused her to look up. Oksana entered the room, and her grim expression confirmed that she'd heard every word of their conversation.

"Hey, sweetheart," Mason greeted. "I just got a call from—"

"Gita," Oksana interrupted, and sat down next to him at the table. "Yes, I heard. No offense, my love, but you were projecting so loudly that I'm sure any vampire within a five-mile radius could have heard you."

Mason frowned. "I've really got to figure out how to control that."

"You're better than you used to be," Duchess assured him. "Especially while you two are having sex… thankfully."

Oksana cleared her throat loudly. "Yes, *thank you*, Duchess." She shot Duchess a glare. "So. Kuala Lumpur. That's not very far from here. When do we leave?"

"Whoa, there. Aren't we getting a bit ahead of ourselves?" Mason protested, holding up a hand. "It's quite a jump from 'my friend's son was just kidnapped somewhere in a city of a million and a half people' to 'when's the next flight out?'"

"Is it really? Why? I mean… what else do we have to do?" Oksana inquired, angling her body towards Mason. She cupped her chin in one hand, the two seeming instantly lost within each other's gazes as they communicated silently.

*Ah, and once again I am the third wheel on the bicycle,* Duchess thought. She made sure to shield the dark observation, aware of how bitter such things made her seem. Besides, as much as the thriving couple-ness of everyone close to her turned her stomach these days, she truly did believe that no one deserved happiness more than Oksana.

She would not let her cold cynicism ruin her comrades' contentment so easily—and *certainly* not Oksana's contentment.

"All right. Fine," Mason said. "So, we're talking about a field trip straight into another hornets' nest. What precisely do we hope to accomplish by going? What's our plan?"

"Hostage recovery isn't nearly as challenging as humans make it out to be," Duchess said in a bland voice. She examined her manicured nails, making a show of it. "I daresay we can do a far better job of it than Malaysian law enforcement is managing right now."

Mason perked up for the first time since the phone call.

"You think we could really get him back? Well, I suppose Malaysian law enforcement can't change into mist or owls," he mused, getting into the spirit of things. "Which is hardly their fault, obviously.

But you're offering to help? Even though it would still be dangerous?"

Duchess shrugged. "Dangerous? Against militant Buddhist *monks*? I'm reasonably certain we can handle them." She let her lips curve into a pointed smirk. "Even though you're still practically a newborn."

Oksana stifled a snort, covering her mouth.

Mason appeared mildly offended at the jab. "Yes, well—I am completely capable of changing form and feeding on my own these days, so you can dispense with the baby vampire jokes any time now." He gave Duchess a narrow look. "Christ. You're starting to make me miss Xander's subtle application of tact and diplomacy."

That riposte did manage to hit a tender spot, but Duchess only lifted a haughty eyebrow. "Mason, you *are* a baby vampire. You still shout half the time when you and Oksana are—"

"*Oh*-kay, I think that's enough of this particular conversation," Oksana interrupted. "I agree that we should visit Kuala Lumpur and see if we can be of any help with Gita's son. Duchess, you're the one who's been saying that some of the reports coming out of Malaysia were alarming, even before this happened—so let's go check things out."

"Agreed," Duchess said readily enough, experiencing a sudden surge of eagerness to be doing something more positive than sitting around, waiting for the next crisis to appear.

"Agreed," Mason echoed, a bit more hesitation in his tone. "But with the caveat that if this somehow turns into another *vortex of chaos*, as you two insist on calling it—we bring in more backup this time. I'm not in a hurry to see anyone else get knifed, shot, poisoned, staked, abducted, or turned into a werewolf if we can avoid it."

Oksana lifted a pointed brow at Duchess, who frowned at her.

*It's a fair point*, her friend sent.

"What are you implying, *mon chou*?" she asked aloud, her tone a bit sour. "Mason is the one who brought this particular crisis to our attention. It's nothing to do with me."

The vortices of violence and unrest seemed to form when one of them got too close to his or her lost mate; something that hardly applied in this instance.

Oksana's eyes narrowed. *You'd tell us, wouldn't you, ti mwen? If you sensed your mate nearby?*

Duchess' frown deepened. "I'll go contact the others and start arranging transportation for us," she said, ignoring the silent question. "Then we should speak to our hosts."

She could feel the others' eyes on her back as she rose and left the room.

-o-o-o-

An hour later, the three of them were sitting at the table again, this time across from Jackson Walker and his wife, Yi Ling.

"You really think this is a good idea, Mace?" Jackson asked, looking at his brother steadily. "You three just got out of one disaster zone. Yet you seem awfully eager to run straight into another one."

Mason shrugged, but his expression was dark. "Gita's a good friend, Jack. And we might be able to do something to get Haziq back safely to his family."

Yi Ling cocked her head. "We were hoping that you would stay here longer. But if your friend needs help, then you should try to help." Her bell-like voice was quiet, but Duchess sensed her lingering unease around them. And yet, Jackson's wife had been the consummate hostess during their stay—even going so far as to donate blood for them. Duchess could not help respecting her for that.

"Our sentiments exactly," Oksana said.

"Well... it sounds like your minds are made up," Jackson said. "For what it's worth, there are still a couple of blood bags in the freezer. You should take them with you, so you don't have to go all '*Interview with the Vampire*' on some poor, un-suspecting Malaysians while you're gone."

"That's very kind of you," Duchess said politely.

Oksana nodded. "We could keep them on dry ice, I suppose. We aren't planning on being there for very long, though."

Jackson sighed, the expression of worry sounding eerily like his brother's. "Well, I guess that's settled, then."

"The girls won't like saying goodbye," Yi Ling murmured, looking at Mason. "They've loved having you here."

Mason smiled. "Oh, I imagine we'll be back in a few days, Yi Ling. It's not that far away, and we're just going to go have a quick poke around. See if we can turn up anything the police have missed."

Jackson huffed, and Duchess got the distinct impression that he didn't believe a word his brother was saying.

# Four

The three of them spent the rest of the day tending Mason's nieces. Apparently, Yi Ling had slowly been growing more comfortable with them, because she and Jackson took advantage of their last chance for babysitting services to sneak away for a day out. Duchess couldn't blame them; these days, quiet moments were hard for anyone to find.

"Duchess!" Abby called from the other room. "Me and Ming want some juice, please!"

"'Ming and I,' Abby," Duchess corrected. "What kind of juice do you want?"

"Papaya!" Ming answered in a bright voice.

Duchess stood and made her way into the kitchen, grateful for a few moments' escape from the happy-couple-bliss that surrounded Oksana and Mason like an aura. *Mon Dieu*, had she always been this twisted up inside, or was it a recent thing? She shook her head, irritated with herself.

Abby bounded into the room. "I have to have the purple cup today," she insisted in a solemn voice.

"Why's that, *petite oiseau*?"

"Because it's a purple kind of day," she answered simply.

"Right," Duchess murmured, and pulled down two cups.

"Lellow day! Lellow day!" Ming, the younger of the two girls, called out as she, too, entered the kitchen.

"She means 'yellow,'" Abby clarified, her tone communicating an air of long-suffering patience with her younger sister.

Duchess smiled at the antics of the two energetic girls, letting their carefree lightness chase away some of her own dark thoughts. After both had been satisfied with their drinks, they returned to the playroom, where Duchess encouraged them to parade past her in a variety of dresses and shoes obtained from both Yi Ling's closet and her own luggage. It was an eclectic fashion show and would no doubt have raised eyebrows on the runways of Paris—but it did ease the heavy weight that pressed down across Duchess' shoulders these days.

Later in the evening, once Jackson and Yi Ling had returned, the two girls clambered into Duchess' lap and demanded one last story before she left. Each night since they'd arrived, Duchess had spent a portion of the evening reading to Abby and Ming from a collection of Grimm's fairy tales.

She flipped through the pages, aided and abetted by the captivated girls. Finally, it was time for them to say their goodbyes. Through the curtained windows of the stylish but homey apartment, Duchess could sense that the sun's rays were sinking safely below the horizon. Soon, they would begin the journey to Kuala Lumpur.

"Please don't go," Abby begged, her small arms wrapped around Duchess' neck. "I don't want you to leave yet!"

Duchess caught herself before the unexpected ache in her chest could enter her voice. The small pain was sharp enough to take her by surprise. Sharp enough to make Oksana look at her with an expression of worry.

"Abby," Duchess answered, squeezing the little girl, "we will return another time. You must stay here and look after your little sister while we're gone."

"And Mommy and Daddy, too?" she asked, leaning back with wide eyes.

"Of course, *petite oiseau*. Your parents, as well," Duchess replied, passing the little girl into Mason's waiting arms. She hugged Ming next. The younger girl was obviously getting sleepy, sucking her thumb with drooping eyes. As soon as everyone had hugged everyone else, Duchess picked up her bag and departed with the others.

Despite her earlier appreciation for the restful break, she found that she was happy to leave the emotional surroundings. Everyone seemed to be on edge with this departure. Singapore's humid night air flowed over her cool skin as they exited the building, and she could smell several humans walking along the road nearby. It would take them hardly any time to travel by mist to Kuala Lumpur, yet Duchess felt strangely rushed.

A few moments later, Oksana and Mason followed her outside, slinging their bags across their backs.

"The girls certainly have the knack of tugging at your heart with those big puppy dog eyes, don't they?" Oksana said, looking troubled.

Mason chuckled, though he, too, looked less than pleased about leaving. "Oh, just wait until Christmas time. Abby practically has me convinced it's a moral imperative that I tell her what I got her in advance."

"That little girl will rule the world someday," Duchess said wryly, "assuming we can save it from the forces of evil for her."

"No doubt," Mason said. "I keep telling Jack that he's going to have to start saving for either an Ivy League college fund or bond money. I doubt there's going to be much of an in-between with that one."

Duchess couldn't help her small breath of amusement, as some of the tension in the air eased.

She hefted her bag and gestured for Mason to hand his over as well. They were traveling light, leaving most of their belongings with Jackson and Yi Ling. Still, there was a knack to transporting inanimate objects while in a shifted form, and although Duchess trusted Mason not to reappear on the other end of the journey wearing only his boxers and one sock, asking him to keep mental track of a knapsack full of clothing and incidentals was probably a bit much at this stage.

"Stay close to me, Mason," Oksana said. "I don't want you to get lost or separated."

"Try not to worry, sweetheart. I'll be fine," he answered, his voice low. "In fact, I'm rather looking forward to this—my first long-distance flight."

He bent to press a kiss to her lips, and when they were still lip-locked fifteen seconds later, Duchess cleared her throat.

"Dawn isn't *that* far off, you two," she pointed out, and felt a brief, unworthy flash of satisfaction at the twin expressions of embarrassment that flared through the bond.

"Right," Oksana said, breaking away from Mason and clearing her throat. "Yes. Traveling now."

Duchess shook her head and took a deep breath, pulling her life force inward with one sharp jerk. She felt the rest of her body follow and hurtled off into the night sky. Oksana and Mason streaked along behind her. She could sense their thoughts and essences more powerfully in this form, and she knew that something about her bond with Oksana had changed. She was so closely intermingled with Mason these days, that at times it was hard to tell them apart.

*That should not matter to you. What business is it of yours?* Duchess thought, irritated with herself. It took almost all of her concentration to shield her thoughts when in this non-corporeal form. Yet, despite this fact, it still felt as though a wall had risen between the two of them. The question she was unwilling to examine too closely was whether the wall was on Oksana's side… or on hers.

Duchess had a sudden—and rather farcical—vision of her and Snag holed up somewhere in a dark room, bemoaning their lack of mates like a pair of old maids. It was a disturbing enough mental image that she vowed to find as many random partners as possible for mind-numbing, meaningless sex and feeding just as soon as she had a free moment in Kuala Lumpur.

A few hours later, Duchess sensed light and life ahead of them. The capital of Malaysia was a massive city—one of the fastest growing metropolitan regions in Asia. She sought out a quiet, shadowed place near the outskirts where they would not be observed and led the way lower. With an outward pressure on her life force, Duchess burst into human form as she leapt lightly down to the ground. Oksana materialized right next to her an instant later.

With an *unff!* Mason popped into existence and tumbled into a heap on the ground. Unable to stop herself, Duchess let out a snort of laughter and shook her head.

*Baby vampires are hilarious,* she thought, making only a cursory effort to keep from broadcasting the observation. Mason, distinctly red in the face, scrambled to his feet. Duchess tossed him his rucksack, and he caught the bag awkwardly against his chest.

"Well, that was certainly humiliating," he said as he brushed himself off.

"Trynn was worse to begin with." Duchess offered the words like an olive branch, burying her amusement. "She still ends up flat on her face half of the time."

Oksana patted him on the back. "I'll tell you about Della's first attempt one of these days. That was... memorable."

Mason managed a rueful half-smile. "All right, you two. Consider my bruised ego sufficiently bandaged." He huffed. "At least my *actual* bruises heal in seconds, now. Come on—let's go. Hotel first, I assume?"

"Yes," Duchess agreed.

"Can you get contact information for Haziq's family from Gita?" Oksana asked. "That's probably the easiest way to start."

"I don't see why not," Mason said. "We're... what? Twelve hours ahead of Haiti? So, it should be afternoon there. I'll call her as soon as we're settled."

Despite the darkness, there seemed to be a large number of people out walking on the streets. The atmosphere was restless. Watchful. Something about it made Duchess' spine tingle. It reminded her of—

"Is it just me, or is anyone else getting flashbacks to that night in Port-au-Prince, right after the earthquake?" Mason asked, interrupting her thoughts.

Before either she or Oksana could reply, two men stepped out of the shadows of an alley, streetlights glinting off the steel blades in their hands. The pedestrians around them scattered, but it was immediately clear that she and her companions, with their obviously foreign features, were the targets. Both humans appeared to be of Chinese descent, a fact that was confirmed when the one on the left spoke with a thick Cantonese accent.

"Oy, *gweilo*," he snapped, his focus on Mason. "Speak English? Give us your money, or we cut up your pretty girls."

Mason blinked. "*Seriously*? No offense, mate, but you really have no idea what kind of shit you're about to step in."

Duchess was not in a great mood by this point, but she still recognized that teaching moments were important—especially for baby vampires. She stepped forward and knocked the knife from the hand of the would-be mugger on the right before grabbing him by the throat and slamming him up against the wall of the alley, where they would be hidden from casual view by other people on the street.

"Practice time, *Docteur*," she said, her eyes blazing into those of the human she was holding. He went very quiet, like a cornered rabbit. "The other one is yours."

She could sense Oksana poised nearby, ready to jump in like a hovering mother hen with one chick. To his credit, though, Mason didn't hesitate. She glanced quickly back at him, to see his eyes glinting like sunlight on blue steel.

"Right," he said. "Back into the alley, slowly. And you want to put that knife down now."

There was the briefest of hesitations, but then shuffling footsteps sounded and something metallic clattered to the ground.

"Good," Mason said. "Now, you and your friend are going to stop robbing people. If you need food or a place to stay, go to social services and ask for help."

Duchess managed not to roll her eyes. Barely.

"It doesn't really work that way, Mason," Oksana said. "You can't influence them to do things they don't want to, once they're away from you. You'd need Snag's kind of power for that."

Duchess dragged her captive around until she could glare at both muggers.

"Run away now," she snarled. "And forget any of this happened."

She let go of the throat she was holding, and both humans hared off like the flames of hell were licking at their heels. When they were gone, she raised an eyebrow at Mason.

"Not too bad. But don't overreach yourself."

Mason scrubbed a hand over his scalp. "I cannot count the number of times in my life when that ability would have come in insanely useful."

"Hotel?" Oksana asked, sounding as tired as Duchess suddenly felt.

"Hotel," she agreed.

They checked into the first place they found that didn't look like an utter shithole, and booked a double since that was what was available. It wasn't completely awful. There was a small bathroom adjacent to the sleeping area. The two beds were full sized. The room was dimly lit but seemed comfortable enough and free of insects.

Mason flopped face down on the far mattress without ceremony. "Ugh. I don't know if it's just the remnants of my humanity, or if I'm a terrible vampire, but I still get tired after dark," he said, speaking into the bedding.

Oksana perched at his side, stretching. She slid a hand up and down the length of his spine, and he made a noise like a contented cat. "Well," she said, "you spent your entire life going to sleep in the evening and waking up in the morning. Your biological clock is probably confused."

"Not true," Mason answered, the words still muffled. "My residency was almost exclusively at night. I was never lucky enough to land the day shifts."

"Then you don't have much of an excuse," Duchess said, "beyond the fact that you just flew three hundred-fifty kilometers in four hours."

"Yeah, you're probably right," he murmured. "I just need a couple of minutes to shut my eyes, and then I'll call Gita."

-o-o-o-

True to his word, Mason dragged himself up a short time later and called Gita, even though he still felt like he'd run here from Singapore on foot rather than flying. His old friend was relieved and more than a little thankful to hear that they were in Kuala Lumpur and planning on making their own investigations. She was also quick to give him every bit of contact information and background that might conceivably come in helpful, which he jotted down on a notepad next to the phone. When he was done, he gave into Oksana's pointed look and fed on some of the blood Jackson's wife had sent with them. Then, he sat down with the other two, so they could discuss their plan of action.

"I really want to get to know the city first," Duchess said, standing alone by the window and looking out at the pouring rain. The skies had opened half an hour previously and showed no signs of slowing anytime soon, despite it not technically being the rainy season. "That would be most helpful to me. I need to get a feel for the place."

Mason looked at her, aware that he was unsuccessful in keeping an air of skepticism out of his reply. "Um, all right. Well… while you're *sensing the city*, I'm going to talk to Haziq's colleagues at the hospital where he worked. Gita told me that he was abducted just after a shift, so maybe one of his co-workers saw something."

Maybe Mason just hadn't gotten used to Duchess' ways yet, but there were times when it felt like she was more *alien* than vampire. What did she hope to accomplish by wandering aimlessly through a city of a million and a half people?

Duchess pulled the notepad toward her with a manicured fingertip and frowned down at it. "You have the hospital's address here?" Her eyebrows went up. "*Mon Dieu, Docteur*—this is the sort of penmanship only a medical professional can get away with."

"Okay, you two, let's have a *bit* of peace on earth," Oksana interjected wearily. "At least in here, all right?"

Not wanting to put Oksana in an awkward position between his and Duchess' sniping, Mason smiled wryly. "Of course, sweetheart. Sorry, Duchess—I'm sure that getting a feel for the city is a good idea. And, yes, poor penmanship is an actual class in medical school. Hadn't you heard? They don't give you a diploma until you pass it."

Duchess looked at him for a long moment, and then sighed. "Forgive my short temper, both of you. We will find your friend's son, Mason."

Shortly before dawn, the three of them went their separate ways— Mason to talk to Haziq's coworkers, Oksana to meet with his family, and Duchess to seek out the militant Buddhist cult thought to be behind the kidnapping. This was actually the first time he and Oksana had been apart for any length of time since Haiti, he realized. He found that being away from her was… strange. Still, knowing that he had his new mental abilities available, Mason tried to subtly reach out and touch Oksana's mind as she left for the central part of the city.

He sensed her mental flinch and knew that, once again, he'd been too heavy handed. *Damn it.*

Her reply was soft and warm. *You're getting better at it, really,* she assured him from over a block away, and he could feel the smile in her mental voice like the memory of sunlight. *Just try to relax. It should be light and easy.*

Mason smiled despite himself. *Easy for you to say, sweetheart. You've been doing this for hundreds of years.*

The impression of an impish wink washed over his mind, and his smile grew wider. *Practice makes perfect,* she said.

It took Mason only a few minutes to fly to Haziq's clinic. Of course, he then made the mistake of returning to human form while still outside. Even though he was only a few steps away from the entrance, by the time he slipped inside, he was completely drenched.

*Note to self: in future, fly inside as mist and change back to human form in a storage cupboard or something. Or else, bring along an umbrella.*

With nothing else for it, he slogged up to the visitors' desk staffed by two nurses.

"Can I help you?" one of them asked in English as he approached. Her accent was very good, giving Mason the impression that she'd been raised or at least trained somewhere in the West.

"Yes, I'm Dr. Mason Walker. I'm a colleague of Dr. Belawan's mother. I was hoping to find someone to talk to about what happened to Haziq a couple of days ago."

The nurse's face grew troubled. She glanced at her colleague nervously and gestured for Mason to step into the hallway.

As he followed her through the doorway, he became aware of the thrum of her pulse beneath the skin of her throat. To his disgust, he felt a sudden urge to feed despite the bagged blood he'd had earlier. He pushed it away ruthlessly.

*Not happening,* he thought. Even after feeding several times from Jackson over the past few weeks, he wasn't sure if he would ever truly get used to the idea of drinking blood from humans. It had honestly been a relief when Xander had floated the idea of no longer hunting humans for blood, though he knew it further complicated their already complicated lives.

The nurse let the door swing shut behind them and glanced at him with anxious eyes.

"Why are you inquiring about Haziq?" she asked, clearly wary.

Mason's brow furrowed. "Do you know something about what happened?"

The woman pressed her lips together. "Answer me first. Why do you come here asking these questions?"

"I thought that would be obvious," he said. "He's a good man, and now he's been kidnapped."

But she continued to stare hard at him, as if expecting a different answer.

After a few moments of awkward silence, Mason rubbed the back of his neck with a weary hand.

"Look," he said, "it's like I just told you, I'm a friend of Haziq's mother. She's extremely worried and I thought that I might ask around, you know? In a hospital as busy as this, someone is bound to have seen something."

"And you think you can do something the police can't?" The woman demanded in a sharp voice.

Mason considered her for a moment. He couldn't read her mind like he could another vampire's, but pain and loss seemed to hang around her like a cloud.

"You cared for him," he said in a soft voice. "Didn't you?"

The woman looked away quickly, but not before Mason saw the tears welling in her eyes.

"Yes," she finally replied, "of course I cared for him. There's not a person in this hospital who didn't care about Haziq. He was an amazing doctor."

The woman turned away and walked towards a small, empty office. He followed her inside, and she flopped down in the chair behind the desk. She gestured for Mason to sit across from her.

"Tell me more about him," he prompted as he took the offered seat.

A single tear trickled down her face as she stared silently out the rain-washed window for several moments.

"Haziq was my friend. I came here through the American Peace Corps and fell in love with Kuala Lumpur. Even after my rotation was over, I opted to stay behind and work in this hospital. Haziq loved this place just as much. He always told me he felt more alive while helping the children here than he had anywhere else. He was a brilliant doctor; he could've made huge money in another country. He knew that, but he still chose to remain here with us."

"You're using the past tense a lot," Mason pointed out. "Do you mean to say you think he's dead?"

The nurse looked at him, moisture glistening in her eyes. "You don't?"

Mason shook his head. "No, I don't. I refuse to believe that's the case until I see incontrovertible proof. Right now, I'm looking into it under the assumption that he's simply missing."

"Then you should be commended for your hope, because the rest of us have none."

"Why do you say that?" Mason asked, not understanding how his friends and colleagues could have given up on Haziq so easily.

"The *Brotherhood*." The words were a whisper, even though they were alone in the small office. It was as though she thought invisible ears might still overhear them.

Mason had no such concerns. "The Brotherhood? That's the group the police think kidnapped him? What about them?"

"They're growing in size and strength every day. More and more people gather at the Thean Hou Temple every night to listen to the monks espousing hatred and violence. Any that oppose them are captured and killed. They hang the bodies from trees in the swamps outside the city as a warning. The police are too scared to stop them."

Mason felt a sinking feeling in the pit of his stomach. "Has anyone here seen Haziq's body?"

The nurse shook her head. "No, not yet. We can't bear to go look, but it's only a matter of time."

# FIVE

"I am sorry to bother you during this difficult time," Oksana said, sitting on the small couch in the front room of Haziq's house. His wife, Jayda, sat ashen-faced in a chair across from her. With trembling fingers, Jayda handed Oksana a cup of tea on a delicate saucer.

"No, no," she murmured in lightly accented English, pausing to sip from her own cup. "I appreciate the company, believe me. Many of Haziq's friends and associates have been by, bringing me food and offering comfort."

Oksana could sense despair from the woman. It was clear she'd given up all hope, despite the police insistence that her husband might still be alive.

"You don't hold out hope of getting him back safely?" she asked Jayda.

Jayda gave her a brief, sad smile and brushed a tear from the corner of her eye. "No, not really. His colleagues think he angered the Brotherhood after he volunteered in the emergency room at the hospital. Several people had been publically tortured at a rally, and Haziq helped treat their injuries. Afterward, he wrote an editorial letter to the Star newspaper denouncing the growing religious violence. So... members of the cult took him from the parking lot as he was leaving work. There were several witnesses—it was obvious they wanted to make an example of him."

Her voice grew ragged on the last sentence, and she wiped her eyes again. Oksana sat back thoughtfully.

"That seems like a reasonable supposition, but I'm not so ready to give up on him. I'm trying to understand the impetus behind this cult. Can you tell me what else you know about them?"

Jayda swirled her cup, staring into the dregs seemingly without seeing them. "It is a bold group, and an angry one. How it started, I really can't say. It seemed like they simply exploded onto the scene overnight. One day it was whispers of a new religious group, and the next it was public torture and executions, extortion, terror… the cult's leaders are well versed in all the tactics of fear, it seems."

"Why do people follow them?" Oksana asked. "What do they hope to gain?"

"The monks shout aloud what some people have been whispering for a long time. They talk about change, which I suppose is needed, but I think they've been really effective at targeting a group that feels like they've been victimized. They paint a picture of revenge paired with new power and wealth. There are a lot of angry people in Malaysia—Chinese immigrants who feel disenfranchised and downtrodden by the Malay majority."

"There are a lot of angry people everywhere, these days. But that does sound like an effective way to throw gasoline on a fire," Oksana mused.

"It is," Jayda nodded. "The world today frightens me. I didn't know how we would be able to keep our children safe, even before this happened to us. Now, I have no idea what I'll do on my own."

"Maybe you won't have to do it alone," Oksana said quietly. "Tell me about the day Haziq was kidnapped."

Jayda sighed. "It was just a normal day, like any other. He left for the hospital early, while I left the children with their nanny and went to work for the morning. I got the call that afternoon. He'd been taken from the parking lot in broad daylight."

"Didn't anyone try to stop the abduction?" Oksana asked, surprised. She'd been imagining a nighttime snatch-and-grab operation. This daylight kidnapping in plain view of witnesses spoke to a whole different level of boldness.

"No," Jayda shook her head. "No one would dare. People are too scared. They're afraid they'd be next. It was sheer luck that someone even bothered to call the police."

"Did you talk to the police yourself? File a missing person report?"

"Yes, I filed one that same afternoon. It seemed very... *perfunctory*, though. I am certain they already know where and how he was taken. And that nothing will come of it."

"You think the police will ignore the report?"

"You misunderstand me," Jayda murmured, her eyes downcast. "I think they will do nothing because they believe he's already dead."

"They've said otherwise, though. Haven't they?" Oksana insisted. It was horrible to see the pain that Jayda was going through, yet Oksana could not give up hope so easily. She would not abandon Haziq if there was even the slightest chance that he was alive.

"Of course they would say that, to try to keep me from becoming hysterical during the interview." Her voice was bitter. "But no one comes back after being taken by the Brotherhood. Haziq is strong, but how can I bear to have hope when no one ever comes back alive?"

"If he's anything like his mother," Oksana replied, "then he's both smart and stubborn."

More tears spilled onto Jayda's cheeks as she looked at Oksana. "That is certainly true. But—"

Oksana cut her off gently. "So, believe that he hasn't given up and that he won't stop fighting. Don't give up on him, because I bet he'll never give up on you. Mason and I won't give up on him either."

Jayda gulped back a sob and set her cup down on the coffee table with delicate care. She stared without blinking at the ground for long moments, clearly trying to rein in her emotions.

"You remind me of him," she whispered eventually. "That's why we're here—because he refused to give up on this city. He said the hospital needed him, and he thrived on helping others."

"That same strength will carry him through this. I know it," Oksana insisted.

Jayda swallowed hard. "I hope you're right, Oksana. I really do. I'm... just trying to be realistic."

Oksana stood and placed her cup next to Jayda's. "I understand. You just worry about yourself and your children for now. Let us worry about finding Haziq and bringing him back to you."

Jayda looked at her. "Hope is a cruel mistress. I appreciate what you're trying to do, but you don't know how it's been around here lately. Bodies in the streets. People disappearing every single day and never coming back."

Oksana suppressed a shiver. She knew all too well about those things... and worse. Again, she wondered if Duchess was being straight with them about her sense of what was going on in Kuala Lumpur. Was it just the same general chaos that was spreading across the globe in a slow march... or something more?

Oksana reached over and gripped Jayda's hand, staring at her with a level gaze. "I do know how it's been, Jayda. And even knowing that, you have my word. My friends and I won't stop until Haziq is found and—spirits willing—returned safely to you."

A flicker of painful hope passed across Jayda's drawn features, and she squeezed Oksana's hand in return. "Thank you. Please, though... try to keep yourselves safe. The last thing Haziq would want is someone else getting hurt while trying to save him."

-o-o-o-

Duchess slipped into a small shop that was mercifully empty of customers. She could hear that the shop owner was just out of sight in the next room, but she did not call for assistance. She merely needed to get away from the sense of chaos swirling around in her head for a few moments.

Pressing her fingers to her temples, she tried to block out the feeling.

As she walked through the city, the undercurrents of turmoil and barely suppressed violence were eerily reminiscent of New Orleans and Haiti. That fact had implications she wasn't ready to examine too closely yet. She'd been eager enough to come here from Singapore, and she told herself it was because she was tired of cooling her heels — doing nothing of use besides watching the news reports.

Was she deluding herself, though? Had she been drawn here for a different reason? Duchess grunted in disgust as she tried to shake free of the cloud of clutching evil present on the streets of Kuala Lumpur.

"Can I help you?" the shop owner asked in Malay.

Duchess looked up, surprised by the man's approach. Such distraction from her surroundings was a bad sign. After spending several hours letting the city's aura permeate her awareness, it was clear her senses were rattled.

"Oh," she answered, clearing her throat. "No, just getting out of the rain."

Unfortunately, her speaking skills in Malay were not quite as good as her comprehension and reading skills, but apparently, she'd at least gotten the gist across. To back up her story, she brushed off water that had soaked her rain jacket.

The owner looked at her and raised an eyebrow.

"We don't often see tourists in this neighborhood," he said crossing to the counter. "Especially with the violence in this part of the city. You'd do well to find a safer place, or at least stay in a group with other people when you venture out."

Duchess took a long slow breath and managed to block out the rest of the chaos, concentrating only on the shopkeeper in front of her. He was middle-aged, but he'd obviously kept up his health and appearance. To her mild relief, she found that his thoughts were slow and calm, matching his speech. She could sense concern, but also a cloak of peace that seemed at odds with his dire warnings.

"I've heard about that, yes," Duchess admitted, feeling him out. "So far, I've been lucky, though. I haven't seen anything."

He nodded thoughtfully. "Hmm. Well, hopefully your luck continues."

Figuring that she might as well take advantage of a person who wanted to talk, she walked toward the sales counter, letting a bit of sensuality color her movements. The man maintained his pleasant and respectful demeanor... but he still looked at her with an appreciative eye. People *always* looked.

*And where would I be if they didn't?* she thought.

"My name is Duchess," she said in a low voice. She allowed some of her hypnotic force to bleed through into her words, making them impossible for him to ignore.

"It is my pleasure to meet you," the man responded with a slight bow of the head. His pupils dilated in the harsh, overhead strip lighting. "I am Raahim, at your service."

"Well, Raahim," Duchess said. "Maybe you could tell me what else I should do to stay safe in this city. I'm not looking for trouble."

Despite the mild daze she'd put him under, a faint smile tugged at his lips—as though he doubted her words. "Am I to take it that trouble often finds you, regardless?"

"Oh, yes," she answered. "Inevitably."

He nodded and leaned towards her over the counter, resting his elbows on the wood.

"Well, in that case, you should avoid crowded places after dark," he advised, staring straight into her eyes. "Especially the local mosques."

"Why?"

Raahim cocked his head. "The Brotherhood has taken issue with men and women of Muslim faith. Our places of worship are too often the targets of brutal attacks these days."

"Really? But Malaysia is majority Muslim. Why doesn't the government step in?" Duchess asked.

"The government fears escalating the tensions into full-blown civil war."

"Fools," Duchess breathed. As though one could look at the world and not understand that without action, things would only get worse as time went on.

"Perhaps they are foolish," Raahim said. "Or perhaps they are correct. As it is, though, things continue to escalate. One attack must always be bigger and more frightening than the last."

"How long has this been going on?"

"Long enough that many of our citizens are becoming numb to the violence. But recently, it has become much worse. One would think that the Brotherhood has lost all fear of reprisal."

Duchess nodded, allowing her long, blonde hair to fall over her shoulders in waves. Raahim's eyes followed the movement in fascination.

"Do you know anything more about it?" she asked, knowing that he was hers now, to do with as she wished. Somehow, the thought did not bring the same satisfaction that it might have brought in the past.

"I do not," he said. "I try to stay out of the politics and extremism—as much as one can these days. I'm a merchant. I simply want to do business and make an honest living."

She could sense that he was telling the truth. And—now that she had extracted as much information from him as she could—it was time to satisfy another need.

"I'm so grateful that you took the time to talk to me," Duchess said, leaning forward with one hand braced on the counter. "I'll try very hard to stay out of trouble—*I promise.*"

Raahim leaned forward as well, closing his eyes as she lifted her other hand to cup his cheek. He sighed in pleasure as her lips latched onto the skin of his throat, fangs extending to pierce the delicate flesh.

-o-o-o-

Some time later, Duchess reconvened with the others in their hotel room to exchange information. Both Oksana and Mason had been busy, taking advantage of the heavy clouds that kept the sun at bay. Between the three of them, a familiar narrative was beginning to emerge.

"… and Jayda is sure that his kidnapping has something to do with her husband's critical editorial piece in the newspaper, so it doesn't look like this was a random abduction," Oksana finished, leaning back in the wooden chair by the desk. "That's pretty much all I've got, I'm afraid."

"That jives with what Haziq's co-workers told me," Mason affirmed from his perch on the edge of the nearest bed. "This group is serious about dissuading anyone from speaking out against them. Now, don't get me wrong—I refuse to give up on him until I see proof that we're too late; that they've already killed him. But these are some scary blokes. It's obvious they don't shrink from murder for murder's sake."

Duchess had resumed her place at the window, staring out into the dark clouds that still swirled over the city. She was silent for a long time, reflecting on the information they'd gathered.

"I think," she said after a while, "that we need to go deeper."

Mason and Oksana regarded her, clearly waiting for her to elaborate.

Duchess looked straight at Oksana and said, "You aren't going to like my next idea."

Oksana sighed in resignation. "Really, *ti mwen*? You shock me."

"There is something more here than is visible on the surface. I want the head of this cult."

A finely swept black eyebrow lifted. "Of course you do."

Duchess lifted an answering brow, not backing down. "I need your help."

"Of course you do," Mason echoed.

Duchess turned a haughty stare on the two younger vampires. "I'm going to infiltrate the cult tonight. It may be a day or so before I can return. While I'm gone, I want you two to get as much information as you can about this *Brotherhood* from law enforcement officials."

"I told you, Jayda doesn't think they'll follow up on what she —" Oksana started.

Duchess shook her head. "I know, *ma petite*. But I still want you to try. Just because the police choose not to act, it doesn't mean they won't have other information that could be useful."

Mason glanced at his watch. "I suppose with the storm clouds overhead and the buildings being packed so closely together, we could go there now if we were careful to keep to the shadows."

Oksana gave Duchess a long, penetrating look. Finally, Duchess could sense her friend giving way.

*I don't like this,* Oksana said, for her ears alone.

*I know you don't,* Duchess replied in the same manner.

"Let's go then," Oksana said, and Mason nodded. The pair gathered a few things and turned to leave, opening the door and stepping into the hallway. Just before Oksana let the door swing shut, she paused to give Duchess a final, lingering stare.

"Don't make us have to come rescue you," she said, her tone deceptively light.

Duchess canted a tight smile in her direction. "Me? I wouldn't dream of it, *ma chère*."

# Six

Night was finally falling, a relief even with the unrelenting cloud cover. Duchess found a deserted alley and solidified from mist into human form. Emerging from the shadows at last, she wandered the streets in the Brickfields neighborhood north of the Thean Hou Temple, where Mason had reported the Brotherhood held frequent rallies. The area had once been vibrant—a cultural center for the Indian and Ceylonese immigrants who had come to work in the late 19th-century brick-making kilns that supplied building materials for the city's explosive growth.

The Buddhist influence here was readily apparent in the large number of temples dotted amongst the Indian restaurants and spice shops. When she'd been here twenty years ago, it had also been home to the hundred-year-old historic YMCA building, several Christian churches of various denominations, and a mosque. The place had teemed with life, exuding that extreme vibrancy which seemed unique to the growing Asian mega-cities in the first decade of the twenty-first century.

Now, the vibrancy was muted under a layer of fear. Again, Duchess was reminded of New Orleans. Of Port-au-Prince. The knowledge lodged in the pit of her stomach, making her feel like she'd tried to swallow solid food rather than blood.

It was far from deserted, but the people around her were tense. A nearly palpable aura of distrust and anger choked the air. There appeared to be a growing current of pedestrians heading south, toward the Brotherhood's base of operations at the temple, so she melted into the groups of people and followed the crowds. A few around her shot nervous or hostile glances at her pale skin and hair, but in the emotionally charged atmosphere it was easy enough to let her power unfold around her, convincing them that they had been mistaken and there was nothing unusual in her being here.

The growing crowd spilled onto Jalan Permai road, dense buildings and gray pavement giving way to vibrant green as palm trees rose around them. The thick growth on either side of the road gave one the illusion of having been transported to another time… another realm. The road widened into a parking area choked with cars, motorcycles, scooters, and lorries, but still surrounded on all sides by trees and brush. The crowd rounded a bend in the road and the temple appeared, lit by torches, its facade and intricate pagoda roof done up in brilliant shades of red, orange, and white.

A raised stage had been erected near the base of the double staircase leading up to the entrance. Duchess slipped into the trees at the edge of the large courtyard and transformed into an owl. From a perch high up in the palm fronds, she surveyed the growing crowd of spectators, easily over a thousand strong with more pouring in every moment. She scanned her surroundings continuously, taking advantage of the elevated position and her enhanced sight and hearing.

A monk with the light of fanaticism in his eyes took the stage and began to speak. All eyes were on him, despite the presence of several other men hanging back in the shadows at the rear of the dais. Unsurprisingly, the monk's speech was soaked in violence, intolerance, and the lust for blood. Some of the people listening shifted restlessly, as though the rhetoric made them nervous or uncomfortable. But a majority of the listeners were clearly there to satisfy their own need for savagery, and the monk delivered it with obvious relish.

Enthusiastic shouts of agreement filled the courtyard, nearly deafening in their intensity. But then, Duchess became aware of something else tickling the edges of her mind. Familiar, but not. And it was shocking enough—once she realized what it was—to make her nearly topple from her perch. That brush of mental energy came from another vampiric presence.

A vampiric presence *that she didn't recognize.*

It wasn't Mason. It most definitely wasn't Oksana, who Duchess could recognize as easily as she recognized her own face in a mirror.

*Another vampire? How was that even possible?*

She concentrated all her mental power on the presence. No, it was not one of the others. Nor was it Snag. This was definitely a vampire she had never met before. She strained to understand the thoughts flickering at the edges of her awareness. They were confused, distant—filtering to her as though through a dense fog. Those thoughts sounded… very young.

And perhaps she had her answer. A young vampire… a *vampire child*. Of course.

*Can you hear me?* Duchess called across the mental connection.

Although this vampire had never fed from her and they did not have the same bond she had with the others of her coven, Duchess was certain he would be able to make out her words over such a short distance. There was no direct response, but Duchess thought his attention flickered in her direction. And the more closely she focused on his life force, the more certain she felt that there *was*, in fact, something familiar about the feel of his mind.

Roars and applause broke out in the watching crowd, snapping her focus away from the shadowy presence. Something was happening on the platform. Still in owl form, Duchess flapped silently to a new vantage point closer to the raised stage, but remaining within the shelter of the trees. The warrior monk turned, and a small form emerged from the shadows behind him. It was the same presence she'd just felt.

A young boy stepped forward, draped in orange robes. He had a very slight build and round, Tibetan features. His head had been completely shaved to match the other monks'.

*Sangye Rinchen.* It had to be.

With his eyes closed, the child lifted his hands towards the sky.

He was silent, but the monk who had whipped the crowd into a frenzy cried, "We will usher in a new era of prosperity and power, once we rid this city and this nation of the worthless filth polluting it!"

The boy opened his eyes. They glowed brightly in the dark—burning like embers, flickering red in the night as he gazed imperiously over the crowd. Duchess could not look away from him. She was both captivated by his presence here and repulsed at his inclusion within this farce of a rally.

Why was he helping the Brotherhood, even tacitly? He was a *vampire*. Xander and his mate Manisha reported that Sangye had been starving himself in London, making him too weak to fight or escape his captors. But he was not weak now. Power nearly crackled from his slight form. Nothing prevented him from transforming into mist and disappearing into the night this very instant. And yet, he did not.

The monk began to speak again, further inciting the crowd's passion. The mob fed off the aura that radiated from the boy. He said no word, but his presence filled the courtyard like the electric potential of an approaching thunderstorm, and even Duchess was not immune. Yet her fascination had nothing to do with the violent rhetoric being spewed from the stage. It was all for the child. He was a study in contradictions—both young and old, familiar and strange, inexperienced and powerful.

*Could he be the answer to all we seek? Or is he a fresh danger to us?*

She desperately needed to talk to him. She had to get him alone, so she could find out what he was doing here, and how he'd come to be here. Because the last time any of their number had seen this child, he'd been in the company of Bastian Kovac, the demon Bael… *and Snag*.

Rushing in would be foolish. She was no reckless youth, to act without thinking. She knew nothing about the child's loyalties or even his mental state. Manisha thought he was the reincarnation of the Dalai Lama, but he was also a little boy—and he'd been whisked away by a demon and a sadistic madman. They'd had him under their complete control for weeks now. She had no way of knowing what they'd done to him… whether he would consider her a friend or a foe.

Common sense took over. She knew that he was aware of her presence, just as she was aware of his. She would try to learn more before seeking to confront him directly. If nothing else, there was still Haziq to consider—she'd learned nothing of use regarding his condition or whereabouts. Not wanting to risk drawing attention, Duchess concentrated and pulled her life force into a tight knot in her chest. She transformed into mist, which would free her to move around without detection.

The rally rose to a crescendo before finally winding down. The child disappeared inside a side door leading into the temple, while the speaker and most of his entourage embarked with considerably more pomp and fanfare.

Duchess circled, still in vaporous form, and spotted a man from the head monk's retinue who was moving in the opposite direction from the others, clear purpose in his stride. He pushed his way through groups of people and did not stop to cheer or clap as the others nearby did.

Under the circumstances, she decided she could do worse than finding out what his errand was. She materialized into human form in the shadows and slipped after him on silent feet. While her beauty normally drew quite a bit of attention, stealth had always been a particular talent of hers when she cared to employ it, and she did so now.

The man slipped into a large complex of buildings about a block from the temple. They were close enough that the sounds of the crowd were still audible behind them. Duchess slipped into a recessed area between two of the buildings, completely hidden in the darkness. With her sharp hearing, she could make out the low voices of two individuals standing in the doorway of the building in front of her.

Most of the older vampires had picked up a number of languages over the centuries, out of some combination of interest, practicality, and boredom. Duchess was no exception, and that hobby came in useful as she came within hearing range of the men's conversation.

"Any new orders?" one of them inquired in Cantonese.

"He wants us to move the new hostage to the far end of the compound," the man Duchess had followed replied. Although they were keeping their voices quiet, Duchess could tell that neither of them was particularly concerned about being overheard.

"I wish he'd make up his mind," the first man grumbled. "This guy is trouble and I'm tired of carting him around."

"Hmm. Got a fighter this time, eh?" the second man said, mild amusement coloring his voice.

"Seems like it. I don't know—I complain about him, but in a way it's kind of nice to see some spirit for once."

The other man chuckled. "Spirit? Don't get used to it. I doubt it'll last long in this place."

Duchess felt her expression sharpen. How many new hostages were the Brotherhood likely to have? Could it be Haziq they were discussing? That seemed like quite a coincidence, on the one hand, but on the other hand, it made sense that if a new prisoner was causing trouble, the cult leader might have him moved to a more secure place of confinement. It was certainly worth following up, since that was the reason she'd come here in the first place.

The two men turned and entered the building, still chatting as they disappeared through the open door. Duchess darted forward with inhuman speed to catch it an instant before it could close and latch behind them. Holding her breath, she reached out with her senses and found that neither man had paused to make sure the door locked properly. They were already moving deeper into the building.

When she was sure that the way was clear, she slipped inside and allowed the door to slip fully shut behind her. Following the receding sound of the humans' footsteps, Duchess moved along behind them cautiously, pausing at every door and junction to ensure she was not seen. The footsteps grew fainter and she paused in the hallway, listening intently.

A door opened and closed somewhere ahead of her, but it echoed strangely, making the location impossible to pinpoint. There was no movement, no voices, nothing to guide her any further. She continued in the direction she'd been going, so focused on detecting any movement in the distance that she didn't pay close enough attention to her immediate surroundings. She had only an instant to register the indrawn breath and the sound of a steady heartbeat inside the room she'd just passed, before a body exploded into action behind her. A metal bar flashed across her vision, settling under her chin with surprising speed and force. Before she could slip free, a strong tug on the bar jerked her backwards through the open door by her neck.

The pressure on her windpipe would have been immediately debilitating to a human. Even as a vampire, it was a struggle to overcome the long-buried human instinct to panic at the feeling of her trachea being crushed. With a movement too quick for the man to avoid, Duchess landed a solid elbow blow to her attacker's stomach and was rewarded with a satisfying *oof* sound as the air left his lungs.

As the man fought not to double over in pain, the pressure on her windpipe eased for an instant. Duchess swung her legs up and planted her feet on the wall next to the door. With all the force she could muster, she propelled her weight backwards, sending them both crashing to the floor.

The man lost his grip on the metal bar as they went down. Duchess took advantage of the reprieve to twist so that she faced her assailant. As his head slammed on the clay tile floor behind him, Duchess jerked away, freeing herself from the close-quarters grappling.

Her limbs were quivering with reaction from the surprise attack, but she pushed power into them from her center. With a snarl, she reached down and hauled the man up by his shirtfront. Her strength flowed around the room, the air crackling with electricity.

"Enough," she hissed, feeling her fangs lengthen.

The man smirked, his dark eyes narrowed. "Not quite."

Duchess cocked her head and as she blinked, he moved. A gun barrel materialized inches from her face.

*Merde*. He was fast for a human.

After a split second's calculation of her chances in a fight while healing from a bullet wound through the face, she released the fabric clenched in her hand and took one step back. His expression was cold as he planted his feet and rolled his neck, vertebra cracking. She widened her eyes, playing the frightened captive as she prepared to mesmerize him.

"That's better," he said in Cantonese. "Now, let's start with who you are and…"

He fell silent, staring at Duchess with a strange, blank expression sliding over his strong features. The gun, which had been pointed at the center of her forehead, dipped slowly towards the floor.

Duchess gaped at him, taken aback. She hadn't exerted her power, yet he was acting like someone else had taken control of his will.

"I have a message for you," he said in a distant monotone.

Her gaze sharpened. "Do you, indeed?"

He was staring blankly into the middle distance, like he could no longer see her standing right in front of him.

*How interesting...*

Duchess reached out mentally, hoping to get a sense of the man's mind, but all she met was a completely blank wall. It was as though he were deep in a trance, without a hint of thought or emotion leaking through. She could sense nothing from him at all.

His lips parted. "Sangye is not the Thirteenth," he said in a monotone. "Bael is attempting to draw the Angel out of hiding, but he does not understand."

Silence descended for a long moment after the flat, distant words faded away. Duchess raised her eyebrows, perplexed.

"Who told you to say that?" Duchess asked cautiously. There were an extremely limited number of people in the world who could have implanted such a message. The most obvious culprit was the boy Sangye. But... did he have the power and skill to do so? Did he even know about the prophecy? A hundred questions swirled around her mind as she stared at the blank-faced human before her.

"Who are you?" Duchess demanded. "How did you know to tell me this?"

The man's arms dropped to his sides, the gun held loosely in his right hand. He made no answer and didn't even blink.

Duchess let out a growl of frustration. "Oh, come now! You've got to give me more than that. What do you know of the Thirteen? What do you know of the Angel?"

He still gave no reply, continuing to stand as if turned to stone.

Duchess felt her temper crackle, anger rising at whoever would plant such a cryptic message in a random human cult member and provide no further useful information beyond a riddle. She reached out and grabbed the man's throat, intending to shake him out of his stupor. Her fingers touched the exposed skin above the collar of his long-sleeved shirt. A sensation like an electric current passed through her, jolting all of her senses and sending her staggering backward a step. She stared down at her offending hand like it belonged to someone else.

"No," she whispered, unable to say anything more as memories rose up like brackish floodwater, choking her.

-o-o-o-

*"No!" she screamed into the darkness. "I will not serve you, demon! I will not kill the father of my child!"*

*"Marie, do as the creature says!" her beloved Bertrand cried, thrashing on the ground. His spine arched in agony. A terrible gurgling noise came from his throat, right before blood erupted from his eyes and ears.*

*She stood over her fallen husband, facing the dark cloud that shifted and swirled around them. Marie could see glowing eyes within the mist and the vague outline of a huge, monstrous form with the head of a toad. A scratching noise filled the air around her, like millions of spiders crawling over plaster walls. The putrid smell of the black fog made her retch.*

*"Please," Bertrand whimpered, his voice growing weak. "Please, Marie, you must save yourself. Think of our child. Please!"*

*Marie wrapped her arms around her swollen stomach, feeling their child moving inside of her. She stared down at the protruding bulge, trying to picture the child within her womb. She knew she'd need every shred of strength she could muster if any of them were to survive.*

-o-o-o-

"No," Duchess repeated in horror, wrenching herself back to the present. "No, I can't. *I'm not ready.*"

# SEVEN

Chan blinked back to awareness as a shock like touching a live power line jolted through him. The woman who had just grabbed him by the throat reeled away from him, looking horrified. Chan fell to his knees, leaning over to catch his breath, one hand planted on the floor. He grasped his chest with the other and tried to master the sudden nausea that threatened to engulf him.

"No," the woman breathed, the word barely audible. "No, I can't. *I'm not ready.*"

Chan was a highly trained CIA operative, and a battle-hardened military veteran. He wasn't about to be knocked on his ass twice in sixty seconds by a slip of a woman with golden hair and dark, fluttering lashes. He lurched upright, putting a few steps of distance between them, and swallowed several times to bring his stomach back under control. After a moment, his watery eyes cleared enough for him to see the blonde woman staring at him with an unnatural, electric blue gaze.

His breath caught. It wasn't the first time he'd seen a person's eyes glowing like laser beams. In fact, he'd just come from the stage, where the nameless Tibetan boy's red eyes had whipped the crowd into new heights of fanaticism. Chan had been able to convince himself, up until now, that the red glow was some sort of stage trick. But the actinic blue light shining from the eyes of the woman in front of him wasn't so easy to dismiss.

He could feel the power leaking from her as much as he could see it. What she had just done should be impossible — no way should this woman have been able to restrain him and lift him from the floor like a rag doll. Even though she was only a few inches shorter than he was, he easily out-weighed her by 30 kilos.

And she was *unarmed*, for fuck's sake. How could she possibly have gotten the best of him? Despite his burning humiliation at having been taken down by an opponent who should have offered no challenge whatsoever, he couldn't seem to stop staring at her like some kind of drooling imbecile. Catching himself, he raised the gun again, and blinked. When had he lowered it?

The moment he did so, the glowing light in her eyes intensified. A gray haze settled over his thoughts, and he shook his head sharply — trying to clear the confusion in his mind. It made his wits feel dull. He brought his free hand up to press at his temple, forcing himself to focus.

"What just happened?" he asked in a tone that was supposed to be stony, but somehow emerged sounding bewildered.

The woman took a long, slow breath before answering. "I believe I'm the one who will be asking the questions."

He raised his eyebrows at her confidence, flicking a quick glance at the semi-automatic pistol just to reassure himself that, yes, he was still holding it, and yes, it was still pointed at her head. She continued to stand there, ignoring the weapon, her eyes burning even brighter. He opened his mouth to snap something... to demand she start acting like someone who was staring down the barrel of a loaded gun.

Somehow, the words tangled up in his brain before he could say them, and his mouth slid shut again. It was really much easier that way, since his brain felt like overcooked mush.

"Who are you?" she asked.

"Chan Wei Yong," he replied, giving her his real name without a single thought, blowing his cover as though it meant absolutely nothing. *What the...?*

"Why are you in Malaysia, Wei Yong?" she pressed, her voice growing low and smoky.

Chan took a moment to breathe. Two decades of intensive training on how to withstand interrogation techniques warred with his primal, deep-seated need to speak. He hung in the balance for a long, tense moment.

"I... I am here... operating in Kuala Lumpur... as a security chief for the Brotherhood of the Cleansing Flame."

"Is that why you're really here?" she asked conversationally, staring into his eyes.

Chan felt a stirring in his consciousness, an unfamiliar sensation. He struggled mutely for a moment before relaxing. Giving in. The words flowed from him as though someone else was speaking using his voice.

"No," he answered with a heavy sigh. "I am here as a deep undercover operative employed by the United States. I'm CIA."

The woman nodded. "Go on..."

Her voice was a purr. He wanted to curl up at her feet and listen to it all night long.

"I've been undercover for a long time," he said, the truth continuing to pour from him in a damning stream of verbal diarrhea. "So long that sometimes it's hard to remember who I really am anymore. There are... so many awful things I've seen and done in the name of maintaining my cover." He blinked. "I used to be one of the good guys. That's what they told me, anyway, but even back then it was bullshit."

"That must be difficult," she said, leaning against the wall by the door. Her arms were crossed over her breasts, her tense posture at odds with her coaxing tone.

"It's all I've known for a long time," he said, feeling more certain of himself now. "I'm a good agent, and I want to serve my country."

"I understand," the woman replied, and the weight pressing on his mind lifted.

Chan took a deep breath, almost a gasp. He looked around, his vision swimming. The woman was still standing a few steps away, staring at him with an expression he couldn't decipher.

"What are you doing to me?" he demanded, his voice barely more than a whisper. His fingers clenched convulsively around the gun. *Shit.* He'd just blurted out his deepest secrets, and the only way to put that information back in the box was...

He steadied his aim, appalled by the fine tremor making the barrel waver. The woman gave him a knowing look. Her eyes glowed again, and the world went wobbly. When it settled, she was in exactly the same place as before, but his hand was empty, and she held the gun next to her hip, pointing down.

"I'm not doing anything to you," she said. "How could I? I'm standing all the way over here."

"You..." He strained to get the words out. "You're doing something to my mind!"

"Try to relax," said the demon temptress.

This seemed patently unfair since she appeared anything but relaxed. Even so, Chan closed his eyes, struggling with the impulse to simply slide down the wall and go to sleep. He wanted to forget about his duties... his handler... and most of all, about the beautiful and terrifying woman in front of him.

"If you're the Brotherhood's security chief, they must trust you with their secrets," she observed.

At that, Chan was able to pry his eyes open. They appraised each other for a long moment before his mouth started running again, still without his approval.

"Not as much as you might think. I mostly learn details by snooping and talking to people behind the scenes. It's my job to gather intelligence and report it back to the US."

"Is your handler nearby?" she asked.

"No. I have a supply of burner phones that I use to contact my superior."

"And no one here suspects you?"

He waved his hand. "It's a cult. They're suspicious of everyone. But they have no reason to suspect me more than anyone else."

"What do you know about them? The leaders—what are their aims?" the temptress asked, moving closer to him in the room's low light. Her eyes still glowed in a way that made Chan's skin tingle with apprehension and, oddly, a growing desire. He felt more aware of his own skin than he had in a long time, even though he still felt like an invisible weight was pressing down on him.

*Did she drug me somehow? What the hell is this?*

Still, the words flowed like water. "Like all such groups, they started small—just a handful of angry, disenfranchised people coming together around an outspoken leader. The monk's name is Tengku Asal, and he is a very powerful speaker. Charismatic. The Chinese immigrants around here feel like they've gotten a raw deal from the government, and Tengku spews rhetoric about cleansing the area of the Muslim nationals."

The temptress nodded. "What about money? Nothing gets this big without deep pockets standing behind it."

He shook his head slowly. "I can't find any concrete information about their source of funding. I do know that the leaders meet frequently with wealthy businessmen from Beijing, but they're careful never to name names." Chan paused. "There's also some guy from Eastern Europe, but I haven't been able to get any info on him. He's basically a ghost, and Tengku is the only one who ever seems to have contact with him."

The woman twitched at his last words and Chan blinked at her.

"*Putain de merde*," she cursed under her breath. "This is all we need." She shook her head and addressed him again. "Enough about that. Tell me about the kidnappings."

"They capture people off the street. Sometimes at random. Sometimes political targets or opponents."

"What happens to these people?"

"It depends. Some are held for ransom. Others are tortured, starved, and eventually killed. The leaders try to get information out of those that they believe have connections."

"Do you know where the prisoners are being held?" The woman's voice held only mild interest, but her expression was that of a jungle cat scenting prey.

Chan struggled again, with exactly the same result as before—which was to say, none at all. "I can take you there now," he said in defeat.

*Yes. Bring her to me. Hurry—my strength is almost gone.*

The deep mental voice echoed inside Chan's skull, making the world go sideways for a moment. When he blinked his vision clear, he found that the woman had gripped his arm through his shirt-sleeve and was squeezing hard enough to bruise.

"What was that?" she asked.

"It's nothing," he answered in a flat tone. "Let's go. I need to take you to see the prisoners now."

Her eyes narrowed, but she gestured toward the door. "Lead the way. I'll just hold onto your gun for you."

He fought his way through the mental fog long enough to ask, "Who are you?"

The woman paused, as though considering her answer.

"Duchess," she said, her expression very controlled. "You can call me Duchess."

Chan nodded, and led the way deeper into the building.

-o-o-o-

The journey through the sprawling condominium complex felt like walking through a dream. The world around him was surreal, everything seeming darker and more threatening than he ever remembered it being before. Even so, he led Duchess towards the prisoners with stealthy steps. She walked at his left shoulder, pausing at the exact moment he did, as if she could predict his movements before he made them.

His body felt sluggish... or maybe everything around him was speeding up? He couldn't really tell. He took them up the stairwell to the higher stories of the building that weren't being used for anything. These levels were deserted, meaning they could avoid prying eyes as they crossed to the other end of the complex—where the repurposed office area was located, with its hidden entrance to the basement level.

"Tell me more about the message you gave me," Duchess said once they'd left the more populated areas.

Chan looked at her. Pale moonlight filtered through the windows of the hallway they were traversing, bathing her features in silver.

*Beautiful,* he thought, only to berate himself a moment later. For fuck's sake... she was doing something to his mind. She had his fucking *gun,* while he was taking her to see the Brotherhood's most secure prisoners. And he was mooning over her because she was *pretty*?

Eventually, his brain caught up with her words. "Message?" he finally asked.

She gave him a searching glance. "You said, 'I have a message for you. Sangye is not the Thirteenth. Bael is attempting to draw the Angel out of hiding, but he does not understand.'"

"I don't know what you're talking about," Chan replied, frowning. "I... don't remember much after hitting my head."

"That didn't seem to keep your mouth from running."

Chan threw a dark look at her.

"You really have no memory of saying that?" she asked.

"I told you I didn't," he said, a bit sharply.

She was silent for a long time, clearly turning the information over in her mind.

"I wonder if he's here," she murmured. "It would make a sort of sense, since the boy is here."

"What are you talking about?" Chan asked, his frustration beginning to grow as his mind became clearer.

Duchess looked startled by his question, clearly not realizing that she'd spoken out loud. "Someone I'm looking for. That message—it sounded like something he would say. Which makes me wonder if he's the one who gave it to you."

"No one has given me any messages," Chan insisted, his voice growing hard even as uncertainty pricked at him.

*Dark eyes, meeting his from a face that looked like it should belong among the dead, not the living. A deep voice emerging from lips that did not move...*

"Suit yourself," she muttered. "There are people ahead of us. What are you going to tell them?"

They were approaching the atrium, with the ground floor offices beyond. It wasn't surprising that other people would be around. Guards patrolled the occupied levels of the building twenty-four hours a day, seven days a week.

"I'm not going to tell them anything," he replied. "They answer to me, not the other way around."

As they passed into the atrium, Chan thought he saw a smile pass across Duchess' face, but it was quickly masked by indifference. He turned his attention to the double doors ahead of them and pushed through. He approached the guards at a comfortable pace. Chan's men stepped aside as he nodded to them, allowing him to pass without question. Even so, he had no doubt that a report of his visit in the company of a female westerner would reach Tengku's ears. He turned towards the highest ranking of his men, prepared to offer some lie to account for her presence, when he realized with a start that she was no longer behind him.

He checked his surprise sharply, only his long experience with covering his reactions keeping him from gasping. His men looked at him expectantly, clearly thinking he was about to issue them some order.

He scanned the area discreetly and muttered, "As you were."

*What the actual fuck? Was he finally losing his grip on sanity?*

Chan didn't know what the hell to do, so he proceeded into the office as he'd originally planned. *Shit, shit, shit.* If he could just clear his head, he might be able to think properly and figure out what the hell was happening to him. He slipped through the heavy door, eager to get away from suspicious eyes. Pulling the door shut behind him, he turned to find Duchess standing right in front of him.

Years of practice covering his reactions be damned—he flinched hard at her unexpected reappearance, taking a step back. His back thumped softly against the closed door.

"What. The. *Hell*?" he demanded, lifting a hand to his head. "Where—? *How*—?"

"Practice," she replied, her tone making it clear that the topic was not up for discussion.

*"That's not an answer!"* he hissed through gritted teeth, not wanting to risk attracting the attention of the guards outside.

Neither was the reappearance of the eerie glow in her blue eyes, but a moment later he found himself leading her to the storeroom and the basement staircase beyond, with no memory of making the decision to do so. Duchess followed silently behind him. He opened the stairwell door and confirmed that the light was turned off, which meant no one was in the dungeon with the prisoners.

"There are no guards down here at the moment," he breathed, "but it's still a good idea to keep quiet."

"Is this where the prisoners are being kept?" she asked, peering into the darkness as though she could see right through it.

Chan blinked a few times. What the hell had he been thinking, bringing her here? He hesitated, his foot dangling over the edge of one of the stairs.

"I don't know why I brought you here," he said in a slow voice, his eyes unfocused. "What's... happening to me?"

"There was something you needed to show me," Duchess prompted, her voice infinitely reasonable. "One of the prisoners, perhaps?"

"Yeah," Chan answered in a haze. "Yeah, I think... that sounds right."

He led her down to the dungeon as though sleepwalking.

"Through here," he said as they exited the stairwell. The stench of filthy bodies and waste rose up to greet them. Duchess gasped sharply and stepped forward, moving with unerring steps to the cell holding the skeletal man with the dark, piercing eyes. His flesh was scarred and grey in the flickering light from a single bulb. He was still chained to the wall, lying on his back and resembling nothing so much as a preserved corpse.

Duchess' steps faltered, her hands gripping the bars of the cell as though she needed the support to remain upright. A small noise slipped free from her throat.

Chan leaned heavily against the moist wall. The damp seeped through his shirt, and he focused on the faint chill as he used all his willpower to try to fight off the wooziness that still assailed him. Around them, the other prisoners muttered and wept, but the figure chained in the cell was completely silent. No dark velvet voice spoke inside Chan's head; no piercing black eyes met his. Time stretched like melting taffy.

A blur of movement startled Chan from his reverie.

"Come on," Duchess hissed, grabbing his shirt and yanking him towards the stairs.

"What?" he asked, frowning at the way his voice slurred.

"Come *on*! Move your feet!"

"Where are we going?" he asked. Something in his mind snapped back into place like a rubber band, making him stumble uncharacteristically.

"Nowhere if you don't keep your legs underneath you," Duchess snarled.

Chan blinked and found himself at the top of the stairs, still being dragged along by the demon temptress.

"You know him, then?" he asked, jerking his head towards the captives. The movement nearly sent him careening back down the stairs as his balance wavered.

"We've got to get out of here," Duchess said, her tone urgent. "You're going to have to walk, it will look too strange if I carry you."

"What are you talking about?" Chan asked, bewildered. Her words sounded like they were coming from underwater. Or maybe he was the one that was underwater.

Pressure tightened in his chest.

They stumbled forward through the offices, bursting out to the atrium and past the confused looking guards. One of them shouted something, but Duchess sent him a hard glare, eyes glowing, and he subsided. The building's exit loomed ahead. Duchess hauled him through it, his limbs barely functioning enough to hold his weight.

"I will drag you the entire way if I have to," Duchess growled, "but this would really be easier if Snag hadn't mind-whammied you nearly into a coma."

"Uhh," Chan replied, trying to remember how to make his legs work. He drew on all his strength and pushed away from her, shaking like a leaf. His muscles burned. He took a few staggering steps before she was back under his arm, helping him along. Their bare skin brushed when she grabbed his wrist to steady him, making everything inside of him sing.

Closing his eyes for just a moment, Chan felt himself being guided across gravel. They were outside. The air in Kuala Lumpur was hardly what you'd call fresh, but it was much better than the musty basement where Tengku was holding his prisoners.

He lifted his heavy head and saw that guards were stationed around the gate to the complex as usual.

*They'll never let us through,* he thought.

Chan was wrong, however. The guards neither moved nor spoke as they passed through the open gate, Duchess still supporting his heavier frame. At any moment, he expected a shout to follow them, but not a sound could be heard except the quiet chirping of nighttime insects.

"How…?" he began, only to fall silent. It was taking every ounce of his concentration to flop one numb foot down in front of the other, over and over.

Duchess didn't answer, and he fell into an uneasy fugue state, his legs moving on autopilot. When he became aware again, they were inside an unfamiliar building, standing in front of a dark, wood-paneled door. Duchess pushed it open and tossed him unceremoniously over the threshold. He fell to the floor in a heap, distantly relieved that it was covered in plush carpet. As his awareness came into sharper focus, he heard a pair of surprised exclamations from elsewhere in the room.

"Duchess! What on *earth*?" A female voice asked.

A man crouched in front of him, his slate-blue eyes peering at him in concern. He lifted one of Chan's eyelids and brought up a cell phone. A bright light flashed in Chan's face.

"He's completely out of it," the man muttered, turning off the light. "What the hell did you do to him? I thought that we agreed about feeding from strangers…"

"I didn't feed from him," Duchess snapped.

"So, what happened to him?" the man asked. "Who is he?"

"Long story," his temptress muttered.

"*Duchess*—" The other woman's voice was sharp.

Chan peered at Duchess as she crouched next to him and lifted him by the arms. To his surprise, she was able to lift him easily, half-carrying him towards a bed. He felt himself being lowered onto the comfortable mattress and sighed in relief. Maybe if he could get a few hours of sleep, things would start to make sense when he woke up. Or, even better, he'd find out this had all been a dream. That would definitely work for him.

He smiled, feeling better about things now that he'd figured out this wasn't real. *Yeah, just a dream…*

"You're not going to be so happy about things in a minute," Duchess said grimly.

She straightened up, glaring at the other two people in the room.

"This is Chan Wei Yong," she said, and Chan twitched at the use of his real name. "He used to be my husband, Bertrand, in seventeenth century France. Now he's an American CIA agent on an undercover assignment inside the Brotherhood. I'll need you both to watch over him for the next day or two. Oh, and I also found out that they're holding the boy, Sangye Rinchen. Snag is there, too, but he made me promise not to rescue him yet."

The twin expressions of shock and increasingly strident demands for an explanation went unheeded.

"I'd apologize for this," she said, looking down at him with an unreadable expression. "But in the end, what would be the point?"

"Wait…" Chan began, wanting answers to at least some of the myriad of questions whirling inside his head. The rest of his sentence was lost as Duchess leaned forward and sank her teeth into his neck.

For a moment, he was lost in the sharp, shocking pleasure-pain of her bite. He gasped and arched, his body straining toward the demon temptress and away from her in equal measure. Deep suction drew his pulsing blood through the wound she'd just inflicted on him. His hazy thoughts grew hazier, lightheadedness making the room grow darker and lighter in time with his pounding heartbeat. She took and took from him, until he was certain he had nothing left to give.

He *burned*. His neck was on fire at the site of her bite and he jerked weakly, trying to sever the connection.

Chan felt her draw even more deeply from the wound at his neck, and the burning began to spread into his head and down his limbs. It was agony, but nothing compared to the feeling that rose in his chest. Something inside him was being ripped in two—the very fabric of his soul rending like torn cloth.

"Stop!" he tried to scream, but the word emerged as a nearly inaudible croak. The feeling of sedation was still lying heavy across his body, and he could only muster enough strength to lift his hands a few inches. They felt detached from his body, useless and numb.

Still, she did not yield. He tried to roll away, but she restrained him as easily as one might restrain a newborn kitten.

"No," he whispered, fire consuming him from the inside out.

Finally, she released him and stepped away.

"I'm sorry," she whispered. "I won't burden you with my presence after this, but for the sake of the world, it has to be done."

"*Ti mwen*, what are you *doing*?" The other woman implored. "You're giving him no choice!"

The reply was hard and cold as ice. "That's because there *is* no choice, Oksana. Don't you see? There is no choice at all—there never has been, for us."

Cool flesh pressed across his slack lips. The smell of copper assaulted Chan's nose, and thick liquid dripped into his mouth. The fire roared higher, demanding to be slaked with blood. Fresh stabs of pain erupted in his mouth as his canines lengthened and sharpened, digging into the flesh of his cheeks.

A few drops of the temptress' blood slipped down his throat, and all rational thought fled. He snapped his jaws around the offered wrist, tearing into pale flesh to get more of that sweet nectar. He drew it into himself in great, gulping swallows. He needed more… more… *more*… needed all the blood in her body… all the blood in the world. There would never be enough blood to douse the flames inside him.

This was hell. It had to be. When his movements grew weaker and more lethargic with every swallow, his mind sliding down to a place of blackness and torment, he was sure of it.

The last thing he heard was the temptress saying, "Look after him," in a voice scraped raw, as though she'd been screaming. A door opened and closed with a slam. After that, he knew no more.

# EIGHT

Snag drifted in a state of unbeing, his mind far away from the wasted remains of his body, which was laid out in iron chains on the floor of the Brotherhood's dungeon in Kuala Lumpur. He had not moved a muscle since Duchess fled with her mate… had it been several hours ago?

No matter. He'd summoned a last burst of strength and ordered her not to intervene in his captivity. For the moment, he was exactly where he needed to be. The young vampire, Sangye, still required his help. Without drawing too deeply on his dwindling reserves, he reached out mentally and touched the connection between the two of them. The boy had sensed her presence earlier that evening. His skills were not so well tuned that he could identify Duchess specifically, but he'd felt another vampire nearby.

After her mate's unexpected appearance at the door of Snag's cell the previous day, he hadn't been surprised to find that Duchess was the one to stumble upon him. There was a hand at play here beyond mere happenstance — this much had become clear to him in the months since Tré found Della in New Orleans.

Israfael was finally waking from her long sleep.

*Elder?* Sangye's youthful voice pierced his musings. They were separated by distance—he a shackled prisoner, while Sangye played the part of Kovac and Bael's puppet. Yet the bond that he shared with the young vampire was strong, tying them together by necessity and blood.

*Are you well, child?* Snag inquired.

*I am tired, Elder.*

Snag sent what strength he could spare, which sadly wasn't much. *We must persevere. Withdraw into meditation and rest your mind, as you are able. You must maintain the strength to keep going.*

Snag felt the boy's hesitation. Snag had never fully explained the depths of his own power, knowing that the information would not be helpful to Sangye, and might be dangerous. It was knowledge that needed to be kept far from Kovac, and even farther from Bael.

*I wish I had your courage, Elder,* Sangye finally replied.

*Courage is merely unwavering focus on one's goal, even when circumstances seem dire. You fed enough to maintain your strength until the monks return you to my side. Draw on the stores of energy you gained from me.*

A pause. *What I am doing for the monks is wrong. Yet I cannot do otherwise.*

Despite Sangye's ancient soul, he was still a frightened boy who lacked practical life experience. He was respectful of Snag's guidance, but Snag knew he did not understand why they were going along with the ploys of their captors. Whereas Snag, a chess expert, was himself a master of ploys.

*Patience, child. Your time will come to stand up for what is right,* Snag counseled.

He felt Sangye sigh in weariness and allowed his own life force to swirl around the boy. It was all the comfort he had to offer.

The door at the top of the stairwell leading down to Snag's basement prison crashed open, and boot steps pounded down the stairs. He let his awareness flow back inside his physical shell as moans of fear erupted from several of his fellow prisoners. The humans kept here had good reason to fear the appearance of the guards. Cruelty was rampant.

With the exception of Snag, everyone in this place was expendable in the eyes of the cult leaders, at least to some degree. More than one had been dragged from the cells and had not returned. The rest were given only enough food and water to survive, and the stench of illness and rot in the basement was nearly overwhelming.

Fortunately for his fellow prisoners, it seemed as though Snag was to be the focus of attention for now, at least to start.

"You," a voice spat.

The voice did not belong to Bastian Kovac, the cult leader called Tengku, the man who was Duchess' lost mate, or any of Snag's friends, so it could safely be ignored. Snag might be encouraging the child Sangye to cooperate with their captors, but that was because he didn't yet know how Sangye's story would end.

He, on the other hand, was in no danger. Bael wanted him alive.

The door to his cell creaked open. A moment later, a hard boot impacted his ribs. Two of the bones cracked, and then immediately started to heal. The process was growing markedly slower these past days. After weeks of feeding Sangye, his body had nearly reached its limits. Once it finally did, matters would be simplified. In the millennia since his turning, the physical had always been little more than a distraction to him.

"Unless you are finally dead, you will show respect to your betters, Silent One," the guard growled. Another flurry of kicks followed.

The man was one of the many guards who patrolled the building where Snag and the other prisoners were being kept. A nobody, caught up in the imagined glory of something larger than he was. Snag let his eyes slip closed, trying to tune him out.

"Maybe you'd pay more attention if I brought you the head of that little freak child on a stake, eh?" A heavy boot landed on Snag's sternum, pressing down. As abuse went, he supposed it would have been more effective on a being that still needed to breathe.

And as for the verbal threat, it probably would have been more effective on someone who didn't know how much the monk Tengku relied on his new pet vampire. Without Sangye, who would awe Tengku's followers with glowing eyes and an otherworldly aura?

Under Bastian Kovac's instruction, Tengku was engaged in a delicate balancing act with his two vampire prisoners. Snag's original plan, hastily conceived in the warehouse in London, had been to accompany the child and convince him to feed until he was strong enough to shift form and escape. Unfortunately, Sangye was naive and softhearted enough to be controlled by threats against Snag's life.

Tengku had convinced the boy that he would behead Snag the instant Sangye attempted escape, and no reassurance Snag gave him would move the child to ignore that threat. Snag, of course, could not leave a young boy alone in the hands of Darkness. And so, their slow dance of danger continued.

Now that Duchess was here—presumably still in the company of Mason and Oksana—the balance would not hold much longer. He only hoped that Sangye would come to understand his true power before it was too late. Snag could perhaps feed the child one more time, but it was quite likely that would be the end of his physical reserves. Once more, he would be relegated to the corpse-like state in which he had spent so much of his long, painful life.

He had faith that Eris and the others would know what to do when that happened, but it would mean the end of his usefulness in convincing Sangye of his power and agency. Tengku was using Sangye as a figurehead to awe the gullible, and Snag was counseling the boy to go along with that manipulation. Because, once the figurehead came to wield more influence over the cult's followers than Tengku did, that figurehead could step forward and wrest control from the warrior monk.

There was only one problem. The child feared that the moment he rebelled, it would mean Snag's death. Snag knew that was an unlikely outcome since the demon Bael had other uses for him, but Sangye refused to entertain even the slight risk.

Stalemate.

On the physical plane, blows and abuse continued to rain down on him until the bored guard grew weary of beating and yelling at an unresponsive body. He left, kicking the bars of another cell hard on his way out, making the poor soul inside cringe and cry out in fear.

Snag lay on the floor and waited for what would come next. He didn't need to wait for long before the skittering of thousands of invisible spider legs across his skin alerted him to the presence of the demon.

There was another reason Snag had encouraged Sangye to feed from him until his body hovered on the edge of complete shutdown. Snag purposely sank more fully into the physical, letting his body pull more of his dwindling energy reserves from his mind to repair the fresh damage done by the guard's boots and fists. Being a simple creature at heart, Bael assumed that additional pain and injury would weaken Snag's defenses against the demon's mental assault.

Fortunately for all of them, Bael was a foolish being in many ways—otherwise, they would have perished long ago. But Bael was incomplete, driven by what he lacked and unaware of what he truly needed. The demon thought to drive his opponent, the Angel Israfael, into the open by threatening the most powerful member of her Council. He sought to finish the job he'd been unable to complete millennia ago, by ripping the Light from Snag's soul while he perceived Snag to be weakened.

Foolish.

Snag let his body draw energy until his consciousness guttered to a mere ember, only dimly aware of Bael's shrieks of frustration as the demon clawed uselessly at the tiny flicker of life, unable to grasp something so small and insubstantial.

Again, a stalemate. And at least now, Snag could get some proper rest until they brought the boy back to drain the last few dregs of his blood. After that, the fight would lie in other hands than his. He only hoped the groundwork he'd laid would be enough to shape the outcome of the battle.

# NINE

Duchess strode out of the hotel room as though the hounds of hell were at her heels, the door slamming behind her. It was wrenched open an instant later. The grip that tightened on her arm and spun her around before she'd made it a dozen steps was not that of a hellhound, however, but that of her closest friend.

Pity — she would have much preferred to face a spectral predator than the look of shocked disbelief on Oksana's face.

"*Duchess*!" Oksana said on a gasp. "What in the name of all that's holy are you *doing*?"

She should dissipate into mist and flee. She should fall into Oksana's arms and beg forgiveness for what she'd just done. She should —

She swallowed hard. "What does it look like I'm doing? I've just located the eleventh member of the Council, and turned him before the forces of Darkness could find him and kill him."

Oksana gaped at her, as though it had some-how escaped her attention before now that Duchess was an ice-cold bitch with no compunctions and no illusions about what her future was likely to hold. She felt a sudden, irrational desire for Xander's presence, which was ridiculous since she'd recently thrown Xander's heartfelt confession of his past sins in his face and more or less spit on him. If there was a way to burn a century-old friendship to the ground without uttering a single word, that was probably it.

She really hoped her friendship with Oksana wasn't about to go the same way.

Oksana blinked, and shook her head—a tiny movement that made it look like she was trying to shake her thoughts back into order. The grip on Duchess' arm relaxed from *bruising* to *steadying*.

"All right," she said, more calmly. "So, you've turned your mate. You've made it harder for Bael to move against him, and maybe it will help calm the vortex of chaos that was already forming around this place. Now come back inside and talk with him. It's clear he has no idea what's going on."

"No," she said immediately.

Oksana's hand tightened again. "Why? *Why*, Duchess?"

A gaping chasm opened in Duchess' chest. "Because he may be the reincarnation of my husband Bertrand, but we have no future together. My situation is not like yours, *ma petite chérie*."

It was the middle of the night, and the hotel hallway was deserted. One of the bulbs lighting it was about to go out—it flickered in an irregular pattern, in time with a faint electrical buzz. Oksana's other hand closed around Duchess' shoulder, and she used the grip to press Duchess back a step until her back met the wall with a light thump. Oksana looked up from her slight disadvantage of height, dark eyes kindling with small points of violet.

"It's time for you to tell me what happened to you, *ti mwen*," she said, very quietly. "In fact, it's well past time."

Duchess' chest caught on another shard of pain. She was older than her friend by the better part of two centuries and had the power to prove it—but to shove Oksana away and flee might well be the action that set their friendship aflame. She was old, yes... and strong. But she wasn't *that* strong.

"Bertrand was a musketeer under King Louis XIII," she began slowly, striving to keep her voice level and dispassionate, "and I was his wife. I was also a spy for the king's greatest enemy—his younger brother Gaston, better known as the Duc d'Orléans. Gaston had designs on his brother's throne, and at the time, the king had no heir. If Louis had died before his wife Anne bore him a son, the throne would have gone to Gaston."

Oksana did not speak or interrupt. Nor did she let Duchess go. Instead, she only nodded, listening avidly.

"My husband was a favorite of the king's," she continued. "He was both brave and courtly, with a pleasant demeanor and a sharp wit. As a favored musketeer, he had the king's ear, though I never knew him to use his influence for selfish or political means. Nevertheless, it made him a powerful figure at court."

Oksana's shrewd eyes widened in understanding. "He was powerful because he had the king's ear. But you were a spy for the king's brother. You had both Bertrand's ear and Gaston's."

Duchess nodded, her eyes growing distant. "Bael thought that if I were his puppet, I might be the key to bringing down the French monarchy. Had he been successful, it would have thrown all of Europe into chaos. Gaston was a fool, and quite possibly insane as well. His ascension to the throne would have been disastrous."

A frown creased Oksana's brow. "If he was such a threat to France, why did you agree to be his spy?"

A harsh breath of laughter choked her.

"For the coin," she said. "Bertrand gambled. He lost all our money at cards, and then some. We were about to—" She cut herself off, appalled at what she'd nearly let slip, and shook her head. "It doesn't matter. I... needed money to buy food and pay Bertrand's gambling debts. There were a limited number of ways for a woman to get that kind of money, and when one of Gaston's lackeys approached me with an offer, it seemed less onerous than whoring, so I accepted."

Oksana finally released her arms, taking a step back.

"I see," she said, no judgment clouding her tone. "But what I don't see is how that affects the current situation. You and Bertrand might have betrayed each other once, a long time ago, but Chan isn't Bertrand. He needs you now, even if he doesn't realize it yet. And, I'm sorry, Duchess—but you need him, too."

"No," she said simply. "Chan is an innocent pawn caught up in this war. Believe me when I say, I am the very last thing he needs."

*I am the very last thing any man needs.*

Oksana continued to look at her with those large, violet-lit eyes, and Duchess could feel the tentative brush of her thoughts, searching.

"There's more, isn't there?" she asked.

Duchess regarded her, silent and unmoving. Not replying. Eventually, Oksana sighed in defeat.

"Fine," she said. "Keep the rest of your secrets for now. But what are we supposed to do with Chan?"

Duchess only shook her head—she had no more answers to give.

-o-o-o-

Chan's darkness was shot through with crimson swirls of memory and confusion. Dimly, he was aware of his physical body. It still felt as though he were being torn open by red-hot claws, exposing the vulnerable flesh inside to devouring flames. He heaved and struggled, but the agony was not something outside of him… not something he could escape by moving.

There was nothing to be done except surrender to the oblivion gathering at the edges of his mind. As he sank deeper, he began to feel a gentle swaying beneath him, like he was seated on a moving surface. His awareness became more dreamlike, and he blinked, finding himself no longer in a dingy hotel room in Kuala Lumpur, but rather in the dazzling sunlight on the edge of a glade of trees.

He looked down and discovered that the swaying motion was due to the fact that he was on horseback, of all things. The animal was plodding along at its ease, one ear cocking toward him in a lazy movement.

"Bertrand!" a voice called.

Trotting hoof beats approached from behind and he turned, somehow recognizing the name as his own despite the fact that he'd never heard anyone address him that way in his life. As he watched, the man on horseback approached him, dressed in leather and linen from a bygone age. A sword hung at his belt, and an antique musket hung in a long holster at his mount's shoulder. A moment later, he recognized the face of his dear friend, Pierre, one of his brothers-in-arms in the service of the King's Musketeers.

"You started your journey early, my friend," Pierre admonished. "You should have waited for me."

"Aye," Bertrand said, shifting his tabard to cover the nearly empty coin purse hanging from his belt. "But I couldn't bear to see the knowing look on your face."

"Hmm… I take it your purse is considerably lighter than before we passed the Red Hen?" Pierre raised an eyebrow. "Why do you gamble so much, *mon ami*?"

"Why, for the thrill of victory, Pierre!" he blustered. "It is much like a battle, in that I must slay my foe. But at least at the card table, he merely walks away humiliated and poor, rather than missing a limb or dead."

"How very altruistic of you to spare your opponents' lives," Pierre replied, allowing their horses to walk side by side. The two geldings were stabled next to each other in the Musketeer garrison, and they sniffed noses in greeting. "Though were I a braver man, I might point out that your analysis assumes your foe is on the losing side."

Bertrand only grunted.

"I doubt Marie will allow you to participate in such escapades once your babe is born," Pierre continued idly, settling back in his saddle and pushing his blue cloak out of the way of the breeze.

"Ah, I have no worries there. My wife is a magician with the coin, even when I manage to hit a spot of sore luck," Bertrand assured his friend.

It was true, and one of the many reasons he adored Marie. Yes, he probably gambled too much. He considered himself to be both lucky and skillful when placing bets, but he was not immune to the occasional downfall. No mortal man was, after all. Lately, he'd been in an admitted slump. He'd hoped that by playing a few rounds with complete strangers in the village they'd just left, he would break his losing streak.

"At the risk of raising your ire, my friend, you and sore luck seem to be close companions these days," Pierre said. "Perhaps it's time to leave these youthful follies behind? You are about to have a son of your own. You're not getting any younger, and it's time to think of accumulating an inheritance for your heir."

"Inheritance… yes," Bertrand answered in a vague tone. Truthfully, he'd given almost no thought to laying down an inheritance for a son, because he was secretly hoping that Marie was carrying a daughter instead.

That might have been an unusual wish, he knew. Much emphasis was placed on producing strong sons to carry on the family name. Yet Bertrand had long ignored traditional customs in favor of pursuing his heart's desires. He was an unusually old Musketeer at the age of thirty-one, and he had only taken a wife within the last few years. He'd courted Marie in secret until finally saving up enough money for a suitable dowry to her father.

Old Monsieur La Fleche had been less than delighted to know that his daughter was marrying a soldier, even one in a regiment as prestigious as the musketeers. He'd hoped, perhaps understandably, for a suitor with a less hazardous job and more financial security, but he'd accepted the arrangement grudgingly after Marie had made her voice heard over the matter.

Rarely meek or mild, Marie was usually one to speak her mind and make her opinions known. This was another thing that Bertrand cherished about his wife. He'd never been able to stomach the simpering women at Court. He needed someone who was bold and courageous, who could match his fire with a blaze that both fed and sated his needs. Marie fit that requirement admirably, and he loved her for it.

He and Pierre rounded a familiar bend in the road that led to the musketeers' garrison. After another ten minutes of riding, they reached the stables—home at last after a grueling two-day journey. They'd been tasked with delivering a message to one of the King's cousins in an isolated palace more than a dozen leagues from Paris. The

King had ordered them to guard the missive they carried with their very lives, if necessary.

Happily, the trip had been uneventful—almost surprisingly so. The message was delivered without incident, and they were able to return home at a more leisurely pace. One that even allowed for a game of cards or three in the village between the cousin's palace and their home environs of Paris.

After unsaddling their horses and turning them over to the stable boys, Bertrand and Pierre slung their belongings onto their shoulders and checked in with Monsieur de Tréville, the garrison's commander.

The grizzled old soldier nodded in satisfaction upon hearing of the letter's safe delivery. "Well done, lads. His Majesty has no more use for you today. Take the time to rest after your journey, and report for duty at mid-morning tomorrow."

They acknowledged the welcome orders and departed soon after.

"Drink?" Pierre asked.

Bertrand smiled and shook his head. "I think not. I'm going back to my apartments to check on Marie. She works too hard when I'm not there to make her rest. Why don't you find René and Jean Paul? Let them buy you a bottle and raise a glass for me."

Pierre gave him a knowing look and nodded, diverting his course towards a tavern frequented by members of the regiment.

Bertrand continued on, trying not to think about the lack of weight in his coin purse. He did feel a twinge of guilt about losing so much at the

Red Hen, but he hoped that Marie wouldn't be too severe with him. Surely she wouldn't be upset—she always managed to come up with the money they needed.

Finally, he came within sight of their small set of rooms on the Rue Férou. He passed through the front door, but the inside was quiet except for the purr of the fat tabby cat Marie kept to discourage the mice. Bertrand continued to the enclosed court-yard at the back of the small building. He found his beloved standing with her back to him, hanging clothes to dry from the line stretched across the open space.

At the sound of his footsteps, she turned and smiled at him. Her blue eyes sparkled, and a few dark curls escaped her chignon, framing her porce-lain features.

Bertrand felt a strange sensation, like he was being pulled from a dream. Something about Ma-rie's face tugged at him. In his thoughts, it was framed by loose waves of golden hair, and her eyes glowed from within, emitting a strange, unearthly light. He shook his head sharply, dislodging the odd daydream and the sense of unease that came with it.

"You've returned!" Marie said cheerfully.

He smiled at her and pulled her into an em-brace, her swollen stomach pressed between them.

"So I have, *mon coeur*," he replied playfully, slipping a pin from her hair so that it fell loose around her shoulders. "You should not be straining yourself so. Are you well?"

"Quite," Marie said with a laugh, and batted his hands away. "You worry too much."

Bertrand reached out and laid a palm on her distended belly, hoping to feel movement from their babe.

"Sleeping, I think," Marie commented, rubbing her sides. "Which is saying something, since I was up half the night with all the kicking."

Bertrand chuckled, wondering if a quick tumble in bed would help her relax enough to nap for a bit. He could push up her skirts and tunnel beneath them, kissing his way up her legs until—

Marie shivered, and glanced around, looking suddenly nervous.

Bertrand frowned. "Marie?"

She looked back at him, smiling widely. *Too* widely. "It's nothing," she said quickly.

"What's wrong? Are you certain you're well?" Bertrand pressed, laying a hand across her forehead to check for fever.

"Yes, of course," Marie said, sounding more herself. "It's silly. I keep feeling this chill breeze blowing over me, that's all. Let's… just… go inside."

Bertrand raised his eyebrows. Of all the excuses Marie could come up with to reassure him, that was perhaps the least effective. Ever since her pregnancy first started to show, she'd been overly warm regardless of the weather. For her to confess a chill when the weather was so balmy seemed somehow ominous.

"You're only making me worry more, you know," Bertrand accused, but he allowed himself to be pulled toward the back door.

All at once, a low, dark cloud rolling in obscured the blue sky. Bertrand whirled and looked up in alarm as curls of blackness descended into the courtyard. *Mon Dieu…* was there a fire in one of the neighbors' houses?

Marie cried out and tried to pull him inside, but Bertrand's feet were rooted to the ground. He could not lift them, nor tear his eyes away from the darkness hurtling in their direction. This was no smoke. In fact, it was nothing from the mortal realm. The fog shifted and thickened, suggesting horrible, demonic forms within. With numb fingers, Bertrand crossed himself and drew his rapier, knowing even as he did it that there was nothing for him to fight. Nothing that could be stopped with steel, at any rate.

His wife tried to call his name, only to collapse into harsh coughing as the fog rolled over them. It was foul, like vitriol. Bertrand felt his nose and lungs burn, the smell of sulfur making his eyes sting and water.

"Marie," he choked out, reaching for his wife through the heavy gloom.

He found her arm, which was cold to the touch and shook violently under his hand.

A voice like nails screeching across slate echoed within the courtyard.

"She has betrayed you," it crooned.

Bertrand looked around wildly, hoping for an opponent he could fight with blade or flintlock. He could see no one else, however, and was forced to conclude that the terrible noise was somehow coming from the cloud itself. Still, he had never been one to quail in the face of danger. Bertrand pulled himself up straight and extended his blade. He moved to stand in front of Marie, who gripped his shoulders from behind, her fingers like claws.

"I would put more faith in such a ridiculous accusation if the man who made it had enough courage to show himself," Bertrand taunted, struggling to keep his voice strong despite the acrid fog choking him.

Cackling laughter reached his ears—a sound that would not have been out of place in hell itself. The fog continued to swirl around them, but part of it grew denser, until it resembled the outline of a huge, misshapen man with the head of a toad.

Bertrand stared, feeling horror sinking into the pit of his stomach.

"As you can see, mortal, I am no man."

"*Mère de Dieu*," Bertrand breathed, the words hoarse.

The dark mist was suffocating him, stripping the flesh from his throat. Marie—he had to get her away from here. He couldn't let her be harmed—

"This whore you are protecting has betrayed you, musketeer," sneered the demonic voice. "Have you not realized that she is a spy for your enemies?"

Bertrand felt Marie flinch hard, and he tried to shuffle her backward, away from the creature. If they could get inside…

The demonic voice laughed. "You think to escape me by hiding behind a wooden door? You cannot escape the truth. How do you think your slut pays for everything, when you gamble away your earnings faster than the king pays you?"

Bertrand was barely listening to the sense of the words, unwilling to entertain the ranting of a minion of hell. Yet in the back of his mind, pieces of a puzzle were falling together despite his intentions not to give the creature any heed.

The money. Marie's growing interest about the goings-on at Court, these last few months. Her occasional disappearances for an hour here or an hour there.

He shook his head, trying to clear it. This didn't matter. Bertrand might have felt a sting of betrayal with this realization, but it paled next to the threat standing before him. The threat to his wife and his unborn child.

"She has betrayed you, and the king you are sworn to serve," the creature hissed. "She seeks to put the Duc d'Orléans on the throne. Every bit of information you've let slip has been passed straight to him. She opens your correspondence and eavesdrops on your orders. You are a traitor to the crown because of her."

Suddenly a gust of wind crashed down on him like a blow from a giant fist. He fell under the onslaught, an unseen force dragging him away from Marie. The mist cleared, and he saw her lying on the ground a few steps away, her skin raw and blistered. She was screaming, clearly in agony. Her eyes glowed and her face was twisted like a wild animal in the throes of death.

"No!" Bertrand yelled, despite the wind sucking the very air out of his lungs. "Stop! Spare her and take me!"

The voice laughed cruelly. "You fool. Don't you see? She will betray you for the last time tonight... by taking your life to save herself."

"No!" Marie screamed into the darkness. "I will not serve you, demon! I will not kill the father of my child!"

"Marie, do as the creature says!" Bertrand cried, latching onto the promise of her being saved. He thrashed, his spine arching in agony. A terrible gurgling noise came from his throat, fresh pain erupting in his eyes and ears. Warm blood trickled down his face.

His vision blurred, and he could barely make out Marie standing over him, facing the dark cloud that shifted and swirled around them. A scratching noise filled the air, like millions of insects crawling. The putrid smell of the black fog was nearly overwhelming.

"Please," Bertrand whimpered, his voice growing weak. "Please, Marie, you must save yourself. Think of our child. Please!"

Marie wrapped her arms around her swollen stomach and stared down at the protruding bulge. When she looked up again, her eyes were glowing with a feral, demonic light. Her body slammed into him, his teeth cutting into his tongue under the impact. Blood trickled down his face as he spat, trying to clear his mouth enough to breathe, even though they were still surrounded by the choking fog.

Hands yanked his head back by the hair, and he felt sharp teeth, like a wild animal's, at his throat. He blinked blood from his eyes and saw darkness descend. From the scent of rosewater, he knew with a jolt that it was Marie's dark hair flowing around him. He could feel her swollen belly pressed against him as she pressed him into the ground.

"Marie!" he rasped. He didn't fight back or try to throw her off, afraid that he might hurt her accidentally.

Evil laughter rang through the courtyard. With trembling fingers, Bertrand reached up and gently brushed the hair away from her face, as he had done countless times before.

"Protect our child, *mon coeur*," he whispered. "*Please*. I don't care what it takes."

Sharp pain pierced his neck, and Bertrand felt his lifeblood spurting from the mortal wound even as his beloved wife tore his flesh wider with her teeth and lapped at the gore like a ravenous beast. Blackness gathered on the edges of his mind, and he slipped gratefully into oblivion.

# TEN

Chan emerged from his dark dream, flailing for purchase in unfamiliar surroundings. Something—*someone?*—was holding him down, but he couldn't make out any details. The light hurt his eyes, and the emptiness inside of him hurt his chest.

"Where am I?" he croaked. "Let me up... *get off me!*"

"Calm down, mate," The male voice was Australian, and heavily accented. "You're safe, but I'm not letting you up until I determine whether you're lucid this time."

There was a light fixture above him, the yellow bulb responsible for the burning glare in his eyes. His entire body felt unbalanced and a dry, parching thirst made his throat burn. He groaned, panic urging him to struggle against the hand splayed over his chest.

"Easy," the man said. "I remember how it is. Lie back for a moment." Something about the man's voice, or maybe his aura, started to percolate through Chan's panic, and he relaxed. The hand gave him a final pat and pulled away. "There, that's better, mate. Sorry about that, just had to make sure you weren't going to do a runner on us."

Chan blinked his vision clear and coughed, trying to form words around the terrible need burning in his belly. "Where... am I?"

"A hotel room in the central city. You've been out of it for the last twenty-four hours or so."

Chan tried to scramble upright. "The last *twenty-four hours*? I've got to get out of here—"

"Yeah, sorry. Not happening, I'm afraid," said the man. "Why don't you rest for a bit, and then we can talk. My name's Mason, by the way, and—"

"You don't understand!" Chan snapped. He felt hot anger lick at his insides like flame, making the burning in his mouth more pronounced. "*I have to leave.*"

Fuck, what was wrong with him? He needed to overpower this man and get out of here. But his limbs felt uncoordinated, and his instincts shied away from the idea of attacking his captor. Which was ridiculous—the guy didn't hold himself like a fighter. Even disoriented as he was, Chan could have taken him down in a minute, but instead, something inside him wanted to roll over and show his belly like a damned puppy.

"Yeah, Duchess mentioned about you being CIA," Mason replied, frowning. "I'm afraid that's going to be a bit of a problem now."

Chan froze, trying to drag his memories into focus. "She told you I'm CIA?" He swallowed, his throat rasping like sandpaper. "That's... that's complete bullshit."

Way to sound completely convincing, there. *Not.* What the *hell* had happened to him?

The Australian gave him a look that could only be called condescending. "Whatever you say, mate."

Chan narrowed his eyes, trying to claw back the upper hand even though he felt like his sanity was holding on by a thread. Why was he so *thirsty*?

"So, I've been abducted and...drugged, from the feeling of it, by a strange woman called 'Duchess' who dumped me in a hotel room with you after concocting this fabricated story that I work with the CIA. And you expect me to just sit here? You're out of your damned mind."

Mason sighed. "I get that you're trying to maintain your cover, but you really don't need to. And, honestly, it's a bit late for that now. Like I said, you're not in danger, and frankly no one here is particularly interested in what government you work for."

Chan stared at him with a level gaze.

"Are you delusional, *mate*?" he asked with mock concern. Then his voice hardened. "Or just an idiot?"

The man's mouth flattened in an expression of mild irritation, right before a disembodied voice filled Chan's head—still with the same Australian accent.

*Neither, actually — but thanks for asking.*

Chan jerked back, as though doing so could somehow stop him hearing disembodied voices in his head.

"Yeah, telepathy," his captor said aloud. "I know, right? Impressive. Sorry if I shouted, by the way—I'm trying to get a handle on that."

Chan stared at him for a long moment. "You cannot be serious."

"Serious as a heart attack," the other man replied with a shrug. "And I say that as a medical doctor. Not that heart attacks are a concern for either one of us any more."

"You're a doctor?" Chan asked, still trying to drag his head back in the game.

"I'm a doctor in the same sense that you're a CIA agent," the guy said infuriatingly. "Which is to say, I was one."

"Then, *doc*," Chan said, laying on the sarcasm, "Maybe you could get me a glass of water after I've been out cold for a *full fucking day*? Because whatever that demon bitch drugged me with is making me burn up."

"Duchess didn't drug you," the man answered, sounding suddenly weary. "And believe me when I say, water won't help."

"Whatever," Chan forced past a throat scraped raw. "Rice wine sounds more appealing anyway."

The guy grimaced. "Yeah, voice of experience speaking here—that would be even worse. Look, I'm probably not the best person to explain this mess to you. I think I only drew the short straw because I'm the youngest.'"

Chan stared at him, trying to convey through his expression how very *done* he was with this conversation. When that didn't seem to work, he said, "Look. You're holding me here, doped up on god-knows-what. It's really very simple—you tell me what the hell is going on and let me go; or, fuck it.

Just let me go and ignore the first part, if that's easier."

Again, Chan railed at himself for his seeming psychological inability to leap up, knock Doctor Outback unconscious, and sprint out the door like all his instincts were screaming at him to do. Helplessness wasn't a feeling Chan experienced very often, but it was one he really, really hated. A memory floated up, of him standing on the porch, watching a car drive away with everything he was supposed to care about inside—

No. *Fuck*, no. Not here, not now.

His captor huffed a frustrated breath. "I wish there was a way to make this easier, but you need to understand a few things before you get up."

"Oh, yeah? That might be easier if you'd answer any of my goddamned—"

"You're a vampire," the man interrupted in a flat tone.

Chan snapped his jaw shut, waiting for the punch line. When the Australian simply continued to stare at him without speaking, Chan gave an incredulous laugh that made his throat hurt even more than it had before.

"Riiiight," he replied, drawing out the word. "Okay—well, if that's all…?"

He started to get up, but found an unyielding hand on his chest again, an irresistible force behind it that held his mind in thrall as much as his body.

"You need to hear me out," his captor said mildly. "This isn't a joke."

"Thought you were supposed to be a doctor." Chan said, forcing challenge into his voice. "Didn't they cover the whole 'vampires don't exist' thing in medical school? Now, get your hand off me and out of my way. I'm leaving."

"Oddly, they didn't cover it, no," the man said, ignoring the last part. "I think the instructors sort of assumed it was a given. So, yeah, it was a bit of a shock for me, too. I was like you in that regard — comfortable in my beliefs. I thought I had my life mapped out... thought I could fill the gap inside me by risking my life for a noble goal. I volunteered in war zones. Figured if I could save enough kids' lives, the world would start to make sense. But it never did. Not until recently, at any rate."

Chan couldn't help the chill that ran through him. The words prickled uncomfortably at the part of him that pushed him to take dangerous assignments. The part that had sabotaged his marriage and destroyed his relationship with his child before it ever had a chance to start.

He was damned if he'd admit that out loud to this guy, though.

"Look," he said reasonably, "I'm sorry you had a difficult life, but I'm a *security guard*. You want to know why? Because they pay me for it. They pay me *really well*, in fact."

"Whatever you say, mate," his jailer answered, clearly not believing a word.

The Australian accented mental voice reverberated inside Chan's head once more, making him suck in a sharp breath. *I realize that nothing short of absolute proof will convince you of the truth, so let me just lay it out there for you.*

Chan's indrawn breath hissed between his clenched teeth as he tried to scuttle backward on the lumpy hotel bed mattress.

*You felt a powerful connection to Duchess, the woman who brought you here. It was almost like an electric shock when your skin touched, right? That's because you knew her in a previous life. And I bet you've been dreaming about the distant past recently, am I right?*

Chan blanched.

*Duchess dragged you back here and drained your blood almost to the point of death. After which, she fed you vampire blood and turned you. You're like us, now. Dependent on human or vampire blood for nourishment. Sensitive to sunlight, which will burn your flesh. Capable of healing from most wounds. Soon, you'll gain the ability to shift form, and to communicate mentally, as I'm doing with you now.*

"How?" He injected disbelief into the single word, but despite himself, he couldn't hold back his growing curiosity.

The doctor snorted. "The others will tell you I'm not the person to ask. I'm still getting the hang of it myself. Mostly, though, you just concentrate on the words you want to convey."

Unable to help himself, Chan concentrated hard for a moment. *Like this?*

The guy winced. "That's the ticket—although you were shouting at the top of your mental lungs just now. I suspect this is some kind of cosmic karma that the others would find completely hilarious."

*Can you hear me now?* Chan asked, trying to make it a whisper. Fascinated despite himself.

"Yes, and that was much better."

"Okay," Chan said cautiously. "What was your name again? Mason, wasn't it? Let's just say for one second that I believe you. I'm not saying I do, but just hypothetically speaking."

"Sure," Mason replied.

"You said I could heal really fast. So why do I feel like complete shit right now?"

"You need to feed again."

"What are you saying," Chan pressed. "I'm craving blood or something?"

The words were disbelieving, but as soon as he said them, a spasm of hunger cramped his stomach, nearly doubling him over.

Mason nodded sympathetically. "Spot on, I'm afraid. You can feed now if you want."

Chan looked at him, appalled. "This is insane. I can't drink *human blood*."

"Human or vampire blood. And, I'm sorry, but it's either that or starve yourself into a coma... assuming you don't lose control and go on a killing spree first. Blood is necessary for your survival. Most of us can't stomach human food anymore, and it does us no good anyway. The good news is, you can feed from one of us until you get used to the idea."

Chan shook his head slowly back and forth. "You said you just recently became a vampire?"

"Yeah, a few weeks ago."

"Why are you the one telling me all of this shit? Why isn't Duchess in here explaining things, since she's apparently responsible for this?"

"She's... busy elsewhere."

"*Busy*," Chan echoed, his voice flat. "Busy doing what?"

"Trying to learn more about the Brotherhood and their prisoners," Mason said, grim. "I'm sorry — you're right that she should be here."

"You do realize how far-fetched this all sounds, right?" Chan asked, massaging his forehead.

Mason snorted. "Preaching to the choir, mate. I know it's a lot to take in all at once, but you can't leave here without understanding what you'll be facing now. You're not human anymore, and until your new instincts are under control, you're dangerous to others."

Chan sat back and closed his eyes. The burn in his throat was getting worse, demanding much of his attention. He gripped his neck with his hand and tried to push the feeling away.

*Yeah*, Mason said silently, *you won't be able to push this away using willpower.*

"Stay out of my head," Chan growled.

"Sorry, mate. It becomes something of a habit after a while."

"Don't any of you have any privacy?" he demanded, a bit of panic starting to claw at him as the idea that this might actually be happening began to take root.

"You learn to shield," Mason said. "There's a way to block the others from hearing your thoughts, and you learn how to ignore background noise, but it takes practice. Again, I'm not an expert yet."

Chan huffed in annoyance and changed tack, focusing on the dream he'd been having right before he woke to find his world turned upside down. As he reviewed the details, he remembered that everyone—himself included—had been speaking French.

*That's impossible,* he thought. *I barely know enough French to ask where the toilets are.*

*It's not impossible,* Mason said.

Chan grunted in irritation, having forgotten that his thoughts were no longer private. He rubbed his hands up and down his arms, his skin feeling unnaturally cool beneath his fingers.

His mind was starting to slide down this rabbit hole without his permission, if for no other reason than the creepy-as-hell telepathy and burning hunger that was now nearly insatiable. Yet, he still felt like *him.* He didn't feel like a monster.

The more he focused on his body, though, the more he began to realize that there were subtle differences. He could hear footsteps elsewhere in the hotel, and he was sure they were made by a man wearing steel-toed boots. He could clearly hear the soft *shush-shush* of blood running through Mason's veins. He could smell that the other man must've had sex recently.

"What's your girlfriend's name?" he finally asked.

"I'm not sure 'girlfriend' quite covers it," Mason replied wryly. "But her name is Oksana."

Chan cleared his parched throat, trying to get himself under control. He realized with a jolt that he was fantasizing about sinking his teeth into

Duchess' throat and drawing out her blood to soothe the burn inside him.

Mason stood up from his chair and moved to sit on the bed next to him. Chan shifted uncomfortably. It made him feel oddly vulnerable and off-balance, two things he didn't enjoy *at all*. Mason, by contrast, seemed perfectly relaxed.

*Maybe he's used to this sort of thing from being a doctor.*

"Yeah," Mason agreed. "Bedside manner is the same whether it's a scared kid on the bed or a pissed-off new vampire, as it turns out. Who knew? Now, you're going to feed from me before you start looking at that third-story window and thinking that jumping out of it to drain some random, defenseless human sounds appealing. I know you'd rather have Duchess here instead of me, but needs must."

Chan looked at him, alarmed. "Excuse me, *what*?"

"Consider it a blood donation. Odd as it still seems to me, I'm more powerful than you. You can't hurt me, but you're likely to kill a human. Feeding will ease your thirst and make you stronger. Vampire blood also has some rather startling healing properties."

Chan was starting to feel ever so slightly light headed. Just the idea of sating his bone-deep need made him salivate in anticipation. "How… would I go about doing that, exactly?" he managed.

"What do your instincts tell you?" Mason asked. He put a steadying hand on Chan's shoulder as Chan closed his eyes and panted, trying to keep control. Something sharp was poking the insides of his cheeks. His eyes flew open again, burning now like the rest of him.

"I want to bite you," Chan whispered, feeling disgust at himself rise as he tried in vain to control the overwhelming desire.

"You don't have to fight it," Mason said evenly. "Just go with your gut on this."

He proffered his arm. Chan took a sharp breath, sensing blood just beneath the surface of the soft skin at Mason's wrist.

*This is wrong. This is so fucked up. This is wrong. This is wrong.*

"It's all right, mate," Mason said reassuringly. "I'm offering, and it won't hurt me. This is natural, there's nothing wrong about it."

Before he could stop himself, Chan lunged forwards, sinking his teeth into Mason's wrist. For a brief instant, he was so horrified by his actions that he started to pull away, but then the first spurt of blood filled his mouth.

It was glorious. The burning in his throat and the terrible longing calmed almost immediately. Chan suckled at the wound he'd created like a babe at the breast, feeling a nearly palpable sense of relief. He hadn't recognized the terrible weight of weakness and exhaustion pressing on him until both began to fade. Life flowed into his limbs, strength returning to his grip.

He moaned like a cheap whore, beyond caring how it must have sounded.

"That's it," Mason encouraged. "You're doing fine. Just like that."

When Chan had drawn so much blood into his stomach that he felt he was about to burst, he sat back and allowed Mason's hand to fall from his grasp.

He slumped, scrubbing a hand over his face — not sure if he wanted a cigarette, or wanted to run screaming from the room. "*Shit.*"

Mason snorted. "Don't mention it." He rubbed at the gashes in his wrist, which healed in seconds right before Chan's eyes.

"That's… wait, *what*?" he asked, dumbfounded.

His erstwhile blood donor chuckled ruefully. "Yeah, it makes being a doctor feel a bit superfluous. If only everyone healed that rapidly."

"Doesn't that hurt you at all?" Chan asked, still straddling the knife's edge between fascination and repulsion.

"What? Feeding you?"

"Yeah."

Mason pondered the question a moment. "Not really. I've got a theory that something in vampire saliva acts like a drug. Being bitten can be… intense… but I wouldn't classify it as the kind of pain a human would feel while being bitten by a rabid dog or something. Mostly, I feel weaker and less energetic, because it's not just blood that you took from me. It's life force."

"*Life force*?" Chan grimaced. "Okay. That really doesn't sound good."

"I can get more, don't worry," Mason assured him. "Besides, it seems to act as some kind of social bonding thing for vampires. It's fascinating, really.

They've all fed from each other over the centuries, either to heal injuries or because no other blood was available. As a result, they… well, *we*… have become very close."

The sound of a disturbance outside the room interrupted their conversation.

Chan leapt smoothly to his feet, his strange, helpless lassitude from earlier gone. Whether it was adrenaline or the blood he'd just consumed, vitality flooded his limbs; his body feeling almost like it was vibrating with energy.

"Oh, hell. Here we go," Mason muttered, wincing. "I wondered how long it would take for all this to kick off. Sorry, Chan… things might get a bit—"

He was interrupted by the hotel room door slamming open hard enough to ricochet off the wall behind it. A small woman with dark skin, a prosthesis where one foot should be, and eyes glowing violet dragged Chan's missing demon temptress into the room.

Duchess swung around, her teeth bared at the shorter woman. "Unhand me," she hissed, "before I forget that we're supposed to be friends."

Chan's eyebrows went up, and he cast a fleeting *what-the-hell* look at Mason. *Okay, then. What happened to 'we've all become very close'?*

The glance he got in return said Mason wasn't any happier about being here than he was, but his telepathic voice had a wry twist to it. *I'm guessing you never had any brothers or sisters growing up?*

Chan hadn't, but he was distracted by the supernatural catfight unfolding on the other side of the room. Energy crackled around the enclosed space, making his skin tingle. He couldn't seem to look away from the blonde woman poised like a predator only a few meters away from him. Heat pooled at the base of Chan's spine, and the twin prick of pointed fangs rasped once more against his inner cheeks.

*Yeah, I know the feeling mate,* Mason said, the words sounding like a mental sigh.

"It's been more than a day. I'm not going to sit by any longer and watch you do this to yourself," snarled the dark-skinned woman, whom Chan assumed was Oksana. She released her grip on Duchess with a sharp shove and positioned herself between the taller woman and the door.

Duchess appeared to be in full-on ice queen mode. She glared at Oksana with glowing eyes the same color as the blue inside a glacier. "I do not answer to you, *petite soeur,* and I never have," she bit out. "Don't presume to lecture me on what I should and shouldn't do."

The words were deadly, her anger calling to something broken and ugly that lived deep inside Chan's soul. It resonated, that sharp-edged fury.

"*Presume?*" Oksana echoed, incredulous. "Here's a news flash for you, *ti mwen.* You're stuck with me, and that means I will always tell you when you're acting like a psychotic bitch."

Duchess growled. Actually *growled,* like a feral animal.

Oksana did not back down. Instead, she crossed her arms, her posture belligerent. "And, in case you need it spelled out, *you're acting like a psychotic bitch right now.*"

"I'm leaving." Each word was bitten off. Duchess' chest and shoulders heaved with emotion, though her voice was stone. "And since none of you in this room can match me in power, you'd do well not to stand in my way."

Something irrational and desperate clawed its way up Chan's throat at the thought of Duchess disappearing again before he could talk to her properly — a tangle of resentment and desire; anger and need.

*Don't go,* he thought at her as hard as he could, the words caught between a plea and a demand.

She froze, her back to him, shoulders stiffening. He tried to reach out to feel her mind, but his thoughts bounced back as though they'd hit a solid steel barricade.

"You turned me into some kind of a monster," he said aloud. "I just guzzled blood from a complete stranger's wrist. I have the right to an explanation about *what the hell is going on.*"

Oksana still had her arms crossed stubbornly, but now she raised a pointed eyebrow at her friend.

Mason crossed his arms as well. "That's fair, Duchess. Wouldn't you agree?"

A weighty pause ensued before Duchess eventually broke it.

"An explanation," she said in a monotone, not turning around. "Very well. Ask me your questions."

Chan had so many questions that they threatened to tumble over each other as soon as he opened his mouth. Surprisingly, the first one that popped out was, "How the hell is it possible that

I'm having dreams about you in French? I barely know any French!"

"You might not know it now, but you did four hundred years ago," Duchess replied, still in that flat tone.

He gaped at her. "What the hell is that even supposed to mean?"

Oksana's mouth was pressed into a grim line. It was she who answered. "You are the reincarnation of her husband, Bertrand, who died in the early seventeenth century. That's why you dream of France a long time ago, and why your skin sparks with energy when the two of you touch."

Shock suffused him. He hadn't told another living soul about the name others had called him in the dream—Bertrand. Unless… could he have been delirious after they brought him here? Perhaps he'd mumbled it while he was unconscious?

Ignoring the feeling that he was taking his life in his hands by doing so, Chan strode up to Duchess and whirled her around by the upper arm. She was wearing a sleeveless tank top over stylish trousers today, rather than the long-sleeved blouse he vaguely remembered from their first meeting. When his hand touched her skin, it was like touching a bare wire. He jerked back even as she flinched, her blue eyes blazing at him.

"Told you," Oksana muttered, but Chan couldn't spare eyes for her.

"What gives you the right to do what you did to me?" Chan demanded, anger finally trumping the other swirling emotions long enough to lend strength to the question.

"You were marked for death," she hissed, her eyes chips of ice. "I turned you into a vampire so you would be safe among us. *I had no choice.*"

"You had a fucking choice," he barked, his face inches away from hers. "You could have minded your own business and let me die like I—"

He managed to cut off the flow of words before he said *deserved*, but from the nearly inaudible gasp and the way Duchess' eyes flared with anger, he might have been less successful at cutting off his thoughts.

His schizophrenic emotions abruptly changed course again, making him want to needle her into unthinking rage rather than this cold, simmering resentment. Against his volition, he pictured himself snarling at the others to leave... slamming her against the wall behind her and ravaging her mouth with lips, tongue, and fangs.

*Yeah, talk about a death wish. Where was this even coming from?*

She continued to glare at him. "Sorry to disappoint you, but this isn't about you. And I don't have the time or the patience for anyone's self-sacrificing, suicidal *connerie*."

Outside of his dream, Chan's fluency in French had deserted him, but she bit out the word in the same way he might have said *bullshit*. Oksana and Mason remained silent during the exchange, while Chan's anger flared higher.

"Not about me, is it?" he shot back, his tone going as cold as hers. "So, I suppose it's just a coincidence that in the dream, you were carrying my child when you killed me?"

The room went absolutely silent, even as Duchess' porcelain complexion paled to chalk. Before Chan could press his momentary advantage, Duchess shouldered both him and Oksana aside as though they were rag dolls before disappearing through the door, which slammed behind her.

# ELEVEN

Duchess slammed the door closed and fled down the hallway, dissolving into mist without even bothering to check for the presence of human onlookers first. She swirled free of the choking confines of the building, emerging into the twilight. Even as vapor, an unbearable weight pressed down on her, threatening to crush her.

A modest park nestled a short distance from the entrance of the hotel, and she circled the deserted space. Away from any witnesses, Duchess rematerialized in human form and dropped to her knees near the base of a tree. She did not bow her head in grief, but stared hard at the waving branches and darkening sky above her, feeling nothing except an all-consuming heaviness.

Her entire existence, even as a vampire, had been different than the others'. Yes, they'd all lost their beloved mates, but Duchess was the only one who had suffered two inconsolable losses in that one horrible day. She had never managed to heal from either of those blows. Each wound constantly kept the other one festering.

She wanted answers. She wanted an explanation for this curse. Justification.

*Why did Bael mark me? Why not the King? Why not Queen Anne?*

But, no. Bael had been attracted to her potential. Her ruthlessness. He'd wanted her as his puppet, to use and discard like all his other soulless pawns.

Breath escaped her lungs in a painful gasp. Her fate was entirely her fault. If she had not chosen to be a spy to manage Bertrand's gambling debts, she never would have attracted Bael's attention They could have lived destitute and blissfully ignorant of the true depths of evil in the world. Maybe Bertrand would have stopped his gambling after their baby was born. Maybe she could have appealed to her father for additional financial support. Maybe she could have just sucked it up and sold her body to strangers to get by.

A familiar presence materialized at the edge of the small park. It was not the presence she might have expected.

Mason stood at the entrance, his hands in his pockets.

"You followed me," Duchess said, not making it a question.

He shrugged.

"You're becoming more powerful already," she observed, her voice sounding distant and detached, even to her own ears.

"Baby vamps have to grow up sometime, I suppose," he said mildly.

Duchess turned back towards the plants and flowers in front of her, half-hoping that Mason would eventually give up and return to the hotel. A vain hope, of course.

He lowered himself onto the soft, fragrant grass — close, but not too close.

"So. Do you want to talk about it?"

Duchess locked her thoughts down tightly. Her reply was cool. "What do you think, *Docteur*?"

*Mon Dieu.* All these centuries, and still, the pain was unbearable.

Mason twirled a blade of grass between his deft fingertips, his attention on the slip of green, rather than on her. "I think that's a heavy burden to carry alone for four hundred years."

Part of her wanted to unburden herself, to throw everything onto him and wait to see if he condemned her for it. *Dangerous*, said a little internal voice. *Not safe to give anyone that much power over what's left of your soul.*

"You know nothing about it. Nothing about what I did," Duchess said, the words trying to strangle her as she spoke them.

Mason did not reply — not even to nod. He merely continued to examine the leaf of grass. *Merde.* She'd seen professional interrogators use strategies that were less effective.

"I was a spy." Again, it felt like the words were ripped from her. "That's what attracted Bael's attention to me. I only did it for the money. I was pregnant, and I wanted to be able to get us out of debt, because Bertrand was an inveterate gambler."

This time, Mason nodded absently.

"I loved him. As a musketeer, he was disciplined in many ways, but there was also a kind of wildness to him. It was difficult to get him to take anything seriously, especially his gambling."

Duchess gathered her thoughts and took a deep breath. "Nevertheless, he was a favorite of the king. Louis talked to Bertrand, and Bertrand talked to me. Then I talked to Gaston, and Gaston—the simple-minded fool—listened."

"Bael thought you were a historical lynchpin," Mason said with unexpected insight. Though perhaps it shouldn't have been unexpected. Affable, Mason was. Unintelligent, he was not.

Duchess nodded bleakly. "That's why he wanted me, yes. He thought he could topple the French monarchy and destabilize the continent by using me. It was a good plan, as such things go. But as with all of us, Bael misunderstood. He underestimated the love Bertrand had for me. I think Bael assumed that he would forsake me when he learned of my betrayal. Many would have, I suppose."

A faint smile curved Mason's lips, but only for a moment. "He didn't, of course."

"No," Duchess answered, her gaze growing distant. "Bael might as well have accused me of accidentally overcooking his dinner, for all the reaction Bertrand showed afterward."

"He sounds like a good, though imperfect, man," Mason said.

"Yes," Duchess agreed. "I hated lying to him, but it was a different time back then. For him to *only* have a problem with gambling was such a minor thing. I thought I could manage the problems it caused. But I only succeeded in making bigger ones. Deadly ones."

"You survived, though. Love was your protection," Mason observed.

"Yes," Duchess breathed back, still staring at the plants dancing in the evening breeze. Twilight was giving way to darkness around them as they spoke. "The only protection that we can have against such a force, it seems."

"And now Chan is here," Mason prodded gently.

"Yes."

Mason sighed. "I think I'm beginning to understand the prophecy better now. At first, I wondered why you all didn't just grab some random people and turn them, if a group of thirteen vampires is all you need to take on Bael. But that's not it, is it? Xander was onto something. Maybe it's the love between soul mates that will be the deciding factor in this war."

*Mère de Dieu, I hope not,* Duchess couldn't help thinking.

"What?" Mason asked, turning towards her. His brow furrowed. "You don't think that love will protect us?"

Duchess met his eyes. "I hope it will protect the rest of you."

"But not you?"

She shook her head, the truth rising up, unstoppable. "Chan will never love me, nor do I deserve it."

Even to Duchess' own ears, it sounded bitter.

"How can you say that?" Mason asked. "He's your soulmate, Duchess."

Duchess chewed on her lip, debating on whether or not to tell Mason the rest of it. She suspected that Oksana already had an inkling, and if so, Mason would find out soon enough. So be it.

"Bertrand asked only one thing of me before I killed him." Her voice was barely more than a whisper.

"What did he ask from you?" Mason prompted, using that quiet doctor's voice.

She held his gaze, despite what it cost her. "He begged me to save our unborn child."

A satisfying flicker of pain passed across Mason's face.

*There,* Duchess thought. *Now you understand how abhorrent I am.*

"How far along were you?" was all he asked.

The phantom sensation of a baby kicking pricked at her memory, and she smoothed a hand over her flat belly—an unconscious gesture. "I was about eight months pregnant when Bael destroyed us."

Mason watched her with a steady gaze. His inner scientist must be intensely curious about the biology of what happened, but he said nothing, waiting for her to continue in her own time.

"My body wasn't able to hold onto her after I was turned," Duchess said. "She did not survive."

"You miscarried?"

"Yes," Duchess answered. "Bael fled after Bertrand willingly sacrificed himself for me. For *us.* I was left shattered and broken, writhing in agony as my newly turned body tried to heal. When I awoke, I found my daughter's tiny corpse on the ground next to me."

Mason nodded.

"I'm so sorry, Duchess," he murmured.

The anger that rose up in response to his quiet words was a relief, and she grasped it around her like a threadbare cloak.

"Save your pity," she snapped. "I don't deserve it. If you must spout platitudes to someone, direct them to Chan, who has been thrust into this war *again*. He is trapped in a situation he cannot escape because of the decisions *I* made."

"You weren't wrong to change him," Mason said, ignoring her jab. "You were absolutely right — Bael would have destroyed him as soon as he became aware of Chan's presence."

"You think I don't know that?" she snarled. "That's not the decision I mean! Because I chose to be a spy four centuries ago, I attracted Bael to us. I made us targets. It's my fault, and I wasn't even able to protect his child — the one thing he begged me to do! Now instead of resting in eternal peace with our daughter, he has been reincarnated into the *same battle*. He'll suffer *again* because of me, lifetimes later!"

"Maybe some of us would rather fight next to our loved ones than rest underground with the worms," Mason said evenly. "Even if those loved ones are convinced they betrayed us somehow in the past."

Duchess fell silent, her chest heaving.

"You can ignore what I'm trying to tell you about Chan," he continued, "but as a doctor, I can assure you that there was nothing you could have done to save your child. You were late term, and Bael destroyed your body as well as tearing your soul in two. Bertrand asked you to do the impossible."

"I killed both of them," Duchess retorted.

"*Bael* killed both of them," said Mason. "And for some reason, all of you seem to have difficulty with that concept. But Chan is not Bertrand. Maybe you'll do him the courtesy of letting him make up his own mind about what's going on."

"You don't know what you're talking about," Duchess said, low and angry.

Mason snorted. "Don't I?" He shook his head. "I think you and Bertrand were on this path long before you chose to become a spy. Much as it still pains me to talk about prophecies, this one was apparently set in motion millennia ago. We all just happened to get caught up in it."

Her throat started to close. "Go away," she whispered.

"Duchess…"

"Leave me alone!" This time, her words sounded like broken glass. "Don't presume to tell me how I should feel about Bael, my past, or this *prophecy*."

A brief pause, and Mason sighed, pushing himself to his feet. He inhaled, as though debating the merits of saying something more, but in the end, he pursed his lips and turned away, heading back in the direction of the hotel.

Duchess reinforced the shields that kept her thoughts from reaching the others. Her emotions were ablaze, trying to burn down those barriers and melt them into slag, but she would not allow that. She built up her defenses taller and stronger, refusing to let anyone see the depths of despair she'd sunk to now that the past had returned to exact its vengeance.

Alone in the balmy night air, she covered her face and wept with all the hopeless desperation of the damned.

# TWELVE

Chan allowed himself to be guided into a chair. Already, his burst of energy was flagging, buried under a growing sense of having done something truly heartless to a person he should have been trying to protect, rather than eviscerate.

He frowned at himself. *Where the hell had that come from?* The woman in question had just admitted to more-or-less killing him and bringing him back as some kind of B-movie monster. He'd drunk someone's blood, tearing mindlessly into flesh until the crimson liquid overflowed his mouth.

He was a fucking *vampire* now, and he was supposed to worry about the feelings of the vampire who'd bitten him? Chan shook his head, trying to clear his thoughts, and pressed the heel of his palm into his left eye socket until he saw starbursts.

He was peripherally aware of some sort of silent exchange between the Aussie guy, Mason, and his vampire girlfriend, before Mason said, "I'll go. She'll probably be expecting you to come after her."

The girlfriend—Oksana—nodded. Chan heard the door open and close as Mason left. There was a soft feminine sigh, barely audible, and then Oksana was dragging a second chair around to face his.

"You still have questions," she said.

Chan let his hand drop and pinned her with a pointed gaze. "You *think*?" he asked, laying on the irony with a trowel.

She sighed again and leaned back in the chair, crossing her left leg over her right. The graceful arch of her prosthetic foot tapped against her other shin in a thoughtful rhythm for a long moment.

"There's more going on right now than is visible on the surface," she began. "Your presence here... our presence here... it's not just random happenstance."

His jaw clenched. "Of course it's not random fucking happenstance. I'm here on a mission, which has now been blown all to hell thanks to your friend the ice queen. Lives depend on my ability to get intel on the Brotherhood in advance of any government move against them. But I guess that's been pretty well screwed now, hasn't it?"

The corner of Oksana's mouth turned down for an instant before she consciously smoothed the expression. It bugged Chan that someone who looked so unassuming could give off such an aura of power. She was attractive, yes, with striking Afro-Caribbean features and the smooth muscles of an athlete—but nothing about her should have said, 'I can rip your head off in one second flat and make sure no one ever finds the body afterward.'

Yet, just as Chan had been unable to attack Mason and make a run for it even though he'd had every chance to do so, he now found himself pinned by dark eyes lit from within by the hint of an unearthly violet glow. If anything, the sensation coming from her was far stronger than it had been with Mason, and it made his spine tingle with unease.

She spoke again. "We'll work to minimize the damage done by the Brotherhood—don't worry. We still need to find out what Snag is up to and get him and the boy out of there somehow."

Chan blinked. "Who or what is Snag? And… what boy? Do you mean the child the monks are using as a sort of figurehead to rile up the crowds?" He remembered the boy's glowing red eyes. "Oh, my god. The kid. Is he… a vampire as well?"

"Yes." Oksana's reply was grim. "His name is Sangye Rinchen. Both he and Snag are vampires, and we need to free them. But Snag ordered Duchess not to act yet, and we don't know why."

He'd… ordered her? When and how would that have happened? Unless…

"This Snag. Is he a creepy, skeletal bald guy who looks like he ought to be dead? Lots of scars on his body?" He had a confused memory of Duchess holding onto the bars on the man's cell like they were the only things keeping her upright. Neither of them had said a word to each other, but there was something else niggling at Chan's mind, just out of reach.

"Yeah." The word was flat. "That's him. You wouldn't know it to look at him, but Snag is the most powerful among us. We need to get him back, because there's a war coming."

He frowned. "The civil war that Tengku and the other monks want to start against the Malay Muslim majority? No offense, but I don't think vampires are going to be much help with that."

"No," she said. "No... that's not the war I mean."

Chan gave her a rueful grimace. "Then I'm afraid you'll have to be more specific. There seem to be quite a number of wars to choose from these days."

She arched a dark brow. "In fact, there's only one. The rest of what you see is only symptomatic of the underlying conflict."

He stifled a snort. "What... are you telling me vampires subscribe to some kind of deep state, Illuminati bullshit? Hate to say it, but I'm part of the so-called deep state, and we're lucky to get our 401(k) paperwork turned in on time. Global conspiracy is sadly beyond our reach."

"The war is between the Light and the Dark," she said, ignoring his sarcasm. "More specifically, it's a battle for control of humanity between the demonic force that originally turned us into vampires — killing those closest to us in the process — and an angelic force that has been in hiding or asleep since the balance was tipped several millennia ago."

Chan stared at her.

"You don't have to believe it," Oksana continued, sounding tired. "For now, you just have to be aware of it. There were six original vampires. Each of us wielded power or influence of some kind in the human world. Bael attempted to turn us into his mindless puppets by ripping the Light from our souls, making us slaves to his Darkness. But in each case, the person closest to us sacrificed their lives to save us from that fate. Rather than becoming soulless creatures for Bael to use as he wished, we became vampires instead."

Chan continued to stare. "This is batshit insane."

Oksana shrugged. "Like I said, you don't need to believe it based solely on my word. Just file it away for later, okay? Anyway, one of our number stumbled on a prophecy stating that Bael would someday be defeated by a council consisting of thirteen of his greatest mistakes. For a long time, we had no idea what that meant. Now, it appears that the prophecy refers to us, the six original vampires, along with the reincarnations of those who sacrificed themselves so we might live."

He tilted his head. "Six vampires and six people who supposedly died for them doesn't make thirteen," he pointed out, unsure why he was even playing along with this shit.

"No," Oksana said. "It doesn't. We're not certain about the thirteenth member. We thought it must be the boy, Sangye, but that was before you gave Duchess the message from Snag."

Irritation rose in him. "I keep telling you all, *no one gave me any goddamned message.*"

She shrugged a shoulder. "It's clear you don't remember it, but as I said, Snag is very powerful. Right after you met her, you told Duchess, 'Sangye is not the Thirteenth. Bael is attempting to draw the Angel out of hiding, but he does not understand.' So now we're not sure. There are other possibilities. Maybe it has something to do with the child Duchess lost when she was turned. Or maybe it's something we just haven't thought of yet."

Unwanted guilt pricked at him with the reminder of what he'd said to Duchess before she went pale and fled the room. Before he could chastise himself again for going soft on these psychotic head cases, Chan heard footsteps approaching in the hallway. Oksana looked up expectantly. The door opened, revealing Mason wearing an unhappy expression.

"How is she?" Oksana asked.

Mason heaved a breath and sat down on the bed. "About how you'd expect," he replied. "She... uh, she asked for some time alone."

Mason's eyes settled on Chan for a moment. Perhaps it was Chan's imagination, but his gaze seemed almost speculative. Before he could begin to wonder what Duchess had said to him, Mason turned his attention to Oksana.

"I don't know that we should try to wait for her," he said. "Maybe we should move forward on our own."

Oksana pressed her lips together. "Maybe."

"Chan?" Mason asked. "Could you lead us to the cult's hostages?"

Chan scratched the back of his neck and nodded. "It depends. I'm not sure if they will have revoked my security access after me being AWOL for more than a day. Are you intending to go after the boy? Or that other vampire?"

"Neither," Mason said. "Duchess says Snag doesn't want us to try to get him yet, although I for one have serious reservations about listening to him under the circumstances. Right now, though, we're searching for a human."

"Who?"

Oksana rose from her chair in favor of sitting next to Mason on the bed. The casual way he wrapped his arm around her shoulders made Chan's chest hurt a little, though he couldn't have said why, exactly.

"A friend of mine contacted me a few days ago to tell me that her son had been kidnapped," Mason said. "His name is Haziq Belawan — a pediatric doctor who works at a hospital in the area. That's why we originally came to Kuala Lumpur — we were looking into his disappearance, in hopes that we might be able to uncover something the police had missed."

"It was only when we started poking around that we stumbled on Snag and Sangye's presences here," Oksana added. "Not to mention yours."

"That seems like a hell of a coincidence," Chan observed.

"Not really," Oksana said, sounding tired again. "Although if we'd known we were about to get sucked into another vortex of chaos, we might have come better prepared."

Mason huffed in grim amusement. "Yeah — silly us. We just thought we were wading into your average, everyday morass of violence and strife."

"'Vortex of chaos'?" Chan asked, not entirely sure he wanted the answer.

"That's what we've been calling it when Bael's forces are centralized in one location," Oksana said, "which to date has always corresponded with one of our lost soulmates being found. It's like his power is funneling towards the person we're seeking. This time it was you."

He was right. He shouldn't have asked. Still…

"So you think all this shit with the cult and the political instability is because he was coming after me? That's bull. Why would he bother? I was already working for the bad guys," Chan pointed out.

"Thought you were working for the Americans," Mason muttered.

Oksana elbowed him. "We weren't sure if he'd become aware of you yet. This vortex is muddled, with Snag and Sangye thrown into the mix."

Chan fell silent and thoughtful again. That must be why Duchess had acted so ruthlessly and changed him into a vampire. She believed this so-called demon would discover his presence and try to destroy him.

*So, maybe she really did think she was saving me,* he mused. *Fucking hell.*

"Saving you, and preventing as much pain and suffering as possible by short-circuiting the vortex," Mason offered aloud.

"This whole 'you can read my mind anytime' thing is getting really old, really fast," Chan observed coolly.

Neither of them looked particularly abashed.

"You get used to it," Oksana said. "And if you don't like it… well, consider that motivation to perfect the art of mental shielding."

Something else had been bothering Chan, and he changed the subject in hopes of getting more sense out of them. "How did your pediatrician friend get tied up in all of this vampire shit?"

Mason's brow furrowed. "From what we've gathered, he made himself a target by speaking out against the Brotherhood in a newspaper editorial, after he volunteered for ER duty to treat some victims of the cult who'd been tortured. He was snatched from the hospital parking lot in broad daylight, not long after."

Chan thought back to the man that he recently restrained as Tengku sliced him open with a knife—Loy Cho. It would make sense that he and others like him would seek medical attention after escaping Tengku's temper. Chan could easily imagine the monk targeting any doctor brave or stupid enough to call him out publicly like that.

He sighed, overcome with the sobering realization that whatever happened from this point on, his old life was over. He'd worked for well over a year on this mission, and for what? He'd been due to check in with his handler almost two days ago. It was likely they were already working on the assumption that he'd been compromised somehow.

Little did they know. What the hell kind of operative couldn't go out in daylight and needed to suck on someone's vein to keep from starving to death?

This had been a dangerous mission from the beginning. He'd undertaken it with the full knowledge that it was under an NOC designation—non-official cover, meaning that the United States would disavow all knowledge of him if he were caught. They wouldn't attempt to extract him, or even recover his body. He'd agreed to that on day one.

*At least this way, once they get around to declaring me missing, presumed dead, my pension and insurance will go to my daughter,* he thought to himself. *She'll have everything she needs.*

His old life was gone. The life that stretched out before him was filled with uncertainty — if you could call being a vampire a *life*. He tried to tell himself that it was an opportunity to shed his old skin and start fresh, but he couldn't shake the sense that he'd failed his mission. He'd been placed in Kuala Lumpur to help bring peace back to the region.

"Maybe you can still help with that," Oksana said, breaking into Chan's thoughts, "but the stakes have gotten higher. Help us bring peace back to the world, and Kuala Lumpur is sure to follow."

"And in the mean time, there's Haziq," Mason added. "Not to mention Snag and Sangye."

Chan sighed. As he saw it, there were a couple of possibilities here. This bunch might be completely delusional. Or — and this was much more concerning — they might *not* be delusional. Chan had seen some seriously weird shit in the last couple of days. Enough to make him think that even if things weren't exactly as Mason and Oksana had lain out, there was still more going on in the world than he'd ever believed.

Right now, all they were asking of him was to help find Tengku's hostages and free them. That was something he'd been itching to do long before a demon temptress kicked his ass and drank his blood.

"All right," he said. "I'll do it."

As he spoke, the door to the room creaked open, revealing Duchess framed in the doorway. Her flawless makeup was gone, and her eyes were suspiciously red and swollen. The yellow glow from a streetlight outside peeked through heavy curtains hanging across the window. It illuminated her face with a strange glow, making her look like a statue of some pale, long-forgotten goddess of grief and vengeance.

"In that case," she said, "we'd better get started."

# Thirteen

The next several hours were spent in planning. Much to her disgust, Duchess found it difficult to stay focused on the here and now as memories and emotions clamored for attention behind her tightly constructed mental shields. Chan and Mason were deep in discussion when Oksana moved closer to her in the dim environs of the room.

"How are you?" she asked, keeping her voice low.

"Never better," Duchess replied, deadpan. "Why do you ask?"

Oksana raised an eyebrow. "Goodness. That was certainly… *believable*."

Duchess lifted a matching brow. "It's what you're going to get, *petite soeur*. Learn to be happy with it."

"You're still angry I dragged you back here. I get it, *ti mwen*. But you *cannot* avoid this situation forever."

"Watch me," Duchess bit back, her tone sharp. An instant later, she realized that the words were a precise echo of what Oksana had told her under similar circumstances in Haiti.

The sound of a throat being cleared interrupted the quiet but tense exchange.

"Chan has a proposal," Mason said. "Unfortunately, I'm a doctor, not an army general, so about all I'm able to offer up is some variation of, 'wow, that sounds really dangerous.' Which means you two will probably want to hear him out and offer more useful feedback."

"Probably so," Oksana agreed. She stood up, though her eyes remained on Duchess for a long beat before she turned her attention to the men. "Go on—run it by us."

"The problem is going to be firepower," Chan said, keeping his eyes averted from Duchess. "Unless you have a stash of weapons hidden somewhere, that is."

"Nope. What you see is what you get, I'm afraid," Mason replied.

"I'd figured," Chan murmured, something about his tone conveying that he thought they were being irresponsible by coming here without bringing along a small arsenal.

"We don't generally need heavy weaponry against humans," Oksana explained.

"As you might recall from our first meeting," Duchess couldn't help adding—petty though it might have been.

Chan flushed, the human reflex not yet subsumed by his new vampiric nature.

"Nevertheless," Chan continued, "It's a matter of logistics. Mason told me that a gunshot wound wouldn't kill one of us, but it could slow us down, requiring time for healing."

"Yes, that's right," Oksana replied. "Short of staking and decapitation, there's very little humans can do to us that would be fatal. But there's plenty that a group of well-armed humans with the force of numbers behind them might do to render us temporarily unable to function effectively — at least if we were in solid form."

Chan's eyes flashed. "Solid form? Explain that."

"It will take time and practice for you to master the skill," Duchess said, "but the rest of us can change form at will."

"Into what? Anything?" he asked.

"Into owls, or a vaporous cloud of mist that's unaffected by bullets," Oksana answered for her.

Chan frowned. "Vapor." His eyes met Duchess' for the first time since he'd started talking. "It's a bit muddled... but when I took you into the bowels of the complex, you disappeared when we got close to the guards, and reappeared a few moments later."

Duchess blew out an impatient breath before dematerializing long enough to swirl across the room and reappear by the window.

"Well, son of a bitch," Chan said. "That's certainly a game-changer."

"Yes," Duchess agreed. "Pity you'll be unable to make use of it, and that Mason is still in danger of leaving an impact crater whenever he tries to shift back into human form and land."

"Thanks for that," Mason murmured, giving her a sour look but not rising to the bait otherwise.

"This would still have been good information to have several hours ago," Chan said pointedly.

The worst part of it was, he was absolutely right.

"Suffice to say," Duchess began, "for three of us at least, getting in is not the issue. It's getting out with Haziq, Sangye, and especially, Snag."

Chan frowned. "I'll grant you Haziq. But shouldn't the vampires be able to sneak out in this vaporous form?"

"Normally, yes," Oksana said. "But something has kept Sangye from escaping in the weeks he's been held prisoner. Without speaking to him, we have no way of knowing if it's due to unwilling-ness or inability. After weeks as a vampire, he *should* have the power to transform, even if he's not skilled at it yet. But it's dangerous to assume things."

"Especially since the poor kid apparently spent the first couple of weeks starving himself rather than feed from any humans," Mason added grimly.

Chan looked taken aback. "Damn. Given how strong my cravings were when I first woke up, that's saying something for a kid that young."

Oksana rubbed her face. "We might have ne-glected to mention that Sangye is thought by many to be the reincarnation of the Dalai Lama."

Chan had been pacing restlessly as they spoke, but now he sat rather abruptly in the closest chair. "*What?*"

"Yeah, you heard right," Mason said. "Proba-bly best not to think about that one too closely."

Chan shook his head slowly back and forth. "Uh… yeah, maybe not. Okay, so we can't count on the kid being able to poof himself out. What about your friend? Why did you say, 'and *especially* Snag'?"

"You saw him yourself," Duchess said. "He's nearly comatose—barely strong enough to move, much less transform."

"This mission is a logistical train wreck. You realize that, right?" Chan observed in a pleasantly conversational tone.

"Welcome to our world," Mason said.

-o-o-o-

In the end, they settled on a plan in which Duchess, Oksana, and Mason would sneak into the Brotherhood's complex as mist, while Chan flexed his new powers of mesmeric influence. It was risky since he'd had no real chance to practice the art, but Duchess figured it wouldn't take much to get him in. He was already a figure of authority over the complex guards; he would merely need to remind them of that fact. What they would do to get back out was considerably more nebulous at present.

There was one additional aspect that needed to be addressed before they left, and it was one Duchess fully intended to leave to the others.

"Oksana," she said, "feed Chan before we leave. I don't want him going for someone's vein at an inopportune moment."

Then, exercising the better part of valor, she left the room before anyone could say anything in response.

Half an hour later, the four of them were walking down the same road she'd taken to the temple on the night she'd found Snag and Chan. While there were a few people headed in the same direction, it wasn't the large tide she'd seen before.

When they arrived in the large courtyard, it was clear that if there had been a rally the previous evening, it was long over. Not surprising, since it was well past three a.m.

They had intended to continue to the complex as quietly as possible; those of them who could do so changing form in the shadows of the trees that bordered the area. As the temple came into view, however, Chan called a halt.

"Something's up," he said. "That's way too much activity for this time of night. The temple should be shut up tight."

Duchess cast her senses outward, aware of Oksana doing the same. "Things inside seem rather… confused," she said. "And there's something I can't quite put my finger on —"

Chan's jaw worked for a moment, then he appeared to come to a decision. "I think we should check it out. If it looks like many of the guards are inside, we can take advantage of whatever is happening and try for the complex. But I don't like not knowing what's going on."

"Agreed," Duchess said. "Most of the activity feels like it's coming from the lower level. Is there a way leading directly into the basement?"

Chan indicated the west side of the ornate structure. "The side door behind the stage leads to the ground level, but there's a partially excavated underground area that can only be reached from a stairway inside."

Duchess met the others' eyes, confirming they were ready. She led the way into the shadows beneath the thick growth of palm trees nearby. Chan pulled the gun she had returned to him from his waistband and double-checked it was loaded.

"Let's do this," he said.

The rest of them transformed into mist and swirled above him, following as he walked with confident strides toward the side door. It was guarded, of course, and Duchess hovered, ready to act. Chan walked up to the guard, one hand raised in greeting. When he got close enough, the man's eyes widened, and he scrambled for his weapon.

"Stop," Chan said calmly, copper light kindling in his eyes. "You don't need to detain me. I'm the security chief. You should let me inside now."

The guard hesitated, shaking his head as though to dislodge an insect. A moment later, his shoulders relaxed, and he stepped to the side, opening the door so Chan—and the rest of them—could go through.

"These aren't the droids you're looking for," Chan muttered under his breath, once the door closed behind him.

Inside, the sounds of people could be heard from further ahead, but the entryway was clear. Even on this lower level, the architecture and decoration was stunning. The place exploded with color, open spaces broken up with alcoves defined by ornate columns and scrollwork. Prayer wheels lined one wall.

Chan led them deeper, only to dart into an alcove when a group of monks appeared at the end of the hallway beyond. Duchess and the others swirled around him, concealing themselves near the ceiling where few people bothered to look.

Whatever had been grating on her senses earlier was getting worse, but she was distracted by a presence she had felt once before.

*Sangye is nearby*, she sent through the link.

*I feel him*, Oksana confirmed. *But there's something else…*

*I think they may be keeping the boy here permanently, rather than at the complex.* That was Chan, his mental voice clear but unpracticed.

The voices of the monks gathered in the hallway moved farther away, and Chan slipped out of his hiding place. They followed him to a door decorated in the same ornate style as everything else. This one was unguarded, and Chan frowned.

*Too easy*, he thought, and drew his gun, flipping off the safety before he opened the door one-handed and peered inside. As he'd described, it was a staircase leading down to a subterranean level, though even down here, the walls were brightly painted and clean, covered with decorations.

Duchess realized what was wrong an instant before Chan emerged into the open space beyond the foot of the stairs. She felt Oksana's jolt of distress at the same moment, but Chan was already striding forward toward the circle of monks surrounding a young boy and a withered figure lying on a stretcher on the floor.

"*Tengku,*" Chan snapped, and one of the monks straightened. Duchess recognized him as the charismatic speaker from the rally the other night.

The monk's mouth split into a sickening grin, and he reached for the hilt of a curved sword at his belt. Duchess and the others swirled into solid form just as Chan shot the monk through the heart. The man staggered back a step, but then he straightened, still grinning. He slid the sword from the sash around his waist, and stepped forward, lowering the blade to hover over Snag's neck.

"What the hell?" Chan hissed, staring at the bullet hole clearly visible through the center of Tengku's chest.

"*Undead,*" Oksana grated, her fists clenching at her sides.

"Bael has turned these people into lifeless puppets," Duchess explained, anger flooding her. "Your bullets won't stop them."

"And your friend's vertebrae will not stop my blade as I decapitate him," Tengku said coolly, staring them down with filmy, bloodshot eyes.

The child Sangye still crouched on the floor next to Snag, looking up at his captors with pleading eyes. "Do not do this," he begged.

Tengku didn't even spare him a glance, his eyes only for the vampires standing before him. The other undead monks stared blankly at them, awaiting orders.

"Your arrival is fortuitous," Tengku said conversationally. "The child will not feed."

Duchess itched to pull the dagger from the sheath at the small of her back and dart forward toward him, but that razor-sharp blade poised over the brittle length of Snag's neck held her back.

"Snag doesn't have a drop of blood left in his body," Oksana said in a reasonable tone. "Look at him. There's nothing there for the boy to feed on."

Tengku's head tilted in slow motion as he regarded her, the movement reptilian. "Then, as I said, your arrival is fortuitous. We will capture the most powerful of you, and the child may feed from a fresh vein. The rest of you will join our ranks, as you should have done long ago."

A sick feeling washed over Duchess as the monks' heads fell back in unison, their mouths opening soundlessly. Tengku lifted his arms, the sword still grasped in his right hand.

"We need to leave," Duchess rasped. "Get out now —"

But it was too late. Tengku laughed, the sound like cracking plaster. "Come, my Master. Your new servants await you!"

Black mist poured in from the edges of the floor and ceiling — a great weight pressing down on Duchess as Oksana and Mason cried out behind her.

# FOURTEEN

Duchess tried to draw enough breath to shout again—to order the others to flee. But the suffocating weight of the blackness smothered her, eating at her flesh with that horrible vitriolic burn. Chan screamed, and a single thought of '*No!*' propelled her toward the place where he'd been standing.

Their bodies collided, and Duchess pressed him to the floor, covering him, for all the good it would do against an attack that was as much psychic as physical. She cast around; her telepathic senses feeling like they were submerged in murky swamp water. She could just about make out Oksana and Mason clinging together. Their love for each other was a faint globe of light pressing back against the darkness within the landscape of Duchess' mind.

They were hanging on—barely—but they were in no position to mount any real resistance. Snag's essence was so faint that she'd lost track of it as soon as Bael descended on them, and Sangye cowered on the floor, obviously terrified. The worst was Chan, though. Even trapped beneath her body, he was still screaming—clutching at his head and trying to throw her off.

Duchess was the strongest. It was her job to protect the others. She tried to place her mental essence over Chan's like a shield. For a moment, his struggles quieted, but then a cruel laugh echoed around the fog-filled space. Duchess cowered as Bael turned his attention on her, hating herself for the instinctive reaction, but utterly unable to prevent it.

*You think to protect your worthless cur of a mate from the darkness that already lies within his soul?* Bael cackled. *He is as good as mine. Go on – try to stop me from plucking free the tiny spark of Light remaining to him. I can hardly wait to see what happens when I reach inside* your *darkness.*

Duchess moaned as fingers tipped in greasy black claws tore into her essence, reaching unerringly for the cancerous tumor of guilt and grief that twined through her rent soul. *No, no, no,* she thought, feeling the fingers grasp at her soul and begin to tear. She was desperate for a lifeline… for someone to reach out a hand and save her, but Chan was too weak, Snag was nearly dead, Sangye was a young child, and Oksana and Mason were barely holding their own.

She would not drag any of them down with her.

Just as she feared Bael would overpower her and destroy the others, a dome of brightness mushroomed outward from the middle of the room, pushing back the black fog in its wake. It flowed over Duchess and Chan as she lay huddled over him, ripping Bael's grasping fingers free of her essence. The demon shrieked in anger, scrabbling for a hold on her soul, but the moment the light enveloped her completely he slipped loose, leaving her soul still anchored inside her chest.

Every square centimeter of Duchess' body ached and burned, but she pushed upright and looked around in confusion, seeking the source of her salvation. For a bewildering moment, she thought the dome of light was centered over Snag, but his life force was the same flickering ember it had been before. Then, her eyes moved to Sangye.

The boy knelt at Snag's side, his head bowed, and his eyes closed. The harmonics of the protective hemisphere of light matched her memory of the brief brushes she'd had with his mind.

He raised his head and opened eyes that glowed red with power.

"You cannot have them," he said quietly, his child's voice pure and clear.

Above them, Bael roared and battered at the edges of the light.

*Filthy whelp! I will destroy them one by one for this!* Bael's voice was incandescent with rage as the sound of millions of insect legs skittered over the dome. *Their blood will be on your head!*

For an instant, Sangye faltered, and the light around them flickered. What had been a solid shell became more like a web, allowing tendrils of Bael's power to slip through. The boy looked down at Snag, clasping his withered shoulder as though somehow drawing strength from the older vampire's presence. His small chest rose and fell rapidly, and after a moment, the light steadied.

"You would seek to destroy them whether I resisted your will or not," Sangye said. "Their blood rests on no one's hands but your own."

Sangye released his grip on Snag and crawled to Duchess, who was still huddled on the ground next to Chan. His eyes met hers, and she knew that Sangye had seen into her soul and understood what lurked there. He knew everything about her, including the centuries-old pain that had been threatening to overwhelm her from the moment Chan first appeared.

As Bael's power continued to coil angrily around the outside of the sphere, Sangye knelt next to Duchess and took her hand.

His fingers were small and thin against her palm, making her heart ache even more for the child she'd lost long ago. She'd always dreamed of holding that tiny hand in hers, just like this.

*It is time to release this pain*, Sangye said silently. *I see who you truly are, Marie de Duschéne. You were not at fault; this creature was. Your child has long been at peace. You should be at peace as well.*

Even with the others nearby, Duchess sensed that these words were for her alone. Tears welled up in her eyes, yet these felt different than the bitter ones she'd shed before. They no longer held the piercing sting of guilt and despair. These tears were... *cleansing*. They felt like a burden being lifted away; like rain clearing the filth that had been left behind.

Sangye reached up and brushed her face, wiping away the rusty moisture that clung to her cheeks.

"You have a chance to make things right again," he whispered. "Do that for me."

Duchess blinked up at him. She didn't know why she was so certain, but it was clear to her that Sangye was saying goodbye.

"What are you saying?" she demanded, gripping his small arm.

He did not answer, but instead rose to his feet. Her grip slipped free as though an irresistible force had simply pried open her fingers.

"Sangye!" she cried hoarsely, trying to rise only to fall back—still too weakened by Bael's attack to move.

He smiled for an instant, but still did not reply aloud as he gazed around at the others with a solemn look in his eyes. Silently, he walked over to Snag and knelt next him. Sangye closed his eyes and pressed a hand to Snag's forehead. As he exhaled, the dome of light around them contracted, as though some of the energy required to maintain it had been directed elsewhere.

As Duchess watched, it seemed to her that a bit of life returned to Snag's desiccated form. He no longer looked like a petrified fossil, but more like a leathery mummy. His life force flared momentarily and settled into a slightly stronger level. No longer a guttering ember, but now the tiniest of flames.

Sangye stood and walked towards the stairs. Tengku and the other undead monks backed away as though the power surrounding him was poisonous to them. With each step, the luminous dome grew larger, until they could not escape it.

"You will not win, boy," Tengku hissed, his back hitting the wall.

"I do not seek to win," the boy told him, before widening his gaze to encompass all the undead creatures. "Be free, all of you. Return to the circle of life, as it was meant to be."

The light slid across Bael's puppets, and they dissolved into dust that fell to the floor, forming half a dozen small piles. Sangye closed his eyes again, small brow furrowed, and the light around him exploded outward, streaking beyond the bounds of the underground room.

Bael shrieked and roared in rage, retreating before the blinding flash of pure and unconditional love. A crack like lightning split the atmosphere, and when it faded, the quiet left behind made Duchess' ears ring. Chan groaned and rolled into a sitting position, clutching a hand to his temple.

Sangye turned to look at them, the red glow in his eyes fading until only his natural brown was left behind. *Dawn is breaking outside*, he said through the bond. *The Brotherhood's followers are gathering, drawn by unnatural black fog in the sky over the temple. I must go now and speak to them.*

Duchess tried again to rise and could not. Sangye gave her another one of those soft, mercurial smiles before turning away and ascending the stairs to the main part of the temple.

*I don't like this*, Oksana sent, her mental voice sounding as weak as Duchess felt.

Duchess dragged herself forward, barely able to crawl. The stairs stretched upward like an unscalable mountain. She was too weak to stand; too

weak to transform. All she could do was pull herself forward a few centimeters at a time. She was
aware of the others following her in a similar
state — all except Snag.

"Sangye, wait," she croaked, but he was already gone.

She reached the base of the stairs and began to
crawl up them. The distant sound of a restless
crowd reached her sensitive hearing. By the time
she reached the top, a bit of strength was starting to
return to her limbs. She staggered upright, using
the doorframe for balance. The inside of the temple
felt nearly empty — everyone was outside.

By staying next to a wall for balance, she was
able to walk, after a fashion, retracing their path to
the side door that led to the raised stage over the
courtyard. She was aware of Oksana some distance
behind her… Mason and Chan even further behind. Ahead, she could hear Sangye's clear,
childish voice.

"*Brothers and sisters, you must change your path,*"
he called. "*Do not believe those who counsel violence
and bloodshed as a way to achieve your aims.*"

The crowd noises changed, from fear over the
black fog roiling in the sky, to confusion over their
figurehead's sudden change of message.

"*Evil came to Thean Hou Temple this night, drawn
by the Brotherhood's message of hatred,*" Sangye continued.

Duchess stumbled forward the last few steps
and threw open the door leading to the stage. Beyond, Sangye stood with his back to her, looking
out across the assembled people. The shadow of

the temple fell over part of the stage, sheltering it from the rising sun. Sangye stood near the boundary of the light, which crept closer nearly imperceptibly. Monks huddled on the temple steps and at the base of the stage, looking as confused and lost as the common people gathered beyond.

Oksana arrived, grasping Duchess' shoulder to help keep herself upright. "What's he doing?" she asked breathlessly.

Duchess shook her head, trying to pinpoint the reason for her growing sense of dread. He was just talking to them. It might be effective to sway at least some of those present—and they needed all such help they could get.

"That darkness took the leaders of the Brotherhood. It took Tengku. He and the others are dead now," Sangye said. "Hear me, brothers and sisters—if you give yourselves to the darkness, you will never again be able to stand in the light. I let the darkness take me. Now, I pay the price, so you may see and avoid the same fate."

Duchess frowned. Sangye's sweet mental voice wove through her mind, and Oksana drew in a sharp breath beside her.

*Tell Kumari Sadhu not to grieve for me,* he said. *If I am needed, I will return.*

Duchess opened her mouth to cry, "No!" even as she coiled her weakened muscles in readiness to spring forward and try to grab him. But a mental roar of anguish and denial from Snag made her stumble. Sangye stepped forward into the sunlight and burst into flame. The flare of agony through the bond sent her to her knees, Oksana falling beside her.

# FIFTEEN

Screams erupted from the crowd, a deafening wall of noise that seemed to physically press Duchess backward. Sangye's small body fell to the stage in a heap, the flames burning brighter before gradually dimming, until nothing but ashes and bones remained.

She was only dimly aware of Oksana's fingers digging into her arm hard enough to bruise. There was a strange keening noise, as well—barely audible beneath the crowd's hysteria. Duchess only realized that it was coming from her when her throat started to ache.

"Why?" Oksana repeated, over and over. "*Why?*"

Mason stumbled to his knees beside Oksana, and Chan caught himself against the doorframe an instant later.

"What was that, what happened?" Mason demanded.

"Sangye is dead," Oksana whispered. "He immolated himself in front of the crowd."

"Oh, dear god, no," Mason said faintly, looking at the pile of smoking ashes with horror.

Duchess slapped her palm over her mouth to stop the noises coming out. The sick feeling of having allowed a child to die... *again*... erased the brief easing of her spirit that she'd felt after Sangye spoke to her. He'd spoken to her, and now he, too, was dead.

"Get yourselves together, you three," Chan said. "This is a delicate situation — we've got a hysterical mob on our hands."

He was right, of course, but that didn't stop an irrational part of her from wanting to snarl at him. How dare he be so logical when Duchess had just failed to save Sangye?

"Can I go out there if I stay in the shadows?" he asked, grim.

"Yes," Mason said. "But be careful. What are you — "

But Chan was already striding onto the stage.

"*Quiet!*" he roared in Cantonese.

A few of the people closer to the stage turned to look at him, and gradually, the realization of his presence on the stage spread through the crowd in ripples, until enough of them were focused on him rather than making noise that he could be heard more easily.

"Your leaders are dead! Tengku and the boy are dead!" he called. "The Brotherhood is collapsing, and government forces will come soon to pick over the bones! They will arrest anyone found here, and anyone speaking publicly in support of this dead cause. Leave here in an orderly fashion. Go home. Go back to your lives! Don't become embroiled in this kind of hatred. Look where it leads!" He pointed. "Those of you at the back, turn around right now and walk away. The rest, follow quietly as soon as the way forward is clear. *Now. Get. Out.*"

He continued to point an imperious finger over the crowd. Slowly, those at the back did as he'd ordered, retreating down the road that led to the temple parking lot and the city beyond. Duchess watched numbly as others followed, until the entire crowd was shuffling toward the exit, muttering and throwing uneasy glances at the stage bearing Chan, and beyond him, Sangye's sad remains.

Chan was trembling visibly when he returned to the doorway, his face pale and his eyes glowing coppery behind the irises. "Fucking hell," he muttered. "I've always hated public speaking."

Duchess knew she needed to pull herself together. She'd left a two-day-old vampire to deal with an unruly crowd alone, and even now, Snag lay defenseless in the temple basement. She made herself rise; relieved that at least her body was recovering from Bael's attack, even if her mind was still reeling.

"We need to prioritize," she rasped, barely recognizing her own voice. "We can't go anywhere until sunset, and then our goal needs to be to get Snag's body to safety."

"What about Haziq?" Mason asked, not sounding appreciably better off than she did.

It was Chan who answered. "I don't know where he's being kept, and Tengku—the obvious person to interrogate—is currently a pile of dust in the basement. If we try to search, we'd have to split up our forces to guard Snag as well. Duchess is right. We'll have to get him out of here and then return, maybe with the police."

"Agreed," Oksana said softly. "Mason?"

"Yes, agreed," Mason said reluctantly.

The sun's killing rays were creeping ever closer to the doorway where they huddled. Duchess gave a last assessing look outside, not letting her eyes linger on Sangye's remains for more than a couple of seconds. The sun continued to consume him... already flaky ash was wafting away in the morning breeze. Soon, nothing would remain at all.

On the steps leading to the main entrance of the temple, many of the monks whose humanity Bael had not taken were wandering around, looking lost, or else seated with their faces buried in their hands. There was no way of knowing whether the guards tasked with overseeing the complex where the hostages were held knew what had happened here. No way of knowing how they would respond if they did.

"We should shelter in the temple basement with Snag," Duchess said. "If any of the monks are inside, we can mesmerize them into guarding the door to the stairwell until sunset. They can send any guards away without arousing suspicion."

Chan nodded. "Once the sun is down, it shouldn't be difficult to hotwire a truck and transport Snag out of here on the stretcher. There are several vehicles in the parking lot used for shuttling supplies in and out."

"Come on, then," Mason said, hoisting himself to his feet. "I don't like the idea of Snag being alone down there for this long."

-o-o-o-

Chan glanced at his watch, relieved that their involuntary daylight quarantine was nearly over. The day had been surprisingly uneventful, the hypnotized monks guarding the door for them only having had to send away a handful of people who'd been searching for anyone high enough in the Brotherhood's food chain to give them orders in a convincing manner.

He slanted a glance at the six piles of dust decorating the floor across the room and wished he could have Tengku back long enough to shake some answers out of him.

Watching the monk laugh off a high-caliber bullet through the chest had unnerved him badly — there was no denying it. Though not as much as… whatever the hell had happened next. His thoughts still shied away from the vision of black fog choking the room, and icy, monstrous fingers shoving through his skin to get at the soft parts inside his mind. He recognized the memories as potential PTSD fodder, and for now he was more than content to let his mental defense mechanisms block them out.

But those monks. Oksana had called them *undead*, and Chan was uncomfortably reminded of the sensationalized news stories coming out of the Middle East. The so-called *zombie plague* that reputable sources still claimed was something to do with radiation sickness after the terrorist bomb in Damascus.

He wasn't so sure about that anymore.

His gaze cut to Duchess. She was curled in a corner of the room, allegedly resting, but even now he could feel her mental distress over what Sangye had done. Whereas Chan was almost more angry with the kid than upset. And maybe that wasn't fair. What he'd done was psychologically shocking enough that it had turned the crowd from zealotry to fear—enough fear that Chan had been able to use it to send them away. He'd tried to channel mental power as he spoke, but he had no idea how much of his success had been down to vampiric influence, and how much to garden-variety psychology.

As long as they left and didn't come back, he guessed it didn't much matter.

He stood and stretched. "Sun should be down," he said. "I'll go liberate a truck for us. Once we're loaded up, do we have a place to go? I doubt your hotel would look kindly on us hauling a half-mummified body into one of their rooms."

"I know a place," Duchess said, still hunched in her corner.

"Need any help with the truck?" Oksana asked.

Chan shook his head. "No, I've got it."

He left the basement, glancing at the blank-eyed monks as he passed, and exited the temple cautiously. The whole place still had an air of waiting for the other shoe to drop, and Chan vowed to make sure that it dropped just as soon as he and the others could get something organized.

The humid dusk closed around him as he went out the side door of the temple. The stage was empty—no trace remained of Sangye's ashes. Only a few people wandered around outside. He ignored them and made his way to the parking lot.

"Chan?" a sharp voice said, a figure emerging from between two vehicles. "You're not supposed to be here. What's going on?"

It was one of the guards—a man who had always struck Chan as more intelligent than some of his fellows. The guard paused warily, his hand going to his sidearm.

"Don't," Chan said, putting some power behind the word. Already, it was becoming easier. "Turn around and walk away. Tell no one you saw me."

Those wary eyes went blank, just as the monks' had done when Oksana told them to guard the stairwell. The man lowered his hand and wandered away without another word.

Dangerous, that kind of power.

When he was gone, Chan broke the window on one of the older trucks and unlocked it. The plastic cover on the steering column was cracked and brittle. He popped it off, breaking it off around the screws holding it in place. It took a moment to sort out the wiring harness in the dim light, but before long he'd isolated the battery, ignition, and starter wires. He pulled out a pocketknife and stripped the ends, twisting the ignition and one of the battery wires together, then sparking the starter wire against the other battery wire.

The engine turned over, coughing until he revved the gas pedal a few times. A sharp twist of the wheel disengaged the steering lock, and he backed the truck out of its spot. There was a low concrete divider between the lot and the temple courtyard, but nothing the twenty-inch tires couldn't drive over. He steered to the side of the building and backed up to the door.

*Limo's here*, he sent, and felt an acknowledgment a moment later. By the time he'd exited the cab and lowered the tailgate, leaving the truck idling, the others emerged with Snag's stretcher and a small escort of mesmerized monks.

They loaded up efficiently and sent the monks away with orders to forget what they'd seen. Duchess took shotgun, directing him into the city, to a neighborhood about a kilometer and a half away.

"Here," she said, pointing to an alley leading behind some shops.

He parked the truck and joined Duchess while the others stayed behind to guard Snag. She led him out of the alley and to the front door of what looked like a general convenience store, signs in Malaysian advertising newspapers, snacks, and hardware supplies in the windows, one of which was boarded up.

"You take me to all the nicest places," he couldn't help saying, and Duchess rewarded him with a glare.

A bell jangled as they entered. Inside a middle-aged man looked up from his magazine and blinked.

"Raahim?" Duchess asked, and the man's face dissolved into an expression that could only be called *soppy*.

*What the hell?* Chan thought, only remembering when he received a second blue glare that he was supposed to be trying to learn how to shield his thoughts.

"I did not expect you to return, *Puan*," the shop owner replied, still making doe eyes at Duchess in a way that raised Chan's hackles.

Duchess' Malaysian was halting, but serviceable. Her eyes glowed as she spoke. "Greetings, Raahim. My friends and I have found trouble after all. We need a quiet place to stay for a day or two. Will your storeroom suffice?"

Raahim's face lightened. "Of course! Please, make yourself at home. There is a door in the back opening onto the alley. I will give you the key."

"Thank you," Duchess said, gracing him with a small smile. "We'll meet you there."

Raahim was already rummaging for the key as the two of them left to get the others.

"Admirer of yours?" Chan asked tartly, berating himself for giving a shit.

"Lunch date," she retorted in a flat tone that didn't invite further conversation.

It took Chan a minute to parse that, but when he did, he bit his tongue. Evidently, Raahim had enjoyed 'grabbing a bite' with Duchess quite a bit more than he had.

Her eyes narrowed at him. "When you drink someone's blood, it makes it easier to influence them. He'll let us stay in his storage room and not even think twice about it."

She wasn't lying. Raahim didn't bat an eyelash at letting them bring a mummified guy on a stretcher into his nice, reputable store. Chan shook his head in mild amazement as the guy bustled around, setting things up for them in the back room without giving Snag a second glance... or even a first one. When they were settled, he left them to it without a word about compensation or time frame. And, thankfully, without anymore puppy dog looks in Duchess' direction.

"What's that saying about absolute power?" Chan mused.

"I know just what you mean, mate," Mason muttered back.

# Sixteen

As soon as everything was settled in the cramped back room of Raahim's neighborhood store, Chan cornered the others.

"I want to get law enforcement moving on the compound while the cult is still in disarray," he said.

"Seconded," Mason replied immediately. "I don't like the idea of someone panicking and deciding to get rid of the hostages. Or abandoning them with no food or water, for that matter."

Chan nodded. "It's still a delicate situation. There were discussions underway about bringing military force into it, with some… international cooperation that I'm not comfortable discussing in detail despite the fact that all of you could probably pluck it from my mind if you wanted to."

"Was this military intervention imminent?" Oksana asked.

"No," he told her. "Though I'm totally out of the loop now, and I don't know what—if any—influence my disappearance and presumed compromised status will have on the decision-making process."

"So, if we can get ahead of the process by inserting civilian law enforcement, we can potentially de-escalate the situation, correct?" Duchess asked.

"Exactly." Chan ran a hand through his hair, idly noting that it needed a trim. Would his hair still grow now that he was a vampire? He shook off the odd thought. "Police action wouldn't have been practical before. Too many people ready to riot, and too many ready to rally around Tengku like some sort of martyr for the cause if he were arrested. But Tengku's dead, and not in a martyr-ish kind of way. My sense of things today was that the Brotherhood's back has been broken. It's just a matter of cleaning up the leftovers."

Mason raised a brow, probably at the idea of Chan considering the hostages 'leftovers,' but Duchess and Oksana nodded.

"There's just one problem," Chan said. "None of us have any standing with the police force. There's no reason they should take us seriously."

Duchess gave him a look that seemed almost pitying, which grated on his nerves more than it probably should have.

"You still aren't thinking like a vampire," she said.

His irritation flared higher. "Really? Wow. It's almost like I only became one a few days ago."

Oksana looked between them and sighed. "She just means that having credentials won't be an issue. You can influence whoever you speak with to shift you up the chain of command until you're talking to someone with the power to organize an immediate raid. Then you can influence that person to make it happen."

Chan stared at her. "You're right, I still don't think like a vampire."

"Apparently it takes a few decades to grow into that level of shameless audacity," Mason muttered.

Chan's lips twitched into a frown. "Look, if it'll get those hostages out, then fine. Let's do it. I know more details about the cult than the rest of you, so I need to go."

Oksana spoke up quickly, before Duchess had a chance to respond. "Mason and I will stay here and see if we can do anything for Snag. Since Mason's a doctor, it only makes sense, and I'd be more comfortable if I was here to watch over the two of them. I'll also try to contact Eris."

Duchess gave her a look that said Oksana was about as subtle as a two-by-four to the side of the head, and Chan couldn't disagree. But, whatever strange motivation Oksana had for trying to force them together, there was no logical reason to argue the plan.

"Fine," Duchess said. "We'll take the truck. I'll call you if we're forced to shelter somewhere from the daylight tomorrow."

-o-o-o-

It was shockingly easy to influence the police to do what they wanted, as it turned out. Chan was caught between being a bit awestruck by Duchess' ice-cold manipulation of the evening shift commander and being irritated with her ice-cold treatment of *him*.

She was locked down tight after her display of anguish that morning when Sangye had killed himself. Not a single thought or emotion leaked through the blank wall she'd erected around her mind. Chan tried to tell himself he shouldn't care. What was it to him if she wanted to treat him with contempt, like some kind of mute appendage following her around until she needed a piece of specific information about the Brotherhood?

It didn't matter. All that mattered was that the fat Kuala Lumpur police commander with the too-tight jacket straining across his belly was on the phone arranging for SWAT teams and uniformed backup. The guy didn't so much as blink when Duchess informed him in her slightly broken Malaysian that she and Chan would be leading the hostage recovery team, and that he would need to provide her with a gun.

Three hours later, they were jouncing along in a dark Kia Pregio van, part of a convoy headed for the old condominium complex held by the cult. They didn't speak, nor did the stony-faced assault force members, dressed in black and cradling their service weapons like swaddled infants.

Chan had already sketched out maps of the place, and the vehicles immediately split up to cover the main entrance of the building as well as the side entrances and the delivery dock. He wished he had a better idea of the status of the hired guards and mercenaries. Most of them must surely know by now that their paymasters were dead. Would they have left? Or gone on a rampage, looting the place and killing hostages?

It was tempting to send Duchess inside in vaporous form to do recon, but they couldn't afford to have too many members of the police teams see something impossible and freak out. It would be difficult to mentally influence them all without also making them too out-of-it to do their jobs properly.

So, they did things the old-fashioned way. As far as the rest of the team was concerned, he and Duchess were specialists from another department. He was armed with his Glock, and Duchess had a 9mm Makarov shoved into her waistband. They were leading the group storming the main entrance, near the offices where Chan had worked as co-security chief with Pula, and also near the secret entrance in the storeroom leading down to the converted storm shelter where Snag and the other 'dangerous' hostages had been held.

Half of the team covered their approach while he and Duchess led the other half through the unlocked glass doors. The offices were empty, raising Chan's hopes that the guards had fled. The light was on in the staircase leading down to the cells, though, and as they thundered down the staircase, Chan heard the unmistakable sound of a gunshot up ahead. A figure in paramilitary gear was moving methodically along the row of cells, shooting the prisoners as he went. He whirled at the approaching racket, giving Chan a good look at his face.

"*Pula*," Chan snarled, and charged him.

The assault team couldn't shoot Pula without risking the prisoners in the cells, but Pula had no such compunctions. He let off a wild shot that missed Chan but hit someone behind him, judging by the sharp cry of pain. The cry wasn't female—

wasn't Duchess—so he ignored it, plowing into the larger man.

Pula slammed against the bars of the cell behind him, the breath knocked out of him despite Chan's comparatively slender build. He swept Chan's feet and they both went down hard. Chan's limbs had new strength after his vampiric transformation, but the downside of the increased power was that he no longer knew his own body. He'd need time to train and relearn his capabilities, but that was no help now.

This fight would come down to brute, animalistic strength rather than finesse. Before, engaging in such a fight with an opponent as big as Pula would have been suicide, but now, his instincts rose, whispering *prey*, and before long he had the larger man pinned with an arm across his throat.

"*You*," Pula choked. "Goddamnit, I *knew* you were a traitor, Chan."

Chan ignored the words. "Where are the rest of the hostages?"

"Fuck you," Pula spat.

Chan felt his eyes burn, and hoped that they were angled away from the assault team sufficiently not to be noticeable. "*Where. Are. The hostages*," he repeated, pressing his will against the other man's.

Pula's face went gratifyingly blank. "Tengku ordered them moved to the cellar under the rear storage building after you disappeared. He thought you would return and try to free them."

"Goddamn right," Chan said. "Where are the rest of the guards?"

"Most of them took off when they found out Tengku and the other leaders were dead," Pula continued in a monotone. "A few are in the temple. I came to kill the hostages since there's no one to guard them or feed them anymore."

Anger surged, and Chan pressed his forearm harder against Pula's throat. "And you didn't think to, I dunno, *release them* instead?" he asked incredulously.

"No."

"Fucker," Chan hissed. "Stay down and let the police cuff you."

With that, he rolled off the other man and rose to his feet, brushing his hands off in disgust.

"Do you know the location of this storage building?" Duchess asked.

"Yes, it's not far," Chan said. "Though if anything, it's even less fit for human habitation than this place."

She nodded. "Two of you secure this room. Three more deal with the wounded and begin removing the surviving prisoners for medical treatment. The rest, come with us."

Once they were organized, Chan led them out of the building. They skirted the side to the open area behind it, where a barn-like equipment storage building with a metal roof stood at the edge of a line of trees.

"I can hear heartbeats," Chan murmured as he and Duchess neared the building, guns drawn.

"Humans below ground, but none in the main building," she confirmed, too low for the police behind them to pick up. Louder, she said, "It looks like they're unguarded, but take care. Someone might still be lying in wait for us underground."

Chan wasn't intimately familiar with this structure, but he'd seen the lean-to against the south wall that presumably led down to the cellar beneath. He and Duchess approached it.

"Bolt cutters," he ordered, examining the padlock holding the latch closed. Someone passed him a pair and he holstered his gun so he could cut through the metal shackle and toss the lock aside. Several rifle barrels pointed into the darkness as he swung the cellar door open on creaking hinges.

"Police!" Chan called. "We've come to free you. If there are any guards down there, put down your weapons and come out with your hands up. You've got about a dozen rifles trained on you."

"There are no guards," a weak female voice called up. "No one has come to give us food or water in more than a day!"

Chan exchanged a glance with Duchess, who shrugged. A guard could certainly be threatening her to make her say that, but Chan didn't think any of the guards would have agreed to stay padlocked inside a dark, musty cellar with a bunch of desperate hostages.

"Give me a flashlight," Duchess ordered.

One of the officers handed her one, and she descended the steep staircase. Chan followed right behind, gun in hand.

At the bottom, they found about twenty people huddled in truly awful conditions. Moisture glistened on the moldy walls, and the floor was half mud, half rotted boards. Some of the hostages were chained, while others weren't. Several were blinking, squinting, or covering their eyes. It was clear that they hadn't seen light in a while.

Duchess took a step forward, further into the gloom.

"Haziq Belawan?" she asked.

Someone moved, and Chan followed Duchess' gaze to a young man who looked to be in his late twenties. His hair was disheveled and matted with dirt, but he appeared to be in fairly good health otherwise.

"Who are you?" he asked in a hoarse whisper.

"An acquaintance of your mother's," Duchess said. "She asked us to help the police find you."

Haziq gaped at them. He pushed himself up from where he was lying on a pile of rags and walked forward. He was filthy, skinny, and looked exhausted.

Chan sniffed the air around Haziq instinctually and somehow came to the conclusion that he had suffered no major ill from his time in captivity. He was weak, certainly, but would make a full recovery — at least physically. Chan had been held prisoner on a couple of memorable occasions in his life. He knew that a part of you could become lost while in captivity. It would be up to Haziq to come to terms with the psychological impact of what he'd experienced.

"We're getting all of you out of here and back to your families," Chan said to the others. Several looked at him fearfully, as though they didn't believe him.

"It's not a trick," he continued. "The police are right outside. Gather any belongings you have. We need to get moving."

It took a moment before anyone moved, and none did so until Haziq had pulled on his battered tennis shoes.

He wrapped his arms around tattered scrubs and stood shivering in the darkness despite the smothering heat. Slowly, several others got up and joined him in the darkness, following his lead.

"That's the idea," Chan approved. "Let's get out of this place."

When all the prisoners had gotten up and were prepared to leave their dungeon, Chan and Duchess led them out. They walked back down the mud hallway and then up the stairs. A few of the prisoners were so weak they had to be helped by others.

"Don't shoot!" Chan called to the police as they emerged, his hands in the air. "We're coming up with the hostages!"

Carefully, they pulled every person up and out of the muddy hole.

One woman trembled with fear, tears streaming down her streaked face. She blinked and turned her head away from the lights being held by police officers.

An older gentleman appeared to be only semi-conscious. Haziq had one of his arms slung around his shoulders and Chan came forward to help him.

"I think he has pneumonia," Haziq whispered, his voice hoarse. "We could barely get him to wake up in the last day or so."

"I'm glad we got here when we did, in that case," Chan replied, easing the gray-haired man up the rotting steps. "We'll get him help right away."

Hands reached out to them from above, pulling the man from their grasp. Chan looked around and saw a stretcher waiting nearby.

"What about the others?" he asked Haziq.

The doctor wiped his brow, smearing dirt from his hands across his sweaty face. Like the others, he squinted in the light from the flashlights. It was clear they'd been held in the dark.

"Um," Haziq replied, sounding tired. "Almost everyone has diarrhea, which is pretty typical under these conditions. We're malnourished and dehydrated, but other than that I'm not sure. One woman might have a broken wrist. She'll need an x-ray."

"You did good, doc," Chan insisted, clapping the man on his bony shoulder.

Haziq smiled vaguely. "Thanks, I think. Who are you, again?"

"My name is Chan. I actually don't know your mother, but I know Duchess."

"I'm afraid I don't recognize that name either, but thank you both for getting us out of that hellhole. How on earth did you get past the guards?"

Chan gave a rueful smile, figuring that 'we're supernatural badasses with mind-control powers' probably wasn't the most useful answer he could give.

"We brought lots of police with us," he demurred. "Besides, the cult is in disarray, and there weren't that many guards left."

"Sir? Are you in need of medical attention?" An officer interrupted, approaching Haziq with a concerned look on his face.

Both Haziq and Chan spoke at the same time.

"No, I'm not."

"Yes, he is."

Haziq turned an aggrieved eye towards Chan. "I'm fine, really."

"He at least needs to be evaluated," Chan answered with a shake of his head.

"No, what I need to do is get home to my wife. I can't imagine what she's been through the last few—"

Chan interrupted him. "We can get her to meet you at the hospital. Come on—tell me you wouldn't order someone else in your condition to be checked out medically?"

Duchess approached, having been helping some of the others into the backs of waiting ambulances.

"What's this?" she asked.

"Haziq thinks he's getting out of an ambulance ride," Chan explained, raising an eyebrow pointedly. Even though he'd only known the doctor for fifteen minutes, he could already tell that he was going to like the guy.

Duchess turned her best haughty look on the disheveled man. "Physician, heal thyself. Or we'll set your mother onto you."

Haziq sighed and ran his hand through his matted hair. He glanced skyward for a moment, as if for patience, and nodded.

"Fine… at least I can shower at the hospital and leave the mess behind for them instead of Jayda. These scrubs should probably be burned in the hazardous waste incinerator," he joked.

"That's the spirit. We'll ensure that your wife gets to the hospital," Duchess told him as they walked slowly towards the last of the ambulances.

Chan could tell that the adrenaline from being rescued was wearing off. Haziq's legs trembled and he stumbled over nothing before righting himself.

"Take it easy, now," Chan said, catching his elbow.

"We will ride with this patient," Duchess told the wide-eyed ambulance driver, who was wise enough not to argue. Instead, she merely gave a mute nod.

"Did you psychologically compel her to agree?" Chan asked curiously.

Duchess snorted. "Oh, no. That was my normal intimidating glare. She was just being smart."

Haziq let the EMTs settle him in the back.

"We'll be there soon," Chan told him. "Just take it easy — the hard part's over."

# SEVENTEEN

A couple of hours later, Duchess entered Haziq's hospital room, seating herself in the chair next to Chan's. The young doctor had been evaluated by emergency room staff and was admitted for fluids, re-feeding, and monitoring over the next few days. He was also being given a round of powerful antibiotics to treat his gastrointestinal issues. Aside from that—and somewhat remarkably—he'd emerged largely unscathed after his time as a prisoner.

"No IVs until I've had a hot shower," Haziq had repeated, over and over again. The nurses pursed their lips in disapproval, but finally gave him clearance to bathe.

"As long as you have an attendant help you!" one of them had called after Haziq's retreating back.

That had been roughly thirty minutes ago. Once he'd disappeared into the bathroom, Duchess excused herself to make some phone calls.

"I finally spoke to Haziq's wife," she said. "I let her know that we'd located him, and that he'd been admitted but was in reasonable condition. She'll be here soon."

"As middle-of-the-night phone calls go, I imagine that was one she was happy to receive," Chan replied, rubbing his face with his hands.

Duchess made note of his clear exhaustion, but did not comment on it.

"I could tell I woke her from a sound sleep," she said instead. "She seemed fairly confused for a moment, but she was wide awake by the time we hung up."

Right on cue, rapid footsteps could be heard in the hallway. At nearly the same moment, Haziq opened the bathroom door.

He was unrecognizable as the same man that they'd pulled out of the cellar. No longer caked with dirt, his hair was clean and damp, standing on end from where he'd tried to dry off with a towel. A hospital robe was tied loosely around his body.

With a bang of the door, Jayda burst in looking around wildly. "*Haziq*!"

Haziq made a low noise of relief, and the two fell into each other's arms. Jayda hurled herself against him with enough force that he staggered backwards a step, his back thumping softly against the doorframe of the bathroom.

Duchess stood and jerked her head at Chan, motioning for them to leave and allow the two some privacy.

"Oh, my beloved… let's get you into bed," Duchess heard Jayda whisper as they walked out. Both of them were weeping openly with the joy of being reunited. Duchess refused to acknowledge the hard lump that tried to lodge in her throat as the door swung shut behind her with a soft click.

Chan sank into a chair in the hallway, his expression tense. Duchess followed suit after the barest moment of hesitation. She felt unsure of herself in a way that she hadn't in centuries—off balance and out of her element.

"What's wrong?" she asked, when Chan's expression of disquiet deepened.

"I'm... not entirely sure," he replied, running his hand over his face. "But I'm not really feeling my best, all of the sudden."

She examined him more closely, a thread of fresh worry worming its way through her. He looked pale, and a fine sheen of sweat covered his forehead.

"I don't know what the problem is," he continued. "Probably just tired. I don't think I'm very good at this whole *being a vampire* thing yet."

Duchess glanced along the hallway, making sure there was no one nearby.

"You need to feed," she said. "You're pale, and your hands are shaking."

Chan grimaced. She could tell that he was still deeply uncomfortable with the concept. "Maybe that's it. How should I know?"

"You know when anything human with a pulse starts looking irresistible," Duchess said dryly. "Some of the others describe it as a burning thirst, but for me, it was always more like hunger. It seems to be a little different for each of us."

Chan pondered this. When he finally spoke, his voice was grim.

"Yeah, I can kind of see both. I feel like I haven't had anything to drink in days. Parched."

"Like dehydration?"

"Yes. But also… predatory. Which is distinctly disconcerting when I'm stuck in a hospital with a bunch of sick and injured people."

Duchess nodded in understanding. "It won't always become so intense, so quickly. Though I must say, I'm impressed by your self-control as a new vampire."

"What's that supposed to mean?" he asked with a frown.

Duchess gave him a pointed look. "You haven't gone after anyone's throat yet."

"Oh," Chan replied, looking taken aback. "That's… a common issue, is it?"

"Don't worry. I wouldn't allow you to hurt anyone," she reassured him.

Duchess was well aware that as a freshly turned vampire, Chan's instincts would be commanding him to hunt. It was a very difficult position to be in—stuck between the remnants of one's humanity and the instinct of a vampire to seek blood.

A dark-haired nurse emerged from one of the nearby patient rooms. She was young and very pretty, with long hair tied back into a high ponytail. Chan's eyes snapped up, his nostrils flaring as his attention focused on her. Copper light kindled in his dark brown gaze.

To her surprise, Duchess felt a bristle of irrational jealousy. She quashed it immediately, appalled at herself. She had no claim on Chan. Aside from preventing unfortunate accidents while he was still a slave to his hunger, it was none of her business who he chose to feed from. What was it to her? It didn't matter whose neck he decided to latch his lips over, biting through soft skin as his victim moaned in a combination of shock and ecstasy.

*Hypocrite*, accused the voice of self-loathing that lived inside her. *How many nameless, faceless men and women have you bedded and bitten to make the pain go away over the centuries?*

A growl escaped her throat. She managed to cover it — poorly — with a cough.

The sound drew Chan's eyes away from the nurse and back to her. He looked guilty, as though he'd been caught in some wrongdoing.

"Shit... I think I'm in trouble. I may need a bit of backup, here." The coppery glow was still sparking in the depths of his irises. His tongue played over his teeth as though checking for sharp points.

"What do you mean?" she asked, distracted by the small movement.

"I shouldn't be thinking about hunting, especially at a time like this. We just got all the hostages back and--"

Duchess dragged herself back to the present concern. "It's only instinct."

"It's still an instinct that I'm not about to indulge *inside of a fucking hospital*," he hissed, low enough that no one else would overhear.

She opened her mouth to reply, but the door to Haziq's room opened, revealing Jayda.

"You don't have to sit out in the hallway like you've been banished," she said, her face radiating happiness. The relief emanating from her was palpable.

Duchess rose and gave her a gentle hug. "How are you doing?"

"Much better now," Jayda replied sincerely.

"How is Haziq?" Chan inquired, looking through the open door. The glow was gone from his eyes, and Duchess marveled again at his will-power in the face of a new vampire's hunger.

"Why don't you come in here and ask me in person?" Haziq's voice called.

Chan huffed in amusement, despite the tension still coiling in his shoulders. The three of them reentered the room, and Duchess' eyes fell on the frail man lying in the hospital bed.

"I'll need to fatten him up," Jayda observed, plumping his pillows behind his head.

Haziq turned an aggrieved eye towards his wife. "My weight is just fine, thank you. Before all this happened I needed to lose a few pounds anyway."

Jayda rolled her eyes and mock whispered, "That's what he keeps saying, but I don't believe him."

"I'm hurt, dearest. You can trust me on these things—I'm a doctor!"

"A very *stubborn* doctor," Jayda shot back.

Everyone chuckled, even Haziq.

"Well, I can't deny that," he admitted wryly.

"Other than being stubborn and in need of fattening, how are you, truly?" Duchess asked. After so much darkness and fear over the past months, it would be a relief to contact his mother Gita with some good news.

Haziq's face clouded over, his smile fading. "I've been worse, but I expect I'll still need a few days to recover. We survived — that's the important part. I hope that the others you took out of the cellar are okay."

"We haven't received any reports to the contrary," Duchess assured him, figuring that he didn't need to know right now about the prisoners the guard had shot in the complex basement.

Haziq nodded, but he didn't seem satisfied. "I wonder if I'd be allowed to visit them?"

"You can talk to the police about that. I expect they'll be here in the morning to interview you about your experiences." Chan explained.

Jayda made a noise of protest. "So soon? My husband needs his rest!"

"I don't disagree," Chan assured her, "but they'll want to get as much information as possible so they can make arrests and post charges."

"I want these barbarians off the streets," Haziq insisted, a fire burning in his eyes.

"Well," Jayda hedged, "I suppose it's necessary, then. But I will insist to the hospital staff that he needs to take it easy until he's completely recovered."

"And so you should," Duchess said, inclining her head. "Has anyone spoken to Gita yet?"

"I tried to call her on the way to the hospital, but she didn't answer," Jayda said. "I'll try again now."

She dialed and held the phone to her ear, smiling when someone picked up on the other end. Without a word, she handed it to Haziq.

"Hello, *ibu*," he said fondly. "I'm safe."

Then, he winced a bit and pulled the phone away from his ear, as Duchess made out a cry of "Haziq!" from the other end, followed by a rapid-fire torrent in Malaysian. Haziq lapsed into the same language, and Duchess could just about follow as he reassured her repeatedly that he was being treated and nothing was seriously wrong with him. Then he switched back to English.

"Two of my rescuers are here right now," he said. "I'm not sure if you know them?"

More words from the other end, and Haziq covered the microphone. "She wants to talk to you."

Chan waved the phone toward Duchess, since he and Gita had never met. Not that Duchess knew her terribly well, either, but they'd at least spoken a few times in the days after Mason had been turned in Haiti. Gita knew who she was, and, more importantly, *what* she was.

"Hello, Gita," she said. "I'm pleased we could bring you some good news today."

"Duchess?" Gita asked. "Is everyone else safe, too? Mason, and Oksana?"

"We're all fine," Duchess assured. "And Haziq will be soon."

"Allah be praised," she breathed in relief. "I can't ever repay you for what you've done. When I found out he'd been taken, I feared the worst."

"You don't owe us anything," Duchess said. "As it turns out, we needed to be here for... other reasons." She very carefully did not let her eyes slide to Chan. "It's good that we could help get Haziq back at the same time."

"Nonetheless," Gita said, "if any of us can do anything to help you, we will. I spoke to both Jayda and Haziq about you, though I'm not certain how seriously either of them took me. Mason told me you would be searching out sources of voluntarily donated blood. Do you have such a source in Kuala Lumpur?"

"No," Duchess said.

"Let me talk to Jayda, then. And thank you again, from the bottom of my heart. I'll speak to Mason as soon as I can and thank him as well."

Duchess gave the phone back to Jayda. She spoke to Gita in Malaysian, her expression growing uncertain as the conversation drew out. Haziq, listening to Jayda's end, gave Duchess and Chan a speculative look. After Gita finished speaking with Jayda and shared a few more words with her son, she ended the call.

Jayda met Duchess' eyes uneasily. "These things Gita says about you. Are they true?"

Duchess let her eyes glow with inner fire for a moment. "They are. You have nothing to fear from us, though."

"But... you do need blood?" Jayda asked.

Duchess felt Chan stiffen beside her. She hoped that he still had control of his growing hunger.

"We do," she said calmly. "But we can procure it from other sources if necessary."

There was a beat of silence, and Haziq asked, "How long since you last donated, dear?"

Jayda thought about it for a moment. "A little over two months. Maybe nine weeks?"

He nodded. "All right. Here's what I propose. There are bags and catheters in this room. No one will think anything of it if one goes missing. I'm too weak to give blood, but I'm perfectly qualified to draw some from Jayda for you if she's willing."

Duchess looked at Jayda, awaiting her decision.

Jayda swallowed. "Just a normal blood draw? Yes, I can do that."

"Thank you," Duchess said. "It's immensely helpful."

Chan was, if anything, wound even more tightly than before. "I think it might be best if I waited outside," he said.

"We'll both wait," she said, not wanting to leave him alone with his cravings increasing. She ushered him out, and he leaned against the wall, running a shaking hand over his face.

"Shit, Duchess. I'm not sure I can hold on for fifteen minutes while he sticks her," Chan said. "As soon as you started talking about blood, I felt like I was going to lose it. Can you—I don't know—mesmerize me into calming the fuck down for a few more minutes, or something?"

She looked at him in concern. His trembling was growing worse, and light was glinting in the depths of his eyes. "That won't work on you now that you've been turned," she said, running through options.

There was no doubt that she could restrain him if need be, but not without making the kind of scene that would necessitate a fair amount of damage control inside a hospital. They did have another option—one that wouldn't have been her first choice, but was undeniably the logical thing to do. She sighed. "Stay here for a moment."

She stuck her head back in Haziq's room. "We'll be back in fifteen minutes or so."

Haziq waved a hand in acknowledgement and went back to swabbing Jayda's arm with disinfectant.

"What are you doing?" Chan asked as Duchess took his arm. His eyes flared brighter.

"Come with me," she said, and dragged him into the first room that didn't have a heartbeat inside, closing the door behind them.

He was starting to get that feral look a vampire got right before they lost control and lunged for the nearest vein... which was all right, she supposed, since the only veins nearby were hers.

"Feed from my wrist," she ordered. "You've done that before from the others, have you not?"

His lips pulled back, revealing fangs beneath. Rather than answer, he leapt at her, crowding her against the closed door. She snarled back, letting her greater power press against him—not liking the idea of him tearing into her flesh like it was some kind of ravishment.

*Or liking it a little too much*, suggested an unhelpful inner voice.

He was growing in strength already, but nowhere near the levels of someone who'd walked the earth for more than four hundred years. The violence of his attack diminished, and he stood poised barely a step away, panting with need. His fiery copper gaze rested on her jugular with clear longing.

"The wrist," she reminded him sternly, and extended an arm.

He continued to stare at her neck with blatant avarice, but after a moment he grasped her arm and his fangs sank into the thin flesh over her pulse. His eyes fluttered closed in utter bliss as her blood welled up, pouring into his mouth. He was lost in his hunger — probably wouldn't remember this at all once he came back to himself.

At least, she certainly hoped that was the case, because then he wouldn't remember the small, needy noise she made as he suckled at her blood, the bond flaring between them. He wanted… so much. And she could feel him. *All* of him. It wasn't supposed to feel like this. It hadn't felt like this when he'd drunk from her after she turned him… had it? No, then her guilt had kept her from feeling anything deeper. Now, though, it seemed she could do nothing *but* feel.

When he finally pulled away, his physical need temporarily sated, it was all she could do to slam her mental shields down on the confusion of hope and fear and want and need swirling between the two of them. The abrupt jolt of the cut connection seemed to bring him back to the present. He blinked rapidly, his eyes returning to their normal deep mahogany.

"What… just…" he began, but she cut him off.

"You waited too long before feeding," Duchess said in clipped tones. She pulled her arm back, and

Chan let it slide free of her grip. "Come on," she told him. "I need to go refill. Then, we're leaving."

# EIGHTEEN

Roughly an hour later, the pair returned to the storeroom inside Raahim's shop, where the others awaited them. The sun would rise soon, but humanity's pre-dawn lassitude had allowed them to pass easily through the nearly deserted streets of Kuala Lumpur. Chan kept throwing Duchess veiled glances, making her skin tingle even as she schooled herself not to respond.

He had no way of understanding the complexities that lay between them. All he knew of her was a few dream images and a single, devastating lucky guess about her pregnancy. Her centuries of mental torment were not his fault. By contrast, his current circumstances and the upheaval of his life were completely her fault. Feeding him had been a mistake—no matter that she'd worried for the safety of the humans in the hospital at the time. For his *own* safety, she needed to keep Chan firmly at arm's length. He was a good man, but she had never been a good woman. She would only destroy him—even more than she already had.

They entered the storeroom's back door to find that Oksana and Mason had been busy. Some effort at cleaning had been undertaken, and Snag now rested on a simple pallet bed raised slightly off the floor. He was as still and deathly looking as before, his eyes closed and his flesh sunken.

"Any luck?" Mason asked immediately, hope lighting his pleasant features.

Duchess reached for a smile. "Yes, we retrieved him, along with the other hostages. Haziq is at the hospital right now with Jayda. It will take some time for him to recover, but they think he'll be fine. He's already talked to Gita."

Oksana grinned and closed the distance between them to pull Duchess into a hug.

"That is wonderful news!" she said. "I'm so glad to hear that."

Mason sagged in relief. "Oh, thank goodness for that. I can't thank you enough. Both of you." He rose as well, crossing to grasp Chan in a heartfelt handshake before clasping Duchess' shoulder.

"His wife seemed over the moon. Nice to get front-row seats to a happy ending for once," Chan said. He walked over to the cot, looking down at Snag with cool pity in his eyes. "Any change with him?"

"No," Oksana said, as she and Duchess joined him. "I'd hoped he'd continue to improve after Sangye injected him with some of his life force." Her voice grew sad at the mention of the young vampire who'd immolated himself to save them, and Duchess felt a painful stab at the reminder.

"By all conventional measurements, he's dead," Mason said grimly. "If I didn't have your assurances that he'd survived a similar state before, I'd say it was hopeless."

"He spent thousands of years like this and recovered," Duchess said.

"At least whatever Sangye did was enough for us to get him out of there without his body crumbling to pieces," Chan murmured, studying Snag's sunken face. "Maybe that was what he told the poor kid to do?"

Duchess and Oksana shared a look before turning simultaneously towards Chan.

"What do you mean?" Oksana asked.

Chan shrugged. "Well... he supposedly gave me a message to give to you, right?"

"Yes," Duchess said cautiously.

"Maybe he did the same for Sangye."

Oksana's eyebrows drew together as she said, "You think Snag planned this entire thing?"

Chan shrugged again. "Anything is possible, I guess. I don't know the guy, but I just find it oddly coincidental that he came back enough to make it easier for us to get him out. Either we were incredibly lucky or..."

"Snag arranged it in advance," Mason finished for him.

Duchess recalled the mental flare of anguish that had seared through the bond when Sangye died. "He certainly didn't plan what came next," she said in a low, angry tone.

Oksana shivered. "No. That much was obvious."

"Manisha's going to be gutted over losing Sangye, poor woman," Mason said. "Xander, too, I expect."

The vampires all stood in silence, staring at the eldest among them, who remained as deathly still as ever.

"So, how do you fix this?" Chan asked, gesturing to Snag. "Just give him a whole bunch of blood?"

"I have no idea," Mason admitted. "His swallowing reflex is non-existent in this state. We tried giving him our blood, but we just can't get it into him in any kind of quantity. I'd be inclined to try it intravenously — or maybe subcutaneously, since all his veins are collapsed. But I'd rather hold off until I can consult with the expert in the field. Snag's completely out of it right now, for all intents and purposes."

"He didn't seem all that 'out of it' when he was screwing with my mind and implanting strange messages," Chan pointed out.

"No, he definitely maintains some awareness," Duchess said thoughtfully. She moved forward and laid a hand on top of Snag's head. His skin was disconcertingly cool and dry, very much like one of his mummified Egyptian contemporaries. Yet as she closed her eyes, she could still sense his life force deep within him. It was faint and flickering, but it was definitely there.

"He's still in there," she concluded.

A bell-like chime broke the thoughtful silence, and Duchess looked around.

"That'll be Eris," Oksana said. "We can't get a decent voice connection, so he's been blowing up my phone with texts." She gave Mason a speaking look. "Excuse us for a few minutes. The signal might be stronger at the front of the shop."

Mason looked momentarily confused, but then he glanced at Duchess and Chan, and his expression cleared. "Oh. Right. I'll... uh... just go see if Eris and I can come up with anything useful in a hundred and sixty characters or less. Back in, um... a while?" he offered before backing out of the door leading to the main part of Raahim's shop.

"Smooth," Chan observed.

"Not really one of Mason's strong points," she conceded, "though he does have several other admirable qualities."

Chan wandered over to a set of shelves and leaned against it, crossing his arms. "Interesting," he said. "So it's not a generalized contempt for all things male, then? Just me, in particular. Aside from allegedly being the reincarnation of your long-dead husband, what exactly did I do to piss on your cornflakes?"

"You didn't do anything," she finally answered in a soft voice. "You're the victim, here."

He snorted. "Tell me something I don't know. There I was, just minding my own business, trying to infiltrate a militant Buddhist cult run by undead zombie monks, then all of a sudden, I'm caught up in a battle for heaven and earth. You know, I've signed up for a lot of crazy shit over the years, but I didn't sign up for *this*."

Duchess nodded, picking at a frayed piece of stitching on her sleeve. She knew he was right. "I did what I had to do to protect you."

"I know you *believe* that. But how is this protecting me?" His words were sharp, but there was genuine curiosity in his tone.

Duchess sighed. "Bael will try to destroy you, either way. He intends to prevent the formation of the Council of Thirteen. At least as a vampire, you're tougher. Harder to kill. And... you're with us, now."

Bitterness filled her voice towards the end. She couldn't help but turn away as terrible memories from the day she was turned rose up in her mind.

"That doesn't explain why you seem to hate me so much. Especially since I've done nothing to you," Chan pointed out.

"I don't hate you, but you should —"

"I should what?"

"You should hate me. You have every right," Duchess said.

Chan frowned. "Why? Because you killed whasisname? Bertrand?"

Duchess could feel her anger rising, coming to her defense. Its return was a considerable relief. "Is that not enough?" she snapped. "But, *non*, that is only the beginning. You are far better off staying as far away from me as possible. I'm a cold, selfish, angry bitch."

Chan pushed away from the shelves, straightening. "Yeah, I already got that part, thanks. The thing that seems to escape you is that in comparison to me, you look like a fucking saint."

Thinking back over her long and checkered history as a vampire, it was quite likely that Duchess had, in fact, fucked a saint at some point. She debated telling him that just to shock him, but he spoke again before she could.

"So... you acted to save me from the devil, without asking first if I wanted to be saved. And now, here we are, bickering like an old, married couple over the mummified not-corpse of a guy who can quite possibly hear every word we say. Now what?"

The sarcasm in his voice dripped between them like acid.

"Now, nothing," Duchess said coldly. "I've told you. Do yourself a favor and stay away from me. I've already torn your soul apart. Come too close, and I'll corrupt what's left of it."

Chan laughed. In fact, he kept on laughing—choked guffaws that eventually made him collapse into the chair Mason had vacated when they arrived, holding his stomach.

Duchess stared at him as though he'd gone mad.

Eventually, he got control of himself, slumping forward in the rusty folding chair with his elbows propped on his knees and the heels of his palms pressing into his eye sockets.

"*You'll corrupt me*," he echoed, and laughed again—the sound edged with something harsh and ugly. "Oh, that's rich. Seriously, you have no idea how funny that is."

"I certainly don't find it as amusing as you appear to," she said in an icy voice.

He sat back, looking her straight in the eye. "I was married, you know. To a truly good and loving woman."

All the air left Duchess' body, in a single, irrational rush of *who is this woman, and how do I find her and kill her*?

"Yeah, it's true," Chan said, meeting Duchess' shocked gaze with his tired one. "You know what happened? I cheated on her. I left her to go on deployment while she was pregnant with my child, and while I was gone, I banged random women that I met in bars. Then I got caught. One of my buddies told Janette what I was doing—as well he should have. I destroyed her life and the life of my unborn daughter. How's that for some cosmic irony? And I'm supposed to be an upstanding member of the armed forces, living my life beyond reproach. Serving my country and my family with dignity, fidelity, and honor, *blah, blah, blah.*"

He trailed away, looking up and shaking his head at the ceiling. "If you had any concept of what I've done to the people I was supposed to protect and cherish, you'd have let the fucking demon have me, and thanked him afterward for the public service."

Duchess could find no words. She'd tried to listen, but her brain had latched onto the phrase 'I was married,' and gotten stuck there. A surge of territorial jealousy threatened to overwhelm her as she imagined him holding another woman. Loving another woman.

*This is insane.* Was Bael possessing her somehow? Had she lost her mind? She'd given up any claim to the heart and soul of the man in front of her when she'd failed him in a muddy Parisian courtyard, surrounded by hanging laundry and the stink of evil. Had she not filled the empty years since his death with as many meaningless sexual trysts as possible? Had she not told him only moments ago to stay away from her, or risk what was left of his tattered soul?

This logical line of thought did nothing to quash the swell of bitter envy she now felt toward this woman she'd never met. Everything inside of her had been ripped open by his words, left glistening and bleeding in the sun.

She realized that she'd been standing in silence for too long and Chan was staring at her. Slowly, the rest of what he'd said percolated into her consciousness, and she blinked, the red rage of jealousy receding.

*Oh.*

It was obvious he expected a harsh response to his secret.

"Your wife and daughter," she said, forcing the words to emerge evenly, rather than as a hiss. "Do they still live?"

His eyes snapped back to her.

"Of course they're still alive! And they have the good sense to live their lives *without me*, which is something you might want to think a bit harder about."

She narrowed her eyes. "If they're alive, then it appears you have a considerably better track record in marriage than I do."

"*Fuck*. Listen to this shit. This is just *perfect*," he growled. "There's nothing you could say to make me forgive myself for what I did to my wife. I don't love her. I never loved her. I'm incapable of love. I don't deserve to be saved, and I *don't* deserve happiness."

"Neither do I," Duchess retorted.

They stood in the quiet, dingy storeroom — staring at one another without blinking, trapped in silence. A tentative knock shattered the strained atmosphere, and a moment later, Oksana and Mason returned. Oksana looked from one to the other of them, her dark eyes missing nothing.

"Eris is going to travel somewhere with better phone coverage. Then he'll try again to contact us so we can talk properly," she said, choosing to ignore the lingering miasma of emotional carnage in the room. "We should try to get some rest until then. We're safe enough here, and it's not like Snag is going anywhere."

Chan snorted. "Yeah. Sure. Makes sense. First rule of an operative—take your rest where you can get it." His voice was flat and distant. "Someone let me know when anything interesting happens."

With things by no means resolved, Duchess found an unoccupied corner and allowed herself to slide down the wall until she was seated on the floor. Wordlessly, she furled her aura and locked her mental shields down tight, suddenly aware of just how exhausted she was after the events of the past few days. Since it was the only escape available to her within the confines of this cluttered room, she turned her thoughts inward and let them drift, hoping for the respite of sleep.

Even if the nightmares came, it would still be better than trying to untangle the bad dream that was her current reality.

# NINETEEN

Duchess awoke a short time later from dreams of red, red blood and the bottomless rage of a mother's loss. She rolled into a crouch, fangs bared and eyes burning, but the vision of that muddy, seventeenth-century courtyard littered with the corpses of her husband and daughter faded an instant later. In its place knelt Oksana, one hand resting on Duchess' shoulder and unwanted sympathy lighting her dark eyes.

"*What?*" Duchess demanded, before her friend could say anything Duchess might regret.

For a moment, Oksana appeared to debate whether or not to comment on the manner of Duchess' awakening, but fortunately, she thought better of it.

"Eris finally got through," was all she said.

Duchess blinked, and her surroundings came into focus, along with the previous night's events. "Oh," she mumbled. "*Très bien.*"

Oksana rose and offered her a hand up. The others were gathered around a wooden crate they'd been using as a makeshift table, though Chan hung back a couple of steps. Oksana's mobile phone lay face up on the rough surface.

"I've got him on speaker," Oksana said, "but we wanted to wake you before we waded too far into things."

Duchess shook off the remainder of her grogginess and joined them around the crate. *"Bonjour, Eris."*

"Good, you're awake," came the tinny and faintly static-riddled reply. "Duchess, I need you to tell me exactly what message Snag left for you. Word for word."

One of the others might have berated Eris for his lack of social graces, but Duchess had little use for such pleasantries. She pushed her hair out of her face and pulled up a chair, settling into it.

"He said, 'Sangye is not the Thirteenth. Bael is attempting to draw the Angel out of hiding, but he does not understand.' The first part is straightforward enough, if somewhat difficult to credit. The second part is characteristically cryptic, unless you have some insight I lack."

"Nothing concrete enough to be useful," Eris replied. "Though we'd better hope he was right about the boy."

Mason frowned, his brows drawing together angrily. "That's a six-year-old child you're talking about, mate. One who burned himself to death out of some misguided attempt to save the rest of us —"

Eris cut him off. "Yes. He was a young child. And now he's a dead child, so if he was, in fact, our thirteenth member, then we have a rather serious problem, don't we?"

Oksana put a hand on Mason's shoulder as she spoke. "I've been thinking about that, Eris. The council is supposed to be made up of thirteen of Bael's greatest mistakes. But Bael turned Sangye purposely — he wasn't a mistake. At least, he wasn't until he sacrificed himself to thwart Bael's attempt on us at the Thean Hou Temple."

Eris was silent for a moment. "It's a fair point," he said thoughtfully. "As for the part about drawing out the Angel, with luck we'll have the chance to ask Snag for clarification directly, now that you've got him back."

"We've tried several times to give him blood orally," Mason reported in a flat voice, having apparently brought his temper back under control. "But, not to put too fine a point on it, his body is a mummified husk. He can't swallow, and if I tried to massage his throat I think I'd just end up pulverizing it. How exactly did you manage it the last time?"

"With a great deal of patience." Even over the cellular connection, Eris' grim tone was evident. "It took me almost a hundred years of squeezing a few drops at a time into him."

Mason's mouth opened and closed a couple of times, and Chan's eyebrows shot up.

"A hundred... *years*?" Mason echoed. "You might've mentioned that up front, Eris. We don't have that kind of time!"

Oksana met Duchess' eyes briefly, her thoughts brushing along their shared bond.

"Oh! That's right..." Duchess said. "Eris, Sangye was able to inject Snag with some of his life force without using the medium of blood. We perceived it as a sort of white light surrounding the two of them."

"It was enough to rouse him from a petrified state to how he is now, so we could move him without his body being in danger of shattering," Oksana added. "But I couldn't puzzle out the mechanism. I'd have no idea how to replicate it."

"I might," Eris said. There was a weighty pause. "I think you'd better bring him home."

"Home," Duchess repeated, surprised. "*His* home, you mean? To Cairo?"

"To Saqqara," Eris clarified. "To the place where I found him. We may have to make a final stand soon, and I can't think of a more appropriate place than where it all started."

"You think the war is starting now," Oksana said, sounding faintly shell-shocked. "Why? What's changed?"

"With the addition of Duchess' mate, Snag remains the only one of us not to be reunited," Eris said.

Duchess felt Chan stiffen more than she saw it. "Her *mate*? What the hell is that supposed to mean?"

Eris did not appear to have heard him as he continued, "If Bael wishes to act to prevent the council's formation, it will have to be soon. Snag is vulnerable right now. We need to regroup and start planning our defense."

Duchess tried to focus on logistics, but her thoughts were still tumbling like leaves tossed by the wind. "Getting Snag to Egypt will be a challenge. It's going to take some creative planning."

"What resources do you have there?" Eris asked. "I can transfer additional money if you need it, or Xander can."

Mason spoke up. "I can try to arrange for medical transport by air." He paused, rubbing at his forehead. "It will be difficult, though. It takes a ridiculous amount of resources, and there will be plenty of questions about who he is, what's wrong with him, and so forth. For obvious reasons, we can't let any other medical professionals near him unless we mesmerize them immediately afterward."

"Can you do it, though?" Eris asked.

Mason sighed. "Maybe. I can try calling in some favors through Doctors Without Borders. If nothing else, Gita owes us pretty big right now for helping free her son."

"Very well," Eris said. "Let me know what you come up with. In the mean time, I'll organize things on this end."

After a brief round of goodbyes, Oksana ended the phone call. "If nothing else," she said, "it will be a relief to be back together. If we're going into the end game, we should face it as a group."

Duchess had to fight not to let her eyes stray to Chan, who was still standing a short distance away from the others. It took a few moments to identify the tight feeling in her chest as the first stirrings of panic, and a few more to realize that it was in response to the idea that Chan might run for the hills the first chance he got, now that the immediate crisis had been resolved.

A mobile phone rang, but not the one sitting on the crate. Mason rummaged in his pocket and came up with the device, answering it.

"Gita," he mouthed by way of explanation, as someone spoke excitedly on the other end.

When the torrent of words finally stemmed, Mason smiled and said, "I'm just relieved we could help out, Gita. I can't take credit, though—it was Duchess and another friend of ours who finally got the police moving and found where the hostages were being kept. Yes… yes, that's right… I'll pass it on for you, don't worry."

Another heartfelt spate of words.

"Actually," Mason said, "There is something I could use help with. We've got one casualty who's in bad shape, and we need to get him back to his home in Egypt if it's at all possible…"

Mason pointed at the phone and then the door into the main part of the shop, which Duchess took to mean he wanted to get Raahim's input on something to do with the logistics. He and Oksana left a moment later, leaving Duchess alone with Chan again. Given what tended to happen when they were alone, this was perhaps not the wisest course of action. It was, however, a chance to ask him the question that she needed an answer to.

She must have looked uncomfortable, because he studied her warily for a moment and asked, "What is it?" in a guarded tone.

Castigating herself internally, she flipped her hair over her shoulder and turned to study the contents of the shelf nearest her. The affected nonchalance felt like a flimsy act even to her. For the dozenth time in the last twenty-four hours, she wondered what in hell's name had happened to her. This uncertain, emotional creature wasn't *her*. Was it?

"You heard Eris earlier," she said, still not looking at him. "We'll be rejoining the others soon in Egypt."

"Yes," he replied, still sounding cautious.

"I understand that you have no reason to want to be anyplace near me, but the simple fact is that you'd be much safer with the group," she said, pleased with how reasonable that sounded. "You've already experienced what Bael intends for all of us, and how impossible it is to fight him alone. Only together do we stand a chance."

"Of course I'm coming," he said, sounding confused.

She was already framing her next argument, so it took a moment for the sense of his words to penetrate. She whirled to look at him. "You are?"

"Well… yes?" He was giving her a strange look. "I mean… I feel like I'm starting a new TV series by watching the season finale, but I'm not a complete idiot. I think I've picked up the gist, which is that even if you and I would tear each other apart if we got too close, I'm still part of this council, or whatever. We're all that stands between the world and that *creature* from the temple. And your guy on the phone thinks the big battle is kicking off soon, right?"

*He's not leaving.*

The words reverberated through her mind, and she tightened her shields before they could escape and possibly echo across his thoughts. He wasn't leaving. Maybe all hope wasn't lost.

Now he looked even warier. "Assuming the others are on board with me tagging along. Or, did I read this wrong?"

"No," she said quickly. "You didn't read it wrong."

"Well, that's a relief," he said. "All of my bridges have been pretty thoroughly burned."

She frowned. "What do you mean?"

Chan laughed. It was a low, pleasant sound, and Duchess cursed herself for enjoying it.

His expression turned wry. "It's not like I can call up the CIA and say 'Oh hey, it's me! Sorry I've been out of touch for days after my check-in deadline. The good news is that the militant Malaysian cult has been defeated and their leader destroyed, sort of. The bad news is that I've been turned into a vampire!'"

She winced. *It had to be done*, she reminded herself.

"They wouldn't believe it, of course," he went on, "but I imagine they'd still have operatives coming after me with orders to eliminate quicker than you could say 'national security threat.'"

"I'm sorry," she said, knowing that he deserved far more than that.

He shrugged. "Honestly, I always expected this gig to result in my death sooner or later. I told myself that at least that way, my little girl would get my government benefits and insurance. Now she'll get them — once the powers that be get around to declaring me dead, anyway — but I still get to walk around and maybe make a difference in the world after all."

He'd said before that he was incapable of love, but listening to him talk about his daughter, she wanted to cry, *'Liar!'*

Instead, she asked, "Your little girl. Do you have contact with her?"

His face and posture had relaxed as they spoke, but now he closed off like a blast door slamming down. "No. And I suppose there's not much chance of that changing now."

He was probably right about that—another wound laid squarely at Duchess' feet.

"Well, then," she said quietly, "let's see what we can do about making sure she still has a world to grow up in."

Oksana poked her head in a moment later. "Hey, you two. We came up with a new plan."

"Oh?" Chan asked, moving towards the door. As he passed by Duchess, his arm brushed against hers. They both froze at the thrum of electricity, but Chan shook it off first, pasting on a neutral expression.

"It was Gita's idea," Oksana said, "though she has no idea how helpful it was."

Mason was still on the phone, jotting notes on a scrap of paper on the counter while Raahim looked on with mild curiosity.

"Mm-hmm," he said. "Yes. Absolutely. We can make sure to get that done tomorrow. Yeah. No problem. Thank you so much, we really appreciate it."

He hung up the phone, quirking a lopsided smile at the others. "We're set for transport, assuming no one was banking on traveling first class."

"I'm impressed," Duchess said, meaning it.

Chan clapped Mason on the shoulder. "Ditto. So, what's the new plan?"

"It was going to take the better part of a week to arrange for medical transport," Mason said. "So, I might or might not have made it sound like Snag was nearly on his death bed, in hopes of hurrying things along a bit."

"Emotional manipulation?" Chan asked, a hint of amusement peeking through his stoic facade.

Mason let out a rueful laugh. "These days, some of my closest friends are sociopaths—just ask Xander when you meet him. Maybe it's starting to rub off."

"You're a mad genius Australian man, my friend," Chan teased.

"*Anyway*," Oksana interrupted, "Gita mentioned that it was a sad state of affairs when it's quicker and easier to find a cargo plane to transport a dead body than to get medical transport for someone who was still alive. At which, point, a light bulb went off above Mason's head, and he started calling around to the various airlines. There's a cargo plane leaving from the Kuala Lumpur International Airport at eleven p.m., and assuming we can make all the arrangements by then, we're on it."

Duchess' eyebrows rose at the elegance of the plan. "Are we indeed? Well played, *Docteur*."

Mason shrugged. "We just need to get a coffin so we can store Snag's body inside of it. Then we take the cargo plane to Mumbai, and Eris can find us a flight to Cairo from there."

Chan let out a small, choked noise, and the others looked at him. "Sorry," he said, his voice sounding a bit strangled. "Is it in really bad taste that I find it hilarious you're going to transport a vampire inside a coffin?"

Mason looked confused for a moment before his eyes widened. "Oh. Bloody hell. I didn't even make the connection."

"If we're lucky," Oksana said, "Eris will find a way to revive him, and Snag can give you that flat, thousand-yard stare as punishment for laughing at him when he was down."

"Just don't dress him in a dark, red-lined cape before you put him inside the thing," Duchess offered wryly. "It's a very good plan, though."

"Thanks," Mason said. "All we need to do is let Eris know so that he can get working on the connection from Mumbai to Cairo. With luck, we can be in Saqqara within forty-eight hours."

"Do you think it will be hard to find a coffin on short notice?" Oksana wondered.

"These days?" Chan replied, growing sober once more. "I really doubt it."

In the end, it was relatively simple. Since they were confined to the shop due to the bright sunlight, Duchess used her mental powers to convince poor Raahim to help them obtain the needed item. Fortunately, both she and Oksana still maintained the habit of carrying a large amount of whatever the local currency happened to be, whenever they traveled. She pressed a fairly obscene amount into Raahim's hand and sent him on his way.

"That mind control thing is still more than a little disturbing," Chan said as he watched the shopkeeper go.

"At least I'm not asking him to commit a crime," she said carelessly. "I'll even let him keep the change."

"It's more the loss of free will aspect," he said. "Maybe I'm just hard-headed."

Without even thinking, Duchess said, "You always have been, yes."

Chan went still, giving her a thoughtful look.

"I'm starting to regain some of those memories, I think," he said. "Or maybe they're just dreams. But it's still really hard for me to believe in reincarnation."

She glanced at him through her lashes, wishing she'd kept her mouth shut. "Haven't you been living among Buddhists?" she asked carelessly, as though it didn't matter.

"Yes. But it goes against everything that I've always believed," Chan admitted. "I've never been a religious man, so I have a hard time with the whole demons and angels thing, too."

"Even after what you experienced in the temple?"

"Call me the CIA's own Doubting Thomas, I guess," Chan replied with a shrug.

"What do you remember from the past?" Duchess asked, still unable to stop the words flowing.

Chan drew his eyebrows together, as if concentrating.

"It's very hazy. But I remember riding a horse—something I've never done, by the way. And I remember you. Your hair was black."

Duchess lifted a brow.

Oksana snorted. "It could be worse. You should have seen her blue period."

She scowled. "It was the nineteen-eighties, *mon chou*. Blue hair was practically *de rigueur*."

Chan smiled, then sobered. "I remember the dark cloud surrounding us. But that part's more difficult to bring into focus."

She tilted her head, watching him carefully.

"Imagine you were trying to remember something when you were really drunk or had been hit in the head," Chan said. "It's like the memories are there and I can kind of see them, but I can't draw the images up clearly in my mind."

"You aren't missing much," Duchess answered in a dark voice.

"I didn't figure I was," Chan agreed.

Silence fell between them, but it was a more relaxed sort of silence than what had come before. Perhaps, Duchess thought, they would be able to forge a truce of some kind. Perhaps they could simply exist in their separate spaces, without constantly grating against each other's sharp edges.

Perhaps one day, thinking about him marrying another woman—fucking her and siring a child by her—would not make Duchess want to tie him to a bed and mark him from head to foot.

By mutual accord, the four of them returned to the storeroom in hopes of grabbing more rest while Raahim acquired what they needed. A few hours later, Duchess' sharp ears caught the sound of the front door being unlocked and the bell chiming as someone entered. A knock sounded on the storeroom entrance, and Raahim stuck his head in, smiling amiably.

"I have arranged for your coffin. It will be delivered to the rear door of the shop in an hour or so. My condolences on your loss," he said, giving them a small bow.

"Thank you," Mason replied. "You've been exceedingly helpful."

Raahim nodded and withdrew.

"Remind me to leave a big wad of money in the till for him before we leave," Mason added.

"Done," Oksana agreed. "Though I do hope the coffin delivery service in this city is prompt. I'm eager to be on our way."

# TWENTY

Chan had never given much thought before to what it would mean not to be able to tolerate daylight. While the group's travel plans went surprisingly smoothly, he couldn't deny a sense of nagging anxiety that a delay or breakdown might leave them exposed to the sun. And while Chan had long been inured to the idea of his own death, going out in a blaze of frying flesh while horrified onlookers screamed their lungs out wasn't quite what he'd envisioned for his final moments.

The others seemed positively blasé about the concept of travel, however, so he tried to take his cue from them.

"There's usually a shadow somewhere that you can huddle in," Oksana said cheerfully, "if worse comes to worst."

They arrived in Mumbai a couple of hours before dawn, fleeing the sun's slow rise as they flew west. Eris had arranged their connecting flight for that evening. After a brief discussion, they left Snag's coffin in the airport's care and booked a hotel room rather than camping out at the gate.

Chan had an uncomfortable feeling the decision was because of his strange lethargy, which seemed to grow worse as sunrise approached. He wasn't used to being the weak link in the chain—the one who needed accommodation.

"Don't give it a second thought, mate," Mason said. "If it means I'm not the baby vamp of the group anymore, I'm all for it."

Chan slept like the dead... or perhaps, like the undead. He awoke to Duchess' hand on his shoulder, a hum of power washing along his nerves even through the material of his cotton shirt. He must have slept the day away. No light slanted through the gaps in the curtains, but Duchess' eyes flared ice blue before she pulled her hand away and moved back a step.

"Mason bought you a suitcase and some basics for travel," she said, a throaty note to her voice that made his stomach tighten. "Clothing, toiletries — that sort of thing."

With a mild jolt, Chan realized that he'd walked away from every single possession he owned in Kuala Lumpur except for the dirty and sweat-stained clothes he was currently wearing. If he'd had an emotional tie to anything left behind, it probably would have been upsetting... but he didn't. His quarters at the complex had been as sterile and devoid of personality as a jail cell.

"Oh," he rasped, still waking up. "Clean clothes? That was nice of him. Do I have time for a shower?"

She nodded, and he stumbled to the *en suite*, turning the water on as cold as it would go. It took him almost ten minutes to realize that only part of the burning inside him was due to his unwanted and completely inappropriate sexual desire. The rest was hunger.

*Shit.*

When he emerged a few minutes later, wrapped in a towel, the other three were deep in conversation.

"I think I need to feed," he blurted, not wanting to be stuck in an airport full of innocent people if the cravings got worse. He had a ridiculous flash of being trapped on the plane, ripping the cabin door off its hinges and drinking the pilot dry while the aircraft plummeted from the sky.

Oksana glanced at Duchess and raised an eyebrow that almost looked challenging. "Sorry, no help here, I'm afraid. I've sworn off hunting, and I still need to feed Mason."

Mason shrugged, with a *'what can you do*?' gesture.

"Duchess refilled at the hotel bar while you were asleep, though," Oksana continued. She was still gazing unblinkingly at Duchess, who returned the look with a flat stare.

Chan didn't want to examine the surge of — *jealousy?* — he felt at the idea of Duchess wrapping her arms around some bland businessman in a dark corner of the bar… pressing her mouth to his throat…

"Your high-beams are on, mate," Mason said.

It took Chan a minute to parse the cryptic observation, at which point he realized the burning in his eyes must mean they were glowing in the room's dim light.

*Double shit.*

He blinked rapidly, hoping that was the magic formula for getting rid of the telltale glow. "Unless you want me savaging some poor loser at the airport, come with me," he growled, and grasped Duchess by the arm, pulling her into the bathroom.

He closed the door behind them and realized a moment later what a bad idea it had probably been. Her scent filled the small room; her eyes flashed with wariness. Goddamn it, she was more beautiful than anyone had a right to be after a day spent stuck in cargo planes and hotels.

His hunger must be affecting his brain-to-mouth filter, as well, because when he opened his mouth, what tumbled out was, "Did you feed from a man or a woman?"

Her haughty eyebrow made him want to pin her against the door and repeat the question right up against her ear. *Fucking hell, what was wrong with him?*

"Since I've bedded so many of both that I long ago lost count, does it really matter?" she asked.

The knowledge that if she wanted to, she could flex her power and throw him off like an annoying fly gave him the courage to succumb to his earlier temptation. Her back thumped softly against the door, her eyes still blazing at him.

"No," he murmured against the pale shell of her ear. "It doesn't matter."

He nuzzled the sweet-smelling skin at the hinge of her jaw and trailed his lips downward, bloodlust rising. When he struck, it was purely on instinct, his fangs piercing tender flesh until the nectar beneath welled up. *God.* It was a hundred times worse than when he'd fed from her in the hospital—or a hundred times better.

She gasped, her hand coming up to fist in his hair. He growled and clamped down harder, his instincts urging him to fight if she tried to drag him away. But she didn't. She merely held him there, his scalp tingling where her grip on his hair pulled against it.

Long moments of blood-fueled bliss passed before she hissed, "*Enough.*"

The power she'd held in check before unfurled, forcing his inner beast into submission. He sagged against her, pulling his fangs free and lapping at the dribble of red trickling down from the twin wounds. By the time he pulled back enough to see them, they'd already closed over.

Even so, she looked... debauched. Wild, for all her new pallor. Chan's cock throbbed beneath the towel, which was in danger of sliding free of his waist. He grabbed it and backed away, unable to look away from her heaving breasts until she spoke, drawing his eyes back to her face.

"Be ready to leave for the airport in twenty minutes," she said, and left the bathroom, closing the door behind her.

-o-o-o-

The flight to Cairo went as smoothly as the flight to Mumbai had, though Chan and the others passed it in far more comfort than the stripped-down cargo plane had offered.

"For such a frail creature," Mason grunted as they shoved Snag's coffin into the back of a rented truck, "he certainly weighs a lot."

"It must be all that ageless wisdom," Oksana quipped, slamming the dented tailgate shut.

"Or possibly the sheer volume of ornamental metal on this casket," Duchess opined. "Perhaps I should have been clearer when mesmerizing Raahim that he did not need to spend all of the money I gave him buying the most ornate coffin available."

Chan glanced at his watch. "Are you sure we can make it to this place we're headed before dawn?"

Duchess smiled, showing a hint of fang. "As long as absolutely nothing goes wrong between here and there."

Oksana gave her a quelling look. "Don't listen to her. It'll be fine. It's not far—less than fifty kilometers, and Eris says the roads aren't bad. There's plenty of time."

"And the likelihood that someone will stop us and start asking questions about the dead guy in the back of the truck?" Chan pressed, still feeling that the others were treating this expedition too cavalierly.

"Middling," Mason said, not sounding concerned. "Which might be a problem for someone without the ability to hypnotize humans into believing everything is just fine."

Chan managed to rein in his skepticism, knowing that even after what he'd seen and done in Kuala Lumpur, he still wasn't thinking like a vampire. He climbed into the cab with Duchess, while the other two piled into the truck bed with the coffin. As it turned out, his insight had been all too keen and before they had traveled more than twenty-five kilometers, they came upon a roadblock.

Duchess slowed sedately to a stop and lowered the driver's side window. Chan was glad of his passable grasp of Arabic as the uniformed soldier approached, flashlight in hand.

"Vehicle check," he said. "What's that in the back?"

Two more guards approached the truck bed, shining lights on the casket with its shiny silver accents.

Duchess didn't so much as blink. "It's lumber for the archaeological dig in Saqqara," she said in the same language, her eyes glowing. "Nothing to worry about."

Chan glanced in the rearview mirror and saw the other guards straighten in momentary confusion. He caught a flash of violet... a flash of cobalt blue. Oksana and Mason, their eyes burning in the night.

"This is nothing to worry about," the soldier next to Duchess' window parroted. He stepped back and gestured the others away from the truck bed. "Please pull forward."

"You're too kind," Duchess muttered, already closing the window as she pulled away from the barricade.

"I don't think I'll ever get used to that," Chan said, shaking his head. "But it's fucking useful as hell."

"There are compensations for being a bloodsucker," Duchess said grimly, "though they may be few and far between."

The process was repeated twice more with only minor variations. Within an hour of leaving the outskirts of Cairo, the truck was pulling onto the dusty, sand-covered roads beyond the western edge of the Nile flood zone. Behind them lay palm trees and buildings; ahead was the Western Desert, silent and devoid of life.

"That was abrupt," Chan observed, his newly enhanced night vision allowing him to take in more of his surroundings than he would otherwise have been able to. The line of demarcation between livable and lifeless was unexpectedly stark.

"The Nile's waters spread so far, and no further," Duchess said philosophically as the truck bounced over the desert roads. "Beyond that, life must be imported, subject to heavy tariffs in the form of both time and effort."

"Yet this is where your friend wants us to gather?"

Duchess adjusted her grip on the steering wheel. "So it would seem. I'm certain he has his reasons."

His attention shifted abruptly to a flat area in the distance before them. "People up ahead," he said tersely. "Several of them."

"Yes, I know. It's Eris and the others."

He looked at her. "And you're sure of that because…?"

She tapped her temple with a manicured fingertip. "Because I can sense them. Just as they will be able to sense us."

He made an effort to relax his tense posture. They closed the last few hundred meters and pulled into what appeared to be a parking lot for tourists visiting the site. A large sign reading 'Closed for Renovations' in English and Arabic partially blocked the entrance, but several trucks were parked there—some with large trailers attached. A couple of smaller cars completed the mix. Their truck's headlights swept across a group of six people watching their approach.

Duchess parked the vehicle between two of the other trucks and turned off the headlights, killing the engine. Chan let himself out of the cab in time to see Oksana vault from the bed. Her prosthetic foot didn't slow her down in the least as she jogged toward the others. Duchess followed at a more leisurely pace.

Chan hung back a ways, watching the reunion without inserting himself into it for now. Mason stayed back as well, and Chan was oddly grateful not to be the only one playing odd man out.

Oksana went first to a small woman with waist-length black hair and sad, dark-brown eyes. "Manisha," she said, hugging the sad-eyed woman tightly, "I'm so, *so* sorry."

Manisha nodded against Oksana's shoulder, returning the embrace for a long moment before drawing away. Oksana turned immediately to the tall, brown-haired man standing next to her and embraced him as well. Meanwhile, Duchess strode over to the other two couples, no sentimentality evident in the reunion as they immediately fell into intense conversation.

"Fire and ice, those two women," Mason muttered next to him. "Typical. C'mon, mate—we might as well run the gauntlet now, so we can get the patient unloaded and under cover before sunrise."

The tall man and the short, dark-haired woman Oksana had embraced were already walking toward them.

"Ozzie, old chap," said the man, in the urbane tones of a BBC voiceover, "good to see you. You've not met Manisha properly yet—Manisha... Ozzie."

"Manisha," Mason said, taking her by the hand. His other hand came up to cover hers. "Please accept my sincerest condolences. I'm so sorry we weren't able to prevent this." His eyes flickered to Chan's. "Manisha and Sangye were acquainted before they got drawn into this mess," he said by way of explanation. "Xander, Manisha, this is Chan Wei Yong."

"Hello," Chan said, still unsure of where he stood within this odd group.

"Hello," Manisha said, accepting his offered hand. "Welcome to... well... *here*."

He shook Xander's hand next, meeting the cool, assessing gaze.

"American, eh?" the British vampire asked. "Well, I suppose Della turned out to be all right, so we'll try not to hold it against you."

"If it's any consolation," Chan said, "the US would probably deny any knowledge of my existence at this point."

Xander released his grip and gave Mason a brief clasp on the upper arm before turning back to the main group, who were approaching. "Ah, here come the others. This is Tré, Della, Eris, and Trynn," he said, pointing out each of them in turn.

Chan filed the names and faces away, used to committing such details to memory. Tré was dark-haired and Slavic, with unusual silver eyes and the bearing of a natural leader. Della was a short, curvy woman with wild waves of chestnut hair and a mole that brought to mind old photos of Marilyn Monroe. Trynn was a slender, suave woman—tall and a bit boyish with cropped black hair. Eris had a nose, chin, and cheekbones straight from ancient Greek statuary, with a dark and wavy shoulder-length mane. His eyes skimmed over Chan for a bare instant before settling on the coffin in the truck.

"Chan," said the leader—the one called Tré. "You are welcome in our family, such as it is. Don't hesitate to ask for whatever you need." His accent carried strong hints of the Black Sea.

Chan needed oh so many things, but they weren't the sorts of things one got for the asking. "Thank you," he said. "Right now, though, I think what we all need is to get this friend of yours under cover before the sun comes up."

"Quite right," Eris said.

Xander helped Chan haul the heavy coffin forward. While his fight with Duchess had disavowed him of any idea that the women here were weaker than he was, a quick look around showed that he, Xander, Tré, Eris, Trynn, and Mason would be the best match in height to carry the casket funeral-style, on their shoulders. They hefted it up and followed Della's lead toward the dark silhouette of the ancient monument.

The indigo sky was beginning to lighten to navy in the east, a low wash of red at the horizon. Chan craned around as much as he was able to take in their incredible surroundings. The ten of them entered the column-flanked grand hallway that led into the site. Chan knew about as much as most westerners probably did about the pyramids at Giza, which were located not far from here. Still, the age of this place was like a palpable aura.

The high stone walls breached by this single entrance weren't familiar to him, but the broken tetrahedral shape of the Step Pyramid within rang a few bells. It was supposed to be ancient—far older than the other pyramids, if his schoolboy memory served. It was certainly damned impressive, even in the murky pre-dawn light.

It was not to the pyramid that they went, however. Other structures dotted the huge, enclosed space, including a handful of tents. Some of the stone constructions were small; some were massive, like the two-story tall barrier topped by carved cobra heads that loomed before them. Stairs led up to the top—uncomfortably narrow for six people and a coffin. Once at the top, an even narrower staircase led downward, disappearing below ground level.

"The South Tomb," Eris said. "That's where we're set up.

## TWENTY-ONE

*Great*, Chan thought, eyeing the switchbacks on the precarious stone staircase with misgivings. They picked their way down it slowly, and his eyes adjusted to the deeper darkness in seconds. At the bottom, he could make out artificial lighting down a tunnel leading away from the landing at the base of the stairs.

"We've got some solar panels set up, along with a bank of batteries for electricity," Xander said by way of explanation. "Mostly, the lights are for the donors, but it really does get quite dark down here at night—even for vampires."

"Donors?" Chan asked.

It was Della who answered. "Humans who tagged along to voluntarily supply us with blood. That's who's in the tents up top. Xander's got some… connections with people who were willing to help us out."

Chan frowned. Vampires had human groupies who followed them around to offer free meals? That was news to him. Although Oksana *did* say something back in Mumbai about having sworn off hunting…

"Oh-*kay*," he said, drawing out the word.

"I've set up a cot in the tomb where I originally found Snag," Eris said. "It seemed an appropriate place to put him."

*And hardly morbid at all,* Chan thought, only remembering that he was surrounded by people who could read his thoughts when both Mason and Xander snorted quietly in amusement.

The tunnels were cool and dusty, the floors worn smooth by the passage of time. Chan caught glimpses of artwork on the walls—sand-scrubbed friezes and carvings, some still with paint clinging to them, the colors leached by dim light. The place was far larger and more maze-like than he would have guessed, not that he'd ever given much thought to the layout and spaciousness of underground Egyptian tomb structures.

Eventually, Della led them into a decently sized room with the promised cot set up in the center. It had its own halogen bulb strung up from the ceiling, throwing light over the stunning murals that decorated every inch of the three unbroken walls. Chan had a confused impression of gods and humans, horse-drawn chariots, lions, hippos, oxen, even crocodiles... all carefully detailed with brilliant pigments that had stood the test of time remarkably well.

*Wow.* He supposed that if you had to spend centuries stuck in a tomb, there were definitely worse ones available.

"Set him down here," Eris said, and they lowered the casket onto the stone floor next to the low cot.

Eris cracked the seal and opened it, pausing to let out a slow breath as he looked down at the figure resting inside. "Oh, my foolish friend. I'd hoped never to see you like this again."

Della tangled her fingers with Tré's, squeezing hard. "He looks dead," she whispered.

"As close to death as our kind is capable of from natural means," Eris said. "But his soul is still clinging to the husk."

In Kuala Lumpur, Mason had suggested placing Snag on a sheet inside the coffin, so they could use it to lift him out more easily. Chan, Eris, Duchess, and Trynn each grasped a corner and used the cotton material as a sort of sling, easing his body up and onto the cot without jostling him.

"Jesus, Snag," Trynn muttered. "What the hell were you thinking?"

Mason spoke next. "Eris, you said you had an idea that might help him recover without taking a century to do it. What did you mean by that?"

Eris stroked his jaw, which was shaded by a couple days' growth of stubble. "You said it yourself. It's life force that he needs. Blood is merely the medium of transfer. The last time I did this was more than sixteen hundred years ago. I was young then, and alone."

"But now, you're much older, and there are ten of us," Trynn said. "Are you saying we all need to feed him?"

"Yes and no," Eris replied—somewhat unhelpfully in Chan's opinion. "As the doctor said when we spoke before, his physical condition limits how much blood we can get into him right now."

"Ah," Mason said, with the air of someone experiencing a revelation. "You're saying we all need to feed *you*, and you'll try to transfer life force to him. You're the oldest, right? The most powerful, except for him?"

"Yes," Duchess replied for him. "Eris, then Tré, then myself, followed by Oksana and Xander."

Chan frowned. "But Sangye was a new vampire, right? And he was just a kid. Yet he was able to do this life transfer thing somehow…"

"He was an old soul, with a greater than usual awareness of his past lives," Duchess said. Both she and the woman Manisha looked very pale and sad at the mention of the boy. "He'd also consumed Snag's blood and life force to very nearly the last drop."

Tré approached the cot, looking down at the mummified figure lying on it. "If you think this has the best chance of working, Eris, then it's what we will do," he said.

"How's the human donor situation?" Oksana asked. "It's been some time since I fed, and Mason has been feeding from me."

"We have a dozen people," Xander said. "I'll admit I didn't expect us to be channeling all our power into a mummy, but we won't keel over from starvation in the next few days, at least."

"How'd you swing this thing with the donors, anyway?" Mason asked.

Xander shrugged. "I paid a quiet visit to the IT department at HelioTeque. One of the kids there is a conspiracy theorist. He ate up our story with a spoon. Turns out he runs a website for other… shall we say, *like-minded individuals*. Several of them volunteered to help us in exchange for proof of the existence of paranormal phenomena, plus an all-expense paid expedition to view the archaeological wonders of Saqqara."

"I don't think I've ever been a *paranormal phenomenon* before," Trynn muttered. "I'm still on the fence about it, honestly."

"It's blood, freely given," Xander said. "And I'm afraid at this point, beggars can't be choosers."

Chan wanted to dig a bit further into the whole blood donor thing. Several of the others apparently thought *not hunting hapless humans for blood* was a pretty big deal. Yet Duchess appeared to have no compunctions whatsoever about drinking from random passers-by like Raahim and the nameless patron at the hotel bar in Mumbai. Now wasn't the time to press her on it, obviously, but he still felt a bit better knowing that there were people available who were giving their blood voluntarily.

"So, are we ready to do this?" Xander asked. "You want us in shifts, Eris, or all at once?"

"All of you," Eris said. "Though it remains to be seen how much life force I can contain at once."

True to his obvious status as *de facto* leader, Tré nodded and stepped forward. "Start with the oldest among us," he suggested, and offered Eris his wrist.

Mason had done the same thing for Chan, but it was still strange to watch—an oddly intimate exchange as Eris bared glistening fangs and sank them into Tré's vein. Eris' eyes glowed gold, and Chan felt power sizzle through the enclosed underground space. Duchess offered herself next, but the expected burn of jealousy didn't materialize in Chan's chest. These people gave off too much of an aura of family for that—even though their back-grounds spanned the globe, not to mention several millennia.

Also, it hadn't escaped him that he was in the presence of four very obvious couples. Except for the half-dead vampire lying on the cot, everyone here had found the person they'd lost, as Duchess had once lost Bertrand. He couldn't deny the taste of bitterness that rose to the back of his tongue up-on realizing that only he and his golden-haired temptress appeared unable to get their emotional shit together.

Eris worked his way through the group one by one. In his turn, Chan proffered his left arm, unsure what to expect after his singular—and life-altering—experience with being bitten. It didn't help that by this point, getting within arm's reach of Eris made it feel like static electricity was skitter-ing along his skin, leaving gooseflesh in its wake.

Screw the solar panels—they could've stuck an electrical plug in the guy and run the lights off *him*, as much juice as he seemed to be channeling right now.

Fangs slid into his flesh. He felt them—of course he did—but it was nothing like the burning agony he'd experienced as Duchess had destroyed his humanity. He was aware of the pull, a deep draw that tugged not just at his blood, but also at his life. At the same time, he became more attuned to the man whose lips were clamped to his wrist. He felt Eris' fear for Snag, his determination to suc-ceed in healing him, his worry over the coming war, and his deep sadness over the loss of a brilliant, innocent child who should never have had to worry about sacrificing himself to save others.

He could feel the other vampires, too, perhaps because Eris had drunk from them as well. All of them were determined, yet painfully aware of the odds stacked against them.

Eris pulled away, and Chan watched the wounds in his wrist seal over as though they'd never been there to begin with. The only lingering effects were a growing fatigue and a nagging emptiness in his stomach. His lips thinned—being drained probably meant he'd need to feed again soon, and no doubt the sun was rising over the desert above their heads. For now, he drew on his years of practice in self-discipline and set the hunger aside.

The only vampire remaining was Trynn. Rather than taking her wrist, Eris pressed a kiss to her lips and drew her head to the side. His fangs pierced her neck, and a small noise escaped her throat that sounded far closer to ecstasy than pain. Chan shifted in place uncomfortably as desire washed through the newly expanded link, twining with his growing hunger. It took every goddamned iota of his willpower not to let his eyes drift to Duchess, who now stood propped against the wall next to the doorway.

When he was done, Eris rested his forehead against Trynn's for a moment before straightening. He sank into the chair that Della had dragged in and arranged next to the cot.

"This is far more life than I can use, old friend," he murmured. "Perhaps it will be of more help to you." With that, he ripped into his own wrist with his teeth. Blood spurted—Chan could only imagine that he must be filled to bursting after drinking from nine other vampires. The thick red liquid dribbled between Snag's jaws, with his lips stretched into a mummy's rictus grin. Only a tiny amount went into him before it overflowed, dripping down the parchment-like skin of his cheeks. Eris's wound was already healing, though. He laid the palm of his other hand over the withered skin of Snag's forehead, his eyes slipping closed. Chan guessed he was trying to replicate Sangye's trick of willing strength into him.

"Let him work, everyone," Duchess said. "This will no doubt take time."

"Yes," Tré agreed. "The rest of us should feed and rest while we have the chance."

"I'm staying," said Trynn. "I'll let the rest of you know if he needs more blood from you."

# Twenty-Two

Duchess fed from a human girl named Shay, replenishing her strength in anticipation of what was to come. Tré and Della took the four of them who had just arrived on a quick tour of the underground space. Duchess had been to the Giza plateau many times, but had never made the trip to the Saqqara necropolis until now. It was an impressive site, though one she was not in any condition to fully appreciate at the moment.

The underground system of tunnels and rooms stretched over a much larger area than one might expect. It had been thoroughly cleared and restored by archaeologists over the last several decades. The condition of some of the artwork was truly exquisite. It was also perfect for their purposes. Meters of stone and sand blocked the unforgiving desert sun above. There was plenty of room for all eleven of them.

Xander had obviously been busy in the day or so between his arrival and their showing up with Snag. He, Eris, and Tré had convinced the guards that normally patrolled the site to take an indefinite vacation. Soon after, truckloads of supplies had started arriving from HelioTeque—enough for the humans camping in the compound above to survive in relative comfort while the vampires below had a safe and private place to lick their wounds and devise some sort of strategy.

Eris' description of a final stand was all well and good, but the truth was that if Bael and his undead forces descended on them right now, they would have no defense. The attack at the Thean Hou Temple had proven that clearly enough.

At the end of the impromptu tour, Della pointed to two small rooms a short distance apart, both of them near the end of the tunnel they'd been exploring.

"Oksana, I've got you and Mason in this one," she said. "Some of the guys from up top already brought your luggage down. Duchess, you and Chan are in that one."

Duchess paused, drawing breath to demur, only to be cut off by Tré's uncompromising mental voice in her head.

*No*, he said. *I don't know what's wrong between the two of you, Duchess. And I don't have to know, if you'd prefer it that way. But you need to fix this. I won't go into a battle with one of my generals waging war against her own troops.*

The words had clearly been directed to Duchess alone, since none of the others reacted. She pressed her lips together, a trapped feeling washing over her that she didn't like one little bit.

*Mind your own business, Tré*, she managed.

Chan was looking at her warily, and she knew she'd been silent too long. He opened his mouth to say something, his brow furrowed.

She interrupted him before he could. "I need to talk to Xander," she said. "I'll be back later."

With that, she spun and headed in the direction they'd come, following her mental sense of him. This was another discussion she dreaded, but facing it was marginally less daunting than facing Chan alone in a small room again, especially after the bathroom incident in Mumbai. As avoidance strategies went, this was at least one which would accomplish something that needed to be done anyway.

She arrived at a closed door, feeling Xander's presence in the space beyond it. Not all of the rooms had doors on them, but it appeared Della had chosen the ones that did for their sleeping quarters. The door in front of her opened before she could lift a hand to knock. Instead of Xander, however, she was met by a less-than-pleased looking Manisha, blocking the opening as she met Duchess' eyes with a hard, brown gaze.

"What do you want?" Manisha asked in a flat, unwelcoming tone. She was dry-eyed, but grief had cut deep furrows in her pleasant features.

Xander appeared behind her, his hands closing over her shoulders. "Manisha. Love. You can lower your hackles. It's all right."

Manisha's eyes didn't stray from Duchess' or soften in the least. "It's not all right. I'm not in a good place right now, Duchess, and I'm certainly not in the mood to stand around while you pass judgment on the man I love. So, again, what do you want?"

Duchess' heart ached at seeing this tiny woman who was obviously drowning in her own grief standing in front of Xander like an attack dog, ready to defend him against a vampire with many times her strength.

"Nothing that will hurt him," she replied honestly.

Manisha lifted her chin. "You've already done that."

"Only after I hurt her, Manisha," Xander said, and guided her back by the shoulders, opening the door the rest of the way. "Come in, Duchess. Let's talk."

Duchess eased inside, leaving the door open. The room was empty except for a mattress on the floor and a couple of pieces of luggage stowed neatly in the corner.

"I've nothing to offer you by way of hospitality, I'm afraid," Xander said. "Not so much as a chair, though I could probably find one without too much effort."

She waved him off. "You needn't play host with me. I've come to apologize. I can do that while standing."

Manisha had retreated to the corner, where she now perched on one of the upright suitcases with the air of someone waiting for an excuse to throw Duchess out.

"Apologize for what?" Xander asked, sounding tired. "You didn't do anything wrong."

"I judged you," Duchess said, "just as Manisha said."

Xander ran a hand through his hair, mussing it. "Judging someone for ruining the lives of hundreds of people, out of nothing but greed?

Including the lives of young children? You shock me, Duchess."

He'd changed, she realized with a faint jolt of unease. She hadn't appreciated how much until she was here, able to feel him through the bond. Xander had always been quicksilver, sliding away from anything that struck too close to the bone. Deflecting. Misdirecting. Now, though, he stood before her, shields down, waiting for her to say whatever she needed to say. Was this what Manisha had done for him? What *love* had done for him?

"I walked out on you," she tried again, when the silence threatened to stretch too long. "I should have stayed."

"I'm all right, Duchess," he said. "Well… perhaps not *all right*. But I'm better than I was. You're worrying me right now, though."

"I'm fine," she said faintly, thinking *no, stop — this is not how the discussion was supposed to go.*

"No one here is fine," Manisha said, and the bitterness in her voice was unmistakable.

"Your pain is bleeding all over the link," Xander said. "I was debating cornering Oksana and trying to shake some information out of her. I still can, if you'd prefer me to take that approach."

The ache that had taken up residence in Duchess' undead heart unexpectedly sprouted tentacles and tried to strangle her. Her head swam, and without realizing it, she slid down the frescoed wall into a heap, covering her face with her hands.

"*Whoa*, now," Xander said, his voice coming from much closer now. Through the gaps in her fingers, Duchess saw him crouch in front of her, lifting one hand but pausing before it made contact with her skin. Even Manisha rose from her perch in the corner and came nearer, sitting on the edge of the mattress.

"I don't... know what to do, Xander," Duchess found herself saying. "What do I *do*?"

Xander's hand closed the final distance and wrapped around her wrist, drawing it away from her face and tangling their fingers together. A fresh wave of guilt at taking his attention away from the person who truly needed it swamped her. Her shields were in tatters; she was broadcasting all over both of them, she could tell —

"Don't be daft," Manisha said, her earlier hostility gone... replaced by what sounded like exhaustion. "I might be angry, but you did apologize, and anyway, you're family."

"Just so," Xander agreed. "Now, will you tell me what's wrong? Your mate is here. He's safe. You found him, but you're sitting curled up in a ball in my room, instead of being with him. What happened, Duchess?"

She still couldn't talk or even draw breath properly, but in a moment of weakness, she let everything flood the bond in a tangle of terrible hopelessness. Her betrayal as a spy... Bertrand's last plea... her dead baby... Chan, confessing to his marriage and its ugly end...

Silence reigned for the space of several heartbeats, deep and smothering.

"Duchess..." Xander began tentatively, a wealth of compassion coloring his rich voice.

"Sounds like you two are perfect for each other," Manisha said, cutting across him. "So, what's the problem?"

Xander craned to look at her. "A little diplomacy here, love?"

Manisha came over and sat against the wall a few inches away from Duchess. "To hell with diplomacy. If one of you had done all sorts of bad stuff, and the other one was a paragon of virtue, then *fine*. Maybe it's a problem." She shrugged. "But if you've both got horrible track records, then you're on even footing. So come clean with him, stop avoiding him, and agree to start fresh."

"But—" Duchess began.

"But nothing. Get over it," Manisha said mercilessly. "There's more at stake here than your desire to castigate yourself for something that happened hundreds of years ago. People have died, and more of them are probably going to die in the coming weeks. You're alive. So is he. What more do you *want*?"

Duchess covered a wince.

"You're no more used to being put in your place than I am—are you, Duchess?" Xander murmured, still holding her hand. "But please take my word that having someone around to take you down a peg as needed does a world of good."

"I hardly recognize you anymore, *mon ami*," Duchess said, staring at their entwined fingers. "You or Oksana."

He snorted. "I can't speak for the snack food addict, but I'm the same rat bastard I've always been, I assure you." He gave her hand a final squeeze and let it go. "Sometimes, though, it does help to see myself through someone else's lens. It's a very nice lens—I'm becoming quite fond of it. Now, though, I need you to tell me one thing. Mind you—I already know the answer. I just want to hear you say it aloud before I kick you out, so Manisha and I can get some rest."

"What's the question?" Duchess asked.

"Chan. Do you care about him?"

"Yes," she rasped. "Of course I do. He's my soulmate, Xander."

He nodded, a ghost of a smile tugging at one side of his mouth. "There. Wasn't that simple? Now stop cluttering up this dead Egyptian person's perfectly nice floor and go talk to him."

## Twenty-Three

Chan was easy enough to find. He was in the room Della had shown them earlier. He was also asleep, with a newborn vampire's aversion to the daylight hours. After a moment's hesitation, Duchess lowered herself to sit cross-legged next to the mattress, watching him.

He was… so different now.

Or perhaps not. The differences were skin deep—his square-jawed Asian features housing a soul that had gravitated unerringly to the elite military force of his day. He reveled in risk-taking, he was fiercely independent, and he scoffed at personal danger. He was willing to give up his life for his daughter if he thought that would serve her better than continuing to live.

Dark brown eyes blinked open, meeting hers. His hand twitched toward a weapon that wasn't there, only for awareness of his surroundings to return an instant later. Copper highlights glinted in the depths of his gaze.

"I've been a fool," she said. "Ask me anything you want, and I will answer. Then tell me about your wife and daughter. I want to know everything."

Wariness flitted across his handsome face.

"Why?" he asked. "What's changed since you went high-tailing it out of here earlier?"

She chewed her lower lip, a nervous habit she hadn't manifested since before steam engines had been invented. "I went to speak with an old friend, and his lover ripped me a few new and richly deserved orifices."

He blinked.

"Okay."

Silence settled over the room.

"So… questions?" Duchess prompted.

"Uh… right." He seemed to flounder for another moment, before settling on, "The others. They all seem so… nauseatingly happy. Are we just the only fucked up ones, or…?"

It was almost funny, how closely the question echoed her mental moaning back in Singapore.

"I suppose you could say there are degrees of emotional damage," she said. "Some of them have rather serious issues. And all of us that you might call the original vampires are guilty of murdering our soulmates in their previous lives."

He nodded. "But they all got over it somehow, apparently."

Duchess nodded thoughtfully. "Perhaps gaining absolution helped them. Their reincarnated lovers are all disgustingly noble and altruistic people. It is, as you say, rather sickening at times."

He pillowed his head on one lean-muscled arm and raised an eyebrow at her. "Not a fan of altruism, huh?"

"Or nobility. It makes me uncomfortable."

Chan let out a low snort. "Maybe you and I aren't completely doomed after all."

The stab of hope she felt at his words was completely ridiculous... probably.

"No more doomed than the world at large, perhaps," she allowed.

Chan winced and rubbed his stomach absently with his free hand, as though it pained him. She frowned at the gesture.

"You need to feed," she realized.

"Yeah," he agreed. "I can keep a lid on it for a few more minutes, though. That said, I'm not sure you should let me near any of the human groupies quite yet. I don't want to hurt anyone, or scare them off, for that matter."

The low flutter in her belly as she contemplated the alternative should not have been unexpected, but it still made her catch her breath. "Feeding from Xander's groupies will... not be necessary," she managed.

The copper glint in his eyes flared, but as promised, he kept himself under control.

"Okay, questions," he said, as though reminding himself. "So, did spying in seventeenth century France pay any better than it does now? Because, yeah, the benefits may be pretty good, but the salary sucks."

She wavered, caught between the assumption that he was needling her and the idea that he might simply be trying to lighten the mood. Instinct urged her to react defensively — slam down the barriers and retreat, or launch a retaliatory attack.

*Stop*, she ordered herself. *Forge a new path, or risk following the old path over the edge of a cliff.*

"That's a sore subject," she said carefully. "I'm certain you can understand why."

"Okay. Sorry. Poor choice of topic," he said, sounding just as cautious. "But you have to understand, I don't give a rat's ass whether you were working for the king of France, or the king's brother, or Cardinal... what's his name? Cardinal Richelieu."

Her brows flew up as genuine outrage suffused her. "*Richelieu*? That snake? As if I would *ever* have soiled myself by working for the Red Bishop!"

Chan laughed aloud—the rich chuckle she'd heard only a handful of times before. "*God.* This is so strange. For me, these people are characters in old novels, or maybe history books. It's hard to wrap my brain around the idea that they were your contemporaries."

She let her outrage drain away, unable to stop her own breath of amusement.

"Once again, though," he continued, "you need to realize—I don't care that you were spying because your gambling addict of a husband lost the household savings on cards. Aside from feeling kind of bad that you were stuck in that situation in the first place, I mean. Because... newsflash. *I'm. A. Spy.*"

She paused, trying to fit the idea that he wasn't outraged by her betrayal of Bertrand's trust into the puzzle that was her relationship with him.

"Maybe so," she said eventually. "But you were spying because you wanted to lend support to your lawfully elected government. You didn't betray those close to you with your choice of career. You weren't spying *on them*."

In an instant, his expression went flat and controlled, the light in his eyes dimming.

"No," he said in a voice gone suddenly hoarse. "I wasn't spying on them. I was cheating on them."

"Tell me," she said softly.

Chan swallowed hard, his Adam's apple bobbing. He looked away, as though wavering over whether or not to tell her.

*Trust me*, she begged silently, unsure if he would be able to hear the plea.

A shudder wracked him, and he dragged in a slow breath. "I've never…" He trailed off and swallowed again. "People know about it, of course. Far more people than I wish knew about it. But I've never just… *told* someone. About the whole mess, I mean. You know?"

She nodded.

"I married Janette right out of high school. Neither of us was ready. I think she loved me, but from my perspective she was just… convenient, I suppose. People expected me to marry her, so I did. God, that sounds every bit as awful as it actually was." He shook his head. "I went straight into the Navy at eighteen. Worked my way up the ranks and got accepted into the SEALs. And the whole time, things between us got worse and worse. I resented her. Convinced myself she was holding me back.

"After SEAL training, I started getting regular deployments. It was so easy to pay for prostitutes in some random, war-torn shithole, in hopes that I might find with them what I never found with her. In between, I'd come home and try to make things work. She was on birth control; neither of us expected her to get pregnant. But she did, and she was about three months along when I shipped out to Afghanistan.

"I tried to talk myself out of doing any more stupid shit after that. But while I might've been part of an elite unit, I was a goddamned coward at heart. I didn't want to be with her anymore, but I was too much of a hairy ball sack to do the right thing and leave honorably. It wasn't three weeks before I was trawling bars, sleeping with anyone female who'd have me.

"Problem was, this time all of the guys in my unit knew Janette was pregnant. A buddy of mine—Ridley—finally had enough of me treating her like shit. He told her everything. Guess I was lucky he didn't try to have me brought up on charges at the same time. But anyway, Janette waited until I got home and asked me straight to my face if it was true or not. I... couldn't lie to her. She walked out the very next day."

Duchess weighed saying *I'm sorry*, but it would have been a lie since she really wasn't.

Instead, she said, "I've spent far more than a single human lifetime fucking my way through the great cities of the world. If I was going to drink from them, I fucked them first. If I wasn't going to drink from them, but I was bored or the clamor of my thoughts was too loud, I fucked them anyway."

His jaw worked for a moment, but then he shook his head and sighed. "Not the same," he said. "You weren't married."

"No, but I'd already deceived my husband in a different way, as we've discussed before. We both betrayed our spouses."

He lifted a shoulder in what might have been a shrug. "Maybe so."

"What happened next?" Duchess pressed. "Janette left, and then…?"

He sighed. "There was an ugly divorce proceeding. I didn't protest the custody arrangements or the child support amount. My parents did the right thing and took Janette's side in the matter. They haven't spoken to me in almost four years. Janette and Ridley got married less than a year after she left me, and he's been raising Courtney as his own daughter. He adopted her when she was three."

"Do you ever see her?" Duchess asked, wistful.

"I was granted visitation rights during the divorce proceedings. But… I took the CIA job not long after." He closed his eyes, and his voice grew choked. "I've been in Kuala Lumpur for nearly eighteen months. I haven't seen her in all that time, and now…"

"Wei Yong," Duchess whispered.

"Now I guess I won't ever see her again."

He rolled to his feet — pacing… agitated. She rose as well, blocking him with a hand splayed over his chest. His eyes were wet.

"Right now," she said, "we have to fight to make sure she still has a world to grow up in. One free of darkness and terror."

He froze, caught by whatever he saw on her face.

"Your eyes," he breathed, and she realized that rusty tears had welled up and overflowed while he was speaking.

"Vampire tears," she said, her voice grown husky. "Yours are the same."

He wiped at his cheeks in surprise, looking at the moisture clinging to his palm. "*Shit.*"

The word emerged broken. It was the most natural thing in the world to wrap her arms around him and pull him to her. He was trembling as he returned the embrace, his spine curving to bring them level. She was a decently tall woman, and he was not an overly tall man, so his lips ended up even with her ear. He breathed in, a ragged sound that reminded her of his growing need for blood.

"Feed," she whispered. "It's all right. Draw strength from me."

He groaned and slid his fangs into her throat, bending her backward in his hold as blood welled from her neck and into his mouth. The position pressed her body against his from breasts to knees, and there was no mistaking the feel of his hardening length against the crease of her thigh.

How often had she held humans like this, either before or after a seduction? Yet she had never been in this position herself... never felt the pull of blood drawing along the length of her body to tug at her sex, or the feeling of strong arms supporting her. She let her head fall back, baring herself to Wei Yong's fangs, and gave into the sensation with no thought of the past or future—only the present moment.

He fed from her until a faint feeling of dizziness started to tickle the edges of her awareness. Even when he pulled back, he didn't release her completely. One arm still wrapped around her back, supporting her, but his other hand caressed her throat, fingertips sliding over the healing punctures.

"It didn't help," he said hoarsely. "I… want more. I want *you*."

Something clicked into place in Duchess' thoughts, making her wonder how this whole thing could possibly have felt so complicated before. "Then have me."

But he shook his head, his hands falling away as he eased her upright, to stand under her own power. "I don't deserve happiness," he told her. "I don't deserve any second chances."

"Neither do I," she said without hesitation. "But we still need to save the world. Would it be so bad if… we tried to do that together? We can always run away from each other later—"

His hands clasped her shoulders. "What happened to Bertrand and your baby wasn't your fault. My sins are worse than yours," he argued.

She shook her head. "You're wrong. They're not. You don't know all of my sins yet."

"I don't need to," he said. "Duchess—"

She placed a finger over his lips, stilling them. "No." Something heavy tore free inside her; an anchor she'd been using to keep from being dragged into the past. "Not Duchess. Call me Marie."

"*Marie*," he whispered, and kissed her.

# TWENTY-FOUR

She'd kissed so many people over the endless years since Bael had taken her life away — and yet, the moment his lips touched hers, her soul recognized him. He kept the kiss light, just a shade beyond teasing. So different then the demanding pull of his mouth on her neck just moments before.

Rather than frustrate her, the slow seduction of his mouth unknotted her muscles one by one, as all the tension she'd been carrying for weeks… for months… for *years* began to unravel and slip away. As long as he was kissing her, she didn't have to fight him. She didn't have to run, or hide, or protect her battered heart and torn soul.

All she had to do was kiss him back.

When he pulled away enough to rest their foreheads together, his undead heart was galloping like a racehorse. She splayed a hand over it, feeling the rhythmic thump against his ribcage. His chest rose and fell rapidly, and she couldn't help the smile that curved the corners of her lips.

"Except for talking, you don't really need to breathe anymore, you know," she told him.

He huffed, and tightened the grip he still maintained on her shoulders. "Tell it to my body. My head is swimming."

She lifted a hand to cup his cheek, daring herself to meet his eyes and really *see* what lay beneath. For so long, sex and seduction had been another wall she'd built around herself. A role she'd played.

*Femme fatale*, vampire edition.

Wei Yong's gaze was deep and dark, but lit from within by the light of his growing arousal. Beneath it lay a sea of hope and turmoil, guilt and determination. He didn't look away, even when the words *what you're doing right now terrifies me* echoed across the deepening bond to her.

*I need to see*, she answered in kind. *I need to see you seeing me, or I'll never believe it's real.*

"I've built a life around not being seen," he murmured aloud. "What's hidden under the surface is too awful."

"That's what I'm counting on. Otherwise, you'd never want me," she said, and kissed him again.

He made a low noise and crushed her body to his, kissing her again, the earlier control he'd shown snapping. Her lips parted, and he took immediate advantage of the opening, his tongue sliding in to tangle with hers. He dueled her with all the skill Bertrand had once shown with a rapier—a single-minded opponent bent on conquest. And for once, she was eager to be conquered.

In all her meaningless liaisons, she had made it a point never to cede control to another. Whether there was one person in her bed or half a dozen, she was always *le capitaine*, leading the troops.

Something of her thoughts must have shone through the bond. "I am so completely okay with that," Wei Yong said against her lips. "But maybe not right this minute."

"Another time," she agreed, breathless despite her earlier chiding about not needing to breathe. "This… is about something different."

"Yes," he said, walking her backward until her back thumped against a wall covered with priceless ancient artwork. "It is."

Her short-sleeved cotton shirt buttoned in the front, and his fingers attacked it with purpose. Lips followed, running over each new centimeter of exposed skin. When the shirt fell open, hanging to the sides, he straightened. His eyes lit upon the front clasp of her bra.

"Whoever designed this is officially my hero," he said, popping it so her heavy breasts spilled out.

Her head thumped back as his lips closed around a nipple, drawing it to a point—teasing with tongue and teeth.

"Practicality is important," she managed, arching as she felt his fangs lengthen.

He divided his attention between her breasts until desire started to make her dizzy, then pulled away long enough to strip his utilitarian black t-shirt over his head and throw it aside. Her trousers and underwear followed. Finally, he shoved his pants and briefs down his hips before crowding against her, dragging her wrists together and pinning them over her head with one large hand.

*Yes*, she thought as he used the other to hitch her left leg up, wrapping it around his hip.

"Sorry," he rumbled, "I know it's too fast, but I swear I'll make it up to you afterward."

In fact, a rough fuck against a wall was the polar opposite of the carefully orchestrated scenes she usually used for distraction... and it was exactly what she needed. She gasped as his hard length breached her, sliding inside to the hilt. Her eyes slid closed, and her mouth fell open.

"*No*," he ordered. "Look at me. I have to see you. I have to know you really want this. Want... *me.*"

Dragging her eyes open in that moment of vulnerability was one of the hardest things she'd ever done—but once she had, she couldn't have shut them again if she'd tried. His expression was raw. It was the look of someone who didn't really believe this was happening, and she had the awful feeling her face reflected the same thing.

Then, he began to move.

After the first few slow thrusts, his movements grew hard, almost brutal. Daring her to look away... to shrink from the ugliness inside him. She bared her fangs, not backing down, using his tight grip under her left thigh as leverage to wrap both of her legs around his waist.

With only his strength and the weight of the wall at her back supporting her, she kept her gaze locked with his and flexed her hips, angling him even deeper with every stroke. Everything burned—her eyes... her heart... her throbbing and greedy *chatte* clutching at his hard flesh with every stroke. Her aching nipples rubbed against his smooth chest as he screwed her into the wall, her wrists still pinned overhead.

The grind of his pelvis drove her ever closer to release, and her mouth watered with the sudden desire to bite him as they both came.

"No," he growled. "Not now. Look at me. I need to watch you."

She didn't want him to see her final barriers crumble. But if she closed her eyes or looked away, it would mean she couldn't see *him* fall apart.

"I will if you will," he said breathlessly, in response to her unraveling thoughts.

His hips snapped forward, hitting her in just the right way to take her over the edge. Ecstasy slammed over her like a breaking wave, and she fought to keep her eyes open even as they blurred with tears of long overdue catharsis. His face twisted, but he, too, resisted the urge to hide himself away as he groaned and spilled inside her.

*I see you,* she thought. *I won't run away if you don't.*

He released her wrists in favor of wrapping his arm around the small of her back. Gravity pulled them down the wall in slow motion, leaving them in a tangled heap on the floor.

"Not going anywhere," he murmured into her hair.

-o-o-o-

Somehow, they roused themselves enough to make it across to the mattress on the floor, shedding the rest of their clothes as they went. Chan was fairly convinced that Mason had been wrong before and heart attacks weren't out of the question even for vampires, given what the organ in question seemed to be doing inside his chest right now.

Could it really be this simple? Agree that they were both terrible people who'd made bad decisions, hurting those they loved, and move on from there... together? He rolled onto an elbow, looking down at the golden temptress who had destroyed his life and maybe—*just maybe*— redeemed it in a single stroke.

"I want to taste every part of you until you're calling out my name and begging for my cock," he said. "And then, I want to fuck you again. I want to keep doing those things over and over until I can convince myself this is real."

She blinked luminous blue eyes up at him. "I want your mouth on me. I want your flesh inside me, so I know this isn't some dream that I'll wake up from... only to find that I'm alone again."

He nodded slowly. "How long do you think those things will take us?" he asked.

Her hand stroked over his temple, settling to cup his cheek. "I don't know. Forever might just about do it."

Chan almost wanted to weep again, but he swallowed the lump growing in his throat and rolled on top of her instead. "Forever sounds good," he whispered against her ear, and started kissing his way down her body, making certain to cover every square inch as he went.

# Epilogue

A brisk knock at the door roused Chan from the most peaceful stretch of sleep he'd enjoyed in years. It creaked open a moment later, and Oksana poked her head in. She ran a practiced gaze over the rumpled bedding on the mattress, not to mention the single sheet that was doing a wholly inadequate job of covering Chan's and Duchess'—*Marie's*—naked bodies.

His blonde temptress jerked awake beside him, scrambling somewhat inelegantly into a sitting position. Her hair was a wild mess, half-covering her face. Oksana grinned at the two of them, slow and evil.

"About damned time," she observed, before sobering. "Now—get dressed. Things are happening. And not just down here in the tunnels."

"Is it Snag?" Marie asked.

Oksana raised an eyebrow. "Snag, plus the small matter of at least a couple of hundred people from Saqqara village who've come to see what's going on."

Marie tensed. "Are they hostile? Likely to cause problems for the donors, or us?"

"Apparently not," Oksana said with a shrug. "Just curious. The kids topside have been talking to them as best they're able, since none of them speak Arabic. Xander and Manisha have also been keeping an eye on things, since they're both sun-proof now."

"Sun-proof?" Chan asked. "What do you mean?"

"Ah, right," Oksana said. "I forgot you didn't know that part. They're both part werewolf, as well as being vampires. So, they shift into wolves rather than owls or mist, and sunlight doesn't burn them."

"That's... handy, I suppose," he managed.

"Very," Marie agreed dryly. "Now, *mon chou*, please stop standing in our doorway exuding smugness, and let us get dressed. We'll be right there."

Oksana's grin returned, wider than ever. "Oh, but I've earned this smugness, *ti mwen*. You've been positively unbearable for weeks now."

With a final cheeky wink at Chan, she left and closed the door behind her.

After they'd pulled on enough discarded clothes to be presentable, Chan asked, "Do you think this means Snag's awake?"

Marie stilled, her gaze turning inward. "Not yet. But his mind is beginning to stir."

She twisted her hair into a loose knot, pressed a quick kiss to his lips, and the two of them hurried through the maze of tunnels toward the chamber where they'd taken the coffin. It appeared they were the last to arrive. The room was full of vampires—all staring toward the figure on the cot, with Eris slumped in the chair beside him.

It was Eris who caught Chan's attention first. Not to put too fine a point on it, the man looked like shit. His hand still rested on Snag's forehead, but where he'd been crackling with life and power when they left him early that morning, he appeared severely drained now. His Mediterranean features had taken on a gray cast, and his gold-flecked eyes were sunken. Those observations distracted Chan from scrutinizing the form on the bed more closely—at least until Marie drew in a sharp breath at his side. He glanced at her, and then followed her gaze to Snag. Or… to the guy lying on the cot previously occupied by Snag's mummified body, at any rate.

What the *hell*?

The man on the bed appeared to be in his forties, with striking Middle Eastern features and deep-set eyes. A dense fuzz of freshly grown black stubble covered his skull—except at the temples, where it was silver-gray. The shadow of a beard hugged his jaw. Winged eyebrows drew together as Chan watched, mesmerized. The man's eyes flickered under closed lids, like someone in REM sleep.

"Is that really him?" Chan whispered, thinking, *how could it be, though*?

"It is," Marie said, low and shocked. "*Mon Dieu. I can feel him. He's waking up.*"

Indeed, Eris slid his hand away just as those piercing eyes opened, glowing with bronze light. Snag sat up, even as Eris sagged.

"*Dóxa to theoí,*" Eris murmured, embracing the newly regenerated vampire in obvious relief.

Trynn piled on from Snag's other side, half-kneeling on the edge of the cot to get to him. Snag's expression appeared mildly quizzical at being sandwiched between the pair. After a moment's pause, he lifted his arms to encircle both of them carefully, as though he'd nearly forgotten how to touch other people in such a way.

Most of the others crowded forward, though Chan hung back near the door with Marie.

"Snag," Tré said in relief.

Snag blinked up at him, a thoughtful movement.

*Menkhef*, he said, the word echoing along the mental bond.

"Menkhef?" Eris asked in confusion, as he and Trynn eased back from the three-way embrace.

Snag brushed Eris' pale cheek with his knuckles and smiled fondly—a nearly imperceptible curve of the lips that was gone almost as soon as it appeared.

*It is my name. Perhaps there is finally a worthy reason to take it up again.* He examined Eris closely for a moment, and his expression settled into a frown. *You have over-exerted yourself on my behalf. You must feed.*

"Here—we've got him," Oksana said, as both she and Tré moved forward to offer their blood. Eris drank gratefully from both of them.

Trynn continued to stare at Snag—*Menkhef?*—in something like awe. The newly awakened vampire was looking at his hands and arms as though he'd never seen them before; turning his hands this way and that as he examined flesh that was now filled out and free of scars. Chan could feel the thrum of power rolling off him—not the cracking overload that Eris had been carrying around after feeding from all of them, but more like a cocooning blanket that enveloped the room in warmth.

Xander crossed his arms, eyes raking the newly imposing figure as he rose from the cot. "If you'd asked, we could have chipped in with a group blood donation long ago, old chap."

Menkhef tested his legs cautiously and straightened to his full height, his molten bronze gaze meeting the younger vampire's.

*It was not yet time.*

Xander raised an eyebrow. "It might have saved lives," he said, and though his tone was mild, his expression was hard.

*It would not have.* Regret tinged the commanding mental voice. He turned to Manisha, Xander's sad-eyed mate, and gathered her hands in his. *Sangye's death lies on my conscience*, he told her silently. *I thought I could shape events to my liking, only to fail in the worst possible way. It was not my lack of power at issue, but my lack of vision.*

Manisha swallowed, and Chan could see rust-colored tears overflow her eyes. "You tried. At least you went with him—you didn't leave him alone with the monsters."

Menkhef bowed his head in acknowledgement. He lifted it, meeting her shiny gaze once more. *He had a message for you, alsghyr. He said, 'Tell Kumari Sadhu not to grieve for me. If I am needed, I will return.'*

At that, Manisha's face crumpled into lines of abject grief, and a sob rose from her throat. Menkhef let her hands slide free as Xander gathered her into his arms. She burrowed into his chest, weeping. Xander's eyes were also suspiciously bright.

Chan felt an ache through his bond with the woman next to him, and knew that she, too, felt responsible on some level for the boy's death — despite what Menkhef had said. He suspected she wouldn't welcome any overt display from him right now, but he tangled his fingers with hers in support, and she squeezed back tightly.

The mood in the room was sober as Menkhef spoke once more. *It is time for us to move out of the shadows — metaphorically, if not literally. Humans are gathering above, at the foot of Djoser's great pyramid. Stand with me as I speak to them and warn them of what is to come.*

Chan turned and looked into Marie's brilliant blue eyes, feeling as though they were standing on the cusp of something. She returned his gaze with a mixture of grief and stony determination.

-o-o-o-

As the sun slipped below the western horizon, an imposing figure climbed the steps leading from the South Tombs to the cobra-head wall overlooking the grand courtyard and the massive pyramid beyond. The man wore only a death shroud, the white cloth wrapped around him like robes.

The people assembled below gasped in shock as they took in the two massive wolves flanking him, matching his measured pace like well-trained guard dogs. A shorter man with inscrutable Asian features and a military bearing followed him, walking next to a woman with eyes the color of the sky and hair like spun gold.

The rustle of wings heralded the arrival of a pair of yellow-eyed owls that soared to a perfect landing on the man's outstretched arms. A moment later, swirls of fog descended to coil around the group, solidifying into four more striking figures—two men and two women. A hush spread over the watching crowd, the air humming with expectation.

The man in the death shroud spoke no word, but his mental voice rolled over the assemblage, filling every mind with its rich timbre.

*My countrymen*, he said. *The end of the world is nearly upon us. The war that is coming is a war of the spirit — not of the body. Each of you will be called to join it, for good or ill.*

He paused, the silence so complete that not even the sound of breathing marred it. His ageless eyes looked down at the faces below, as though committing each one to memory. Eventually, he spoke again — a final question.

*Ask yourself now, children — which side will you embrace? Love… or hate?*

*finis*

The *Circle of Blood* series concludes in *Book Six: Lovers' Victory*.

To get the free prequel to the *Circle of Blood* series sent directly to your inbox, visit www.rasteffan.com/circle

Printed in Great Britain
by Amazon

42697225R00169